Edward E Hale

SHORT STORY CLASSICS

(AMERICAN)

VOLUME ONE

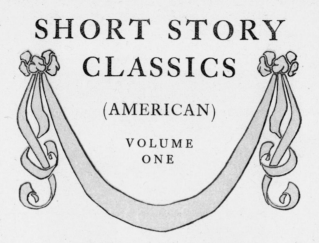

EDITED BY

William Patten

WITH
AN INTRODUCTION
AND NOTES

P. F. COLLIER & SON
NEW YORK

CONTENTS—VOLUME I

CONTENTS—VOLUME II

CONTENTS—VOLUME III

CONTENTS—VOLUME IV

CONTENTS—VOLUME V

PREFACE

THE time has seemed ripe for the publication of a new series of American short stories. There have been two notable collections. The first of these, "Little Classics," was published by Houghton, Mifflin & Co. in 1875, and was edited with rare acumen and judgment by Rossiter Johnson. Strictly speaking, it is not a collection of short stories, as it contains also numerous prose and poetical extracts, which give it more the character of a general anthology. The success of the undertaking is attested by the numerous editions that have been called for. No additions have been made to the collection, however, since the first edition appeared in 1875, and consequently the younger generation of writers, who have done so much to create the present-day interest in short stories, is unrepresented.

The second collection is that published by Charles Scribner & Sons in 1884. It is almost a model of its kind. The selections included in it indicate, almost without exception, the unerring taste and discriminating appreciation of the unnamed editor. Without making any claims to a chronological arrangement, it covers the field well, and, though there are some omissions which would have made it more thoroughly representative on the historical side (W. H. H. Murray, George Alfred Town-

send, and J. T. Trowbridge, for example), on the whole it leaves little to be desired. The popular success of the collection is shown by the many editions that have been printed. Nothing, however, has been added to the Scribner collection since 1884, so that it, like the Houghton, Mifflin & Co. edition, contains nothing by those writers who have come into prominence since then.

How large this unrepresented element is may be judged by the fact that the Collier collection is the only one containing stories by Richard Harding Davis, Booth Tarkington, Jack London, Clara Morris, John Fox, Jr., Edwin Lefevre, F. Marion Crawford, Henry Wallace Phillips, Mary E. Wilkins Freeman, Margaret Deland, Mary Stewart Cutting, Myra Kelly, Elia W. Peattie, Virginia Tracy, Robert W. Chambers, Robert Grant, Henry Harland, Charles G. D. Roberts, Lafcadio Hearn, Joel Chandler Harris, Lorimer Stoddard, George Ade, Finley P. Dunne, J. A. Altsheler, I. K. Friedman, Samuel Hopkins Adams, and Guy Wetmore Carryl.

Some measure of the interest that COLLIER'S takes in the short story as a literary form was shown by its Prize Story Contest. On February 1, 1904, COLLIER'S announced that it would give three prizes, one of five thousand, one of two thousand, and one of one thousand dollars, for the best story submitted under terms which ensured absolute anonymity in a competition to close June 1. Over eleven thousand authors, including many of the best known writers in America, contributed *more* than twelve thousand stories during the four months in which the contest was open. By the predominant opinion of the judges—Hon. Henry Cabot Lodge, Mr. Walter H. Page, and Mr. William Allen White—the first prize was awarded to Mr. Rowland Thomas's story, "Fagan." "Many Waters," by Margaret Deland, was awarded the second prize. "The Promised Land," by Raymond M. Alden, received the third prize. In addition to the prize winners, COLLIER'S purchased sixty-five stories from the best of those entered in the contest, paying an average price of over three hundred dollars for each.

A great short story is not produced every year, and among the editors there was no expectation that there would be found among the prize winners three masterpieces like "The Murders in the Rue Morgue," "The Diamond Lens," or "The Man Without a Country." Mr. Page, in writing of the awards, said: "So many writers seemed to mistake good material for good stories that I wonder if this be not a common mistake in our time. Surely it is a fundamental mistake to forget that story-telling is an art, a difficult art, too. A man who has a stirring fact or a thrilling experience has not a story until he has used it in some proper way—has constructed it, has built it."* Mr. White made the same point in the article he wrote about the awards—"And yet one who looks for the first time over a load of manuscripts and

---

*Collier's, February 11, 1905.

sees how many people there are in the world who seem to believe that they can write a short story, and then observes how few there are who do write a short story well, is forced to the conclusion that, in so much as art consists in surmounting difficulty to produce beauty, short story writing is indeed a fine art."*

Following on the steps of the Prize Story Contest, Collier's announced on April 8, 1905, the offering of four quarterly prizes of one thousand dollars for stories of not over six thousand words in length. As the prizes are in addition to the regular price paid for every accepted story, the prize winner receives in each case approximately thirteen hundred dollars. All stories received within a given quarter become eligible for a prize. Out of about four thousand manuscripts which came up for consideration in the first quarter, seventeen were accepted. The first prize was awarded to Eleanor H. Abbott of Lowell, Mass., for "The Sick-A-Bed Lady."

All the authors who have been approached with reference to the use of their stories in the present collection have manifested a lively sense of interest that is most gratifying. The same is true of most of the publishers. It seems only fair to admit that two or three of the selections are not as thoroughly representative in quality as could be wished. In these instances we were unable to purchase from the publishers the right to reprint the par-

*ticular stories we wanted, though we were willing to pay
whatever was demanded.*

*It will be readily noted by even the most casual reader
that the point of view in selecting the stories has not been
governed by any narrow interpretation as to what con-
stitutes perfection in form. In the case of the older
stories, time, that fine sifter of judgments, has in many
cases placed its seal of approval on certain stories, and
they have come to be accepted as classics. Hence, their
use became inevitable in any collection that attempted to
be representative. When it came to the later stories, the
endeavor has been made to select those stories which
seemed to possess the same classic, or enduring, quality.*

*I am glad of an opportunity to acknowledge my in-
debtedness to Mr. Norman Hapgood, Mr. Charles Bel-
mont Davis, Mr. Albert Lee, and Mr. Samuel Hopkins
Adams, for much valuable assistance, and to Mr. T. A.
Janvier, Mr. Richard Harding Davis, Mr. Booth Tarkington, Mr. Thomas Nelson Page, Mr. Robert W. Chambers, Mrs. Rebecca Harding Davis, Mrs. Mary E. Wilkins Freeman, Miss Virginia Tracy, Mr. Joel Chandler
Harris, Mr. Edwin Lefevre, Mr. Henry Harland, Mr.
John Fox, Jr., Mr. C. G. D. Roberts, Mr. I. K. Friedman, Mr. F. P. Dunne, Mr. George Ade, Mr. Samuel
Hopkins Adams, and Mr. Joseph A. Altsheler, for permission to use their stories.*

*Special thanks are due to Mrs. W. H. H. Murray for
permission to use her husband's story, "A Ride with a*

Mad Horse in a Freight-Car"; to Mrs. O. G. T. Kiliani for permission to use her father's story, "Who Was She?"; to Mr. H. H. Boyesen for permission to use his father's story, "A Good-for-Nothing"; and to Mr. H. Prentice Bailey of the "Utica Observer" for permission to use Harold Frederic's "Brother Sebastian's Friendship."

Acknowledgments are made in connection with the various stories to Messrs. Charles Scribner's Sons, McClure, Phillips & Co., Macmillan & Co., Houghton, Mifflin & Co., G. P. Putnam's Sons, Little, Brown & Co., J. B. Lippincott Co., Funk & Wagnalls, John Lane Co., D. Appleton & Co., and H. S. Stone & Co. for the permissions they courteously granted.

W. P.

INTRODUCTION

THE SPIRIT OF THE SHORT STORY

FROM the time of Poe and Hawthorne the nature and limitations of the short story have formed a favorite subject of discussion among writers and critics of fiction. And the controversy has been all the more valuable because no definite conclusions have ever been arrived at. Had there been a general agreement as to definition, the short story might now be as dead as the sonnet.

The superabundant vitality of the American short story has made such a consensus impossible. The form develops organically under the very microscope of the observer. As seen in the legendary tale of Irving, it appears to have possessed certain essential features which were sloughed off as rudimentary organs in the next stage of development under Poe and Hawthorne. And by the time a definition had been reached which fitted, with a few provoking exceptions, the stories of this period, new processes were extruded and a new habitat was chosen by the short story in the era of Bret Harte. Then, in the present day of the psychological story writers, of whom Henry James is the type, the organism seems to resolve itself simply into a brain with its attendant nervous system. Last of all, in the symbolic stories in which some of our younger writers, such as Arthur

Colton, are experimenting, we see the form pluming itself for a flight away from the confines of form into the region of pure spirit.

And spirit, in the broad sense in which the French use the word, superior intellectual, moral, imaginative, or even humorous quality, is the essence of the short story. And the sole "proof" of this spirit is its effects, the exhilaration of the brain, the warming of the heart, the tingling of the blood, or the tickling of the midriff, or whatever seat there be of risibility.

Nevertheless, it is profitable to know the working theories upon which certain masters of the short story constructed their great works. However protean the form of the short story may be when its entire history is considered, in the use of a single author, or during the brief domination of a school of short-story writers, its structure has often been very clearly defined.

Thus Irving built his tales upon the rambling architectural plan of the legend or narrative. The spirit is *continuity,* rather than congruity of incident. Its effect on the reader is contented charm, like that produced by a devious brook which one is satisfied to have run on forever. For the thrill of expectation, like that produced by rapids converging to certain downfall, the readers of Irving's day turned to the romances of Scott, such as "The Bride of Lammermoor," published the same year (1819) as "The Sketch Book." And for the satisfaction of the yearning imagination, like that yielded by a still mountain tarn glassing the infinite heavens, the poetry of the

Lake School sufficed, although it must be confessed that in Wordsworth's "Peter Bell," published in 1819, the tarn had contracted to something very like a puddle. There was no thought among the readers of "Rip Van Winkle," Irving's best and most typical tale, that the short story was destined shortly to attain the swiftly moving currents and catastrophe of the novel, and, but a little later, the quiet depths of poetic symbolism.

Nathaniel Hawthorne, whose publication of his collected stories, "Twice-Told Tales," in 1837, antedates Edgar A. Poe's first collection, "Tales of the Grotesque and Arabesque," which appeared in 1840, may be considered the next American author after Irving to add materially to the development of the form and spirit of the short story. Indeed, in certain features, he brought it wellnigh to perfection. What Rossiter Johnson said of him in 1875 is true to-day. "As a writer of short stories which are not mere episodes, but which have all the elements of a complete romance, condensed and therefore intensified, Hawthorne has no equal."* So, too, stands unqualified the statement of Leslie Stephen, made in the same year: "No modern writer has the same skill in so using the marvelous as to interest us without unduly exciting our incredulity."†

That Hawthorne consciously developed the legend of the time of Irving into the "complete romance," referred to by Mr. Johnson, and studied with the care

---

* "Little Classics."   Houghton, Mifflin & Co.
† "Hours in a Library."   G. P. Putnam's Sons.

of a *cordon bleu* that proper admixture of the marvelous to which Mr. Leslie alludes, is proved by his preface to "The House of Seven Gables." "The romance," says Hawthorne, "while, as a work of art, it must rigidly subject itself to laws, and while it sins unpardonably so far as it may swerve aside from the truth of the human heart, has fairly a right to present that truth under circumstances, to a great extent, of the writer's own choosing or creation. If he think fit, also, he may so manage his atmospherical medium as to bring out or mellow the lights, and deepen and enrich the shadows, of the picture. He will be wise, no doubt, to make a very moderate use of the privileges here stated, and, especially, to mingle the marvelous rather as a slight, delicate, evanescent flavor, than as any portion of the actual substance of the dish offered to the public. He can hardly be said, however, to commit a literary crime, even if he disregard this caution."

These general remarks, especially the last one, show Hawthorne to have been far in advance of his age in regard to the province of the story writer. They are specifically enforced by his description of "The House of Seven Gables," a typical "short story" of the author, though a long one, and therefore generally put in the class of the novel, whence Hawthorne expressly excluded it. He writes: "The point of view in which this tale comes under the romantic definition lies in the attempt to connect a bygone time with the very present that is flitting from us. It is a legend, prolonging itself, from an epoch now gray in the distance, down into our own broad day-light, and bringing along with it some of its legend-ary mist, which the reader, according to his pleasure, may either disregard or allow it to float almost im-perceptibly about the characters and events, for the sake of a picturesque effect."

In one story ("The Great Stone Face") Haw-thorne dared to condense this almost imperceptible mist of the marvelous into the visible forms of alle-gory, clouding only to define the round orb of the truth he sought to show forth. As one of the most imaginative though simply written of his stories, it may be classed among his most characteristic and best.

Edgar A. Poe made a far broader and more sys-tematic, though no more profound, study of literary form than did Hawthorne. Indeed, to him may un-reservedly be accorded the credit of creating the art of constructive criticism in this country. In a review of the tales of Hawthorne* he has this to say of the distinctive characteristics of the short-story form: "As the ordinary novel can not be read at one sitting, it deprives itself, of course, of the immense force de-rivable from *totality*. . . . In the brief tale, how-ever, the author is enabled to carry out the fulness of his intention, be it what it may. During the hour of perusal the soul of the reader is at the writer's con-trol.

"A skilful literary artist has constructed a tale. If

---

* "Literary Criticism." 1842.

wise, he has not fashioned his thoughts to accommodate his incidents; but, having conceived, with deliberate care, a certain unique or single *effect* to be
wrought out, he then invents such incidents, he then
combines such events, as may best aid him in establishing this preconceived effect. If his very initial
sentence tend not to the outbringing of this effect,
then he has failed in his first step. In the whole composition there should be no word written of which
the tendency, direct or indirect, is not to the one pre-
established design. . . . The idea of the tale has
been presented unblemished because undisturbed; and
this is an end unattainable by the novel."

These ideas of totality of effect, unlimited freedom of theme and compression of narrative, as main
characteristics of the short story in opposition to the
novel, Mr. Brander Matthews has exhaustively ampli-
fied in his essay, "The Philosophy of the Short
Story," which was first published in 1885, and, in
view of later developments of the short-story form,
subsequently modified by a cancellation, an addendum,
and a postscript.*

Prof. Matthews has made one wholly original con-
tribution to the discussion. This is his comparison
of the short story and the sketch, the gist of which is
to be found in the statement that, "while a sketch may
be still-life, in a short story something always happens." This is simply a modern statement of Aris-
totle's rule that the end of drama (action) must be

---

* "Pen and Ink." Charles Scribner's Sons.

a closing incident—a reversal of situation, a revelation of identity, or an affliction (as opposed to infliction).* If the last passive sense is included by Professor Matthews, his point is an obvious one. If this is excluded, his point is erroneous. Some of the best of modern short stories practically omit the active verb "to do," and are written in the moods and tenses of "to be and to suffer." Such are certain stories of character by such psychologists as Robert Grant and F. J. Stimson ("J. S. of Dale") and transcripts from uneventful rural life by Mary E. Wilkins Freeman, Hamlin Garland, and other realists.

Certainly the wisest observation which Professor Matthews makes in his essay is his confession that it is impossible to confine the short story strictly to any metes and bounds. "With the more complete understanding of the principle of development and evolution in literary art, as in physical nature, we see the futility of a strict and rigid classification into precisely defined genera and species. All that is needful for us to remark now is that the short story has limitless possibilities: it may be as realistic as the most prosaic novel, or as fantastic as the most ethereal romance."

George W. Cable, one of our most accomplished writers of short stories, in two articles, "After-Thoughts of a Story-Teller"† and "The Speculations of a Story-Teller,"‡ also presents a liberal view of the

---

* περιπέτεια, ἀναγνώρισις, or πάθος.
† "The North American Review," January, 1894.
‡ "The Atlantic Monthly," July, 1896.

function of the writer of fiction. He is writing of both the novelist and the short-story writer. "Knowledge and training," he says in the first article, "are not so essential to the story-teller as feeling and sympathy. "It is not sight the story-teller needs, but second sight. We do not need to have seen everything in order to feel it, but we do need to feel whatever we would have a reader see." And he supplements this view in the second article. "As the geologist's great treasury of verities lies mainly in the rocks and clays everywhere underfoot, the story-teller's lies so largely in the common soil of the human heart that the power of his imagination, the range of his sympathies, and the stature and beauty of his spirit, far more than any store of knowledge or finish of training, will determine his art."

Mr. Cable, however, does not esteem the short story so highly as do Professor Matthews and most of the literary critics who have written upon the subject. He says, in the "North American" article: "Somebody a while ago started the notion that it is as difficult and creditable to write a short story as a sustained novel. Oh, my! Is a little boat as hard to build as a big ship? Is a melody as great a musical achievement as a symphony?"

Taking Mr. Cable's own comparisons, we would ask him in return: Is not the building of a line of successful defenders of the America's cup considered a more difficult and creditable task than the construction of a series of record-breaking ocean liners? Who knows the name of the Hamburg-American ship designer? Who does not know the name of Herreshoff? And is not Rouget de Lisle's "Marseillaise," voicing so completely, and, as it were, instantaneously, the spirit of revolution, a more astounding performance than even the "Ninth Symphony" of Beethoven — the acknowledged masterpiece of its order of musical compositions?

If the author of "Posson Jone" and "Jean-ah Poquelin" somewhat underrates that province of his art wherein he excels by reason of his unusual ability to depict special types of character, in favor of that branch wherein chief rank is reserved for the creators of broader and more synthesized representations of human nature, another story writer of his class, the author of "The Luck of Roaring Camp," has unduly exalted the short-story form. Rightly solving "the secret of the American short story," Mr. Bret Harte drew unwarranted conclusions as to its place and influence in our future literature.

In an article, "The Rise of the Short Story,"* Mr. Harte said: "The secret of the American short story is the treatment of characteristic American life, with absolute knowledge of its peculiarities and sympathy with its methods; with no fastidious ignoring of its habitual expression, or the inchoate poetry that may be found even hidden in its slang; with no moral determination except that which may be the legitimate outcome of the story itself; with no more elimination than may be necessary for the artistic conception, and never from the fear of the 'fetich' of

* "The Cornhill Magazine," July, 1899.

conventionalism. Of such is the American short story of to-day—the germ of American literature to come."

Unbiased observation of the present tendencies in American fiction will, we believe, prove the view of Mr. Harte untenable. The novel and the short story possess common attributes, those of fiction in general. These naturally exceed in number and importance the points of difference. Writers can attain excellence in them by practice in either the short or long form of fiction. They have usually begun with the short story because of its brevity, and have then utilized the lessons thus learned in novel-construction. They would have learned the same lessons had they begun with the novel. Then again it may freely be admitted that the American short story became famous before the American novel. All this only indicates priority and not paternity of the short story in the field of American fiction. In fact, paternity may be said to be impossible, as the transference of an essential short story characteristic into novel composition would simply result in a lengthened short story.

On the contrary, it is the novel that is influencing, and will influence more and more, the short story. This influence is primarily one of spirit, leading, however, to changes of form to accommodate the new spirit. Fortunately these modifications all make for greater freedom. The novel by its greater length has been able to develop delineation of character to a degree hitherto unattainable by the short story. Yet it has made delineation of character a chief end in all fiction, brief as well as extended. So the short story masters have set to work, by using all the arts of compression—the most subtle suggestion and delicate contrast—and by casting aside every formal convention that nothing may hinder this concentration, to outdo the novelists in psychology, as they have done in every other feature of fiction. While a masterpiece of this new form will require a somewhat greater length than that now permitted the average magazine short story, popular demand may in time secure for it even the sacrifice of advertising space. Yet the length can not be greatly increased, for the short story must retain its present characteristic of compression. It can grow but little outward. Hence, to use a fine phrase of W. D. Howells in his article, "Some Anomalies of the Short Story,"* it must "deepen inward." Its trend of development must be toward that fourth dimension, spirit.

But these are subliminal æsthetics, and the reader may question whether the essential nature of the short story will be preserved and can be discerned under such incorporeal conditions. We will let Mr. Howells answer this inquiry: "In that dim, subjective region, where the æsthetic origins present themselves almost with the authority of inspirations, there is nothing clearer than the difference between the short-story motive and the long-story motive. One, if one is in that line of work, feels instinctively just the size and carrying power of the given motive. Or, if the reader

---

* "The North American Review," September, 1901.

prefers a different figure, the mind which the seed
has been dropped into from Somewhere is mystically
aware whether the seed is going to grow up a bush or
is going to grow up a tree, if left to itself. Of course,
the mind to which the seed is intrusted may play it
false, and wilfully dwarf the growth, or force it to
unnatural dimensions; but the critical observer will
easily detect the fact of this treason. Almost in the
first germinal impulse the inventive mind forefeels
the ultimate difference, and recognizes the essential
simplicity or complexity of the motive. There will
be a prophetic subdivision into a variety of motives
and a multiplication of characters and incidents and
situations; or the original motive will be divined indi-
visible, and there will be a small group of people immediately interested and controlled by a single, or
predominant, fact. The uninspired may contend that
this is bosh, and I own that something might be said
for their contention, but upon the whole I think it is
gospel."

RIP VAN WINKLE

BY WASHINGTON IRVING

Washington Irving (born April 3, 1783, in New York, died November 28, 1859) was aptly characterized by Thackeray as "the first ambassador whom the New World of Letters sent to the Old." It was "The Sketch-Book," published by Irving under the pseudonym of "Geoffrey Crayon," in 1819, while he was living in England, that won not only consideration, but respect and admiration for American literature in the courts of foreign culture. In this work appeared "Rip Van Winkle," Irving's most famous story. Charles Dudley Warner calls the tale "one of those strokes of genius that recreate the world and clothe it with the unfading hues of romance; the theme was an old-world echo, transformed by genius into a primal story that will endure as long as the Hudson flows through its mountains to the sea."

RIP VAN WINKLE

BY WASHINGTON IRVING

WHOEVER has made a voyage up the Hudson must remember the Kaatskill Mountains. They are a dismembered branch of the great 'Appalachian family, and are seen away to the west of the river, swelling up to a noble height, and lording it over the surrounding country. Every change of season, every change of weather, indeed every hour of the day, produces some change in the magical hues and shapes of these mountains; and they are regarded by all the good wives, far and near, as perfect barometers. When the weather is fair and settled, they are clothed in blue and purple, and print their bold outlines on the clear evening sky; but sometimes, when the rest of the landscape is cloudless, they will gather a hood of gray vapors about their summits, which, in the last rays of the setting sun, will glow and light up like a crown of glory.

At the foot of these fairy mountains, the voyager may have descried the light smoke curling up from a village, whose shingle roofs gleam among the trees, just where the blue tints of the upland melt away into the fresh green of the nearer landscape. It is a little village of great antiquity, having been founded by some of the Dutch colonists, in the early times of the province, just about the beginning of the government

(3)

of the good Peter Stuyvesant (may he rest in peace!),
and there were some of the houses of the original
settlers standing within a few years, built of small
yellow bricks brought from Holland, having latticed
windows and gable fronts, surmounted with weather-
cocks.

In that same village, and in one of these very houses
(which, to tell the precise truth, was sadly time-worn
and weather-beaten), there lived many years since,
while the country was yet a province of Great Britain,
a simple, good-natured fellow, of the name of Rip Van
Winkle. He was a descendant of the Van Winkles
who figured so gallantly in the chivalrous days of
Peter Stuyvesant, and accompanied him to the siege
of Fort Christina. He inherited, however, but little
of the martial character of his ancestors. I have observed that he was a simple, good-natured man; he
was moreover a kind neighbor, and an obedient henpecked husband. Indeed, to the latter circumstance
might be owing that meekness of spirit which gained
him such universal popularity; for those men are most
apt to be obsequious and conciliating abroad who are
under the discipline of shrews at home. Their tem-
pers, doubtless, are rendered pliant and malleable in
the fiery furnace of domestic tribulation, and a curtain
lecture is worth all the sermons in the world for teaching the virtues of patience and long-suffering. A termagant wife may, therefore, in some respects, be
considered a tolerable blessing; and if so, Rip Van
Winkle was thrice blessed.

Certain it is that he was a great favorite among

all the good wives of the village, who, as usual with
the amiable sex, took his part in all family squabbles,
and never failed, whenever they talked those matters
over in their evening gossipings, to lay all the blame
on Dame Van Winkle. The children of the village,
too, would shout with joy whenever he approached.
He assisted at their sports, made their playthings,
taught them to fly kites and shoot marbles, and told
them long stories of ghosts, witches, and Indians.
Whenever he went dodging about the village, he was
surrounded by a troop of them hanging on his skirts,
clambering on his back, and playing a thousand tricks
on him with impunity; and not a dog would bark at
him throughout the neighborhood.

The great error in Rip's composition was an in-
superable aversion to all kinds of profitable labor. It
could not be from the want of assiduity or perseverance; for he would sit on a wet rock, with a rod as
long and heavy as a Tartar's lance, and fish all day
without a murmur, even though he should not be
encouraged by a single nibble. He would carry a
fowling-piece on his shoulder, for hours together,
trudging through woods and swamps, and up hill and
down dale, to shoot a few squirrels or wild pigeons.
He would never refuse to assist a neighbor even in
the roughest toil, and was a foremost man at all country frolics for husking Indian corn, or building stone
fences. The women of the village, too, used to employ him to run their errands, and to do such little odd
jobs as their less obliging husbands would not do for
them; in a word, Rip was ready to attend to any-

body's business but his own; but as to doing family
duty, and keeping his farm in order, he found it impossible.

In fact, he declared it was of no use to work on his
farm; it was the most pestilent little piece of ground
in the whole country; everything about it went wrong,
and would go wrong in spite of him. His fences were
continually falling to pieces; his cow would either go
astray, or get among the cabbages; weeds were sure
to grow quicker in his fields than anywhere else; the
rain always made a point of setting in just as he had
some outdoor work to do; so that though his patri-
monial estate had dwindled away under his management, acre by acre, until there was little more left than
a mere patch of Indian corn and potatoes, yet it was
the worst conditioned farm in the neighborhood.

His children, too, were as ragged and wild as if
they belonged to nobody. His son Rip, an urchin be-
gotten in his own likeness, promised to inherit the
habits with the old clothes of his father. He was generally seen trooping like a colt at his mother's heels,
equipped in a pair of his father's cast-off galligaskins,
which he had much ado to hold up with one hand, as a
fine lady does her train in bad weather.

Rip Van Winkle, however, was one of those happy
mortals, of foolish, well-oiled dispositions, who take
the world easy, eat white bread or brown, whichever
can be got with least thought or trouble, and would
rather starve on a penny than work for a pound. If
left to himself, he would have whistled life away, in
perfect contentment; but his wife kept continually din-

ning in his ears about his idleness, his carelessness, and the ruin he was bringing on his family.

Morning, noon, and night, her tongue was incessantly going, and everything he said or did was sure to produce a torrent of household eloquence. Rip had but one way of replying to all lectures of the kind, and that, by frequent use, had grown into a habit. He shrugged his shoulders, shook his head, cast up his eyes, but said nothing. This, however, always provoked a fresh volley from his wife, so that he was fain to draw off his forces, and take to the outside of the house—the only side which, in truth, belongs to a henpecked husband.

Rip's sole domestic adherent was his dog Wolf, who was as much henpecked as his master; for Dame Van Winkle regarded them as companions in idleness, and even looked upon Wolf with an evil eye, as the cause of his master's going so often astray. True it is, in all points of spirit befitting an honorable dog, he was as courageous an animal as ever scoured the woods—but what courage can withstand the everduring and all-besetting terrors of a woman's tongue? The moment Wolf entered the house, his crest fell, his tail drooped to the ground, or curled between his legs, he sneaked about with a gallows air, casting many a sidelong glance at Dame Van Winkle, and at the least flourish of a broomstick or ladle, he would fly to the door with yelping precipitation.

Times grew worse and worse with Rip Van Winkle, as years of matrimony rolled on: a tart temper never mellows with age, and a sharp tongue is the only

edge tool that grows keener with constant use. For a
long while he used to console himself, when driven
from home, by frequenting a kind of perpetual club of
the sages, philosophers, and other idle personages of
the village, which held its sessions on a bench before a
small inn, designated by a rubicund portrait of his
Majesty George the Third. Here they used to sit in
the shade, of a long lazy summer's day, talking list-
lessly over village gossip, or telling endless sleepy
stories about nothing. But it would have been worth
any statesman's money to have heard the profound discussions which sometimes took place, when by chance
an old newspaper fell into their hands, from some
passing traveler. How solemnly they would listen to
the contents, as drawled out by Derrick Van Bummel,
the schoolmaster, a dapper learned little man, who was
not to be daunted by the most gigantic word in the
dictionary; and how sagely they would deliberate
upon public events some months after they had taken
place.

The opinions of this junto were completely controlled by Nicholas Vedder, a patriarch of the village,
and landlord of the inn, at the door of which he took
his seat from morning till night, just moving sufficiently to avoid the sun, and keep in the shade of a
large tree; so that the neighbors could tell the hour
by his movements as accurately as by a sun-dial. It
is true, he was rarely heard to speak, but smoked his
pipe incessantly. His adherents, however (for every
great man has his adherents), perfectly understood
him, and knew how to gather his opinions. When

anything that was read or related displeased him, he was observed to smoke his pipe vehemently, and to send forth short, frequent, and angry puffs; but when pleased, he would inhale the smoke slowly and tranquilly, and emit it in light and placid clouds, and sometimes taking the pipe from his mouth, and letting the fragrant vapor curl about his nose, would gravely nod his head in token of perfect approbation.

From even this stronghold the unlucky Rip was at length routed by his termagant wife, who would suddenly break in upon the tranquillity of the assemblage, and call the members all to naught; nor was that august personage, Nicholas Vedder himself, sacred from the daring tongue of this terrible virago, who charged him outright with encouraging her husband in habits of idleness.

Poor Rip was at last reduced almost to despair, and his only alternative to escape from the labor of the farm and the clamor of his wife was to take gun in hand, and stroll away into the woods. Here he would sometimes seat himself at the foot of a tree, and share the contents of his wallet with Wolf, with whom he sympathized as a fellow-sufferer in persecution. "Poor Wolf," he would say, "thy mistress leads thee a dog's life of it; but never mind, my lad, while I live thou shalt never want a friend to stand by thee!" Wolf would wag his tail, look wistfully in his master's face, and if dogs can feel pity, I verily believe he reciprocated the sentiment with all his heart.

In a long ramble of the kind, on a fine autumnal day, Rip had unconsciously scrambled to one of the highest parts of the Kaatskill Mountains. He was after his favorite sport of squirrel-shooting, and the still solitudes had echoed and re-echoed with the reports of his gun. Panting and fatigued, he threw himself, late in the afternoon, on a green knoll covered with mountain herbage, that crowned the brow of a precipice. From an opening between the trees, he could overlook all the lower country for many a mile of rich woodland. He saw at a distance the lordly Hudson, far, far below him, moving on its silent but majestic course, with the reflection of a purple cloud, or the sail of a lagging bark, here and there sleeping on its glassy bosom, and at last losing itself in the blue highlands.

On the other side he looked down into a deep mountain glen, wild, lonely, and shagged, the bottom filled with fragments from the impending cliffs, and scarcely lighted by the reflected rays of the setting sun. For some time Rip lay musing on this scene; evening was gradually advancing; the mountains began to throw their long blue shadows over the valleys; he saw that it would be dark long before he could reach the village; and he heaved a heavy sigh when he thought of encountering the terrors of Dame Van Winkle.

As he was about to descend he heard a voice from a distance hallooing, "Rip Van Winkle! Rip Van Winkle!" He looked around, but could see nothing but a crow winging its solitary flight across the mountain. He thought his fancy must have deceived him, and turned again to descend, when he heard the same cry ring through the still evening air, "Rip Van Winkle! Rip Van Winkle!"—at the same time Wolf bristled up his back, and giving a low growl, skulked to his master's side, looking fearfully down into the glen. Rip now felt a vague apprehension stealing over him: he looked anxiously in the same direction, and perceived a strange figure slowly toiling up the rocks, and bending under the weight of something he carried on his back. He was surprised to see any human being in this lonely and unfrequented place, but supposing it to be some one of the neighborhood in need of his assistance, he hastened down to yield it.

On nearer approach, he was still more surprised at the singularity of the stranger's appearance. He was a short square-built old fellow, with thick bushy hair, and a grizzled beard. His dress was of the antique Dutch fashion—a cloth jerkin strapped round the waist—several pairs of breeches, the outer one of ample volume, decorated with rows of buttons down the sides, and bunches at the knees. He bore on his shoulders a stout keg, that seemed full of liquor, and made signs for Rip to approach and assist him with the load. Though rather shy and distrustful of this new acquaintance, Rip complied with his usual alacrity, and mutually relieving each other, they clambered up a narrow gully, apparently the dry bed of a mountain torrent. As they ascended, Rip every now and then heard long rolling peals, like distant thunder, that seemed to issue out of a deep ravine or rather cleft between lofty rocks, toward which their rugged path conducted. He paused for an instant, but supposing it to be the muttering of one of those transient thunder-showers which often take place in mountain heights, he proceeded. Passing through the ravine, they came to a hollow, like a small amphitheatre, surrounded by perpendicular precipices, over the brinks of which impending trees shot their branches, so that you only caught glimpses of the azure sky, and the bright evening cloud. During the whole time, Rip and his companion had labored on in silence; for though the former marveled greatly what could be the object of carrying a keg of liquor up this wild mountain, yet there was something strange and incomprehensible about the unknown, that inspired awe and checked familiarity.

On entering the amphitheatre new objects of wonder presented themselves. On a level spot in the centre was a company of odd-looking personages playing at nine-pins. They were dressed in a quaint outlandish fashion: some wore short doublets, others jerkins, with long knives in their belts, and most of them had enormous breeches, of similar style with that of the guide's. Their visages, too, were peculiar: one had a large head, broad face, and small piggish eyes; the face of another seemed to consist entirely of nose, and was surmounted by a white sugar-loaf hat, set off with a little red cock's tail. They all had beards, of various shapes and colors. There was one who seemed to be the commander. He was a stout old gentleman, with a weather-beaten countenance; he wore a laced doublet, broad belt and hanger, highcrowned hat and feather, red stockings, and high-heeled shoes, with roses in them. The whole group reminded Rip of the figures in an old Flemish painting, in the parlor of Dominie Van Schaick, the village parson, and which had been brought over from Holland at the time of the settlement.

What seemed particularly odd to Rip was, that though these folks were evidently amusing themselves, yet they maintained the gravest faces, the most mysterious silence, and were, withal, the most melancholy party of pleasure he had ever witnessed. Nothing interrupted the stillness of the scene but the noise of the balls, which, whenever they were rolled, echoed along the mountains like rumbling peals of thunder.

As Rip and his companion approached them, they suddenly desisted from their play, and stared at him with such a fixed statue-like gaze, and such strange, uncouth, lack-lustre countenances, that his heart turned within him, and his knees smote together. His companion now emptied the contents of the keg into large flagons, and made signs to him to wait upon the company. He obeyed with fear and trembling; they quaffed the liquor in profound silence, and then returned to their game.

By degrees, Rip's awe and apprehension subsided. He even ventured, when no eye was fixed upon him, to taste the beverage, which he found had much of the flavor of excellent Hollands. He was naturally a thirsty soul, and was soon tempted to repeat the draught. One taste provoked another, and he reiterated his visits to the flagon so often that at length his senses were overpowered, his eyes swam in his head, his head gradually declined, and he fell into a deep sleep.

On waking, he found himself on the green knoll from whence he had first seen the old man of the glen. He rubbed his eyes—it was a bright sunny morning. The birds were hopping and twittering among the bushes, and the eagle was wheeling aloft, and breasting the pure mountain breeze. "Surely," thought Rip, "I have not slept here all night." He recalled the occurrences before he fell asleep. The strange man with the keg of liquor—the mountain ravine—the wild retreat among the rocks—the wobegone party at nine-pins—the flagon—"Oh, that wicked flagon!" thought Rip—"what excuse shall I make to Dame Van Winkle?"

He looked round for his gun, but in place of the clean well-oiled fowling-piece, he found an old firelock lying by him, the barrel incrusted with rust, the lock falling off, and the stock worm-eaten. He now suspected that the grave roisterers of the mountain had put a trick upon him, and having dosed him with liquor, had robbed him of his gun. Wolf, too, had disappeared, but he might have strayed away after a squirrel or partridge. He whistled after him, and shouted his name, but all in vain; the echoes repeated his whistle and shout, but no dog was to be seen.

He determined to revisit the scene of the last evening's gambol, and if he met with any of the party, to demand his dog and gun. As he rose to walk, he found himself stiff in the joints and wanting in his usual activity. "These mountain beds do not agree with me," thought Rip, "and if this frolic should lay me up with a fit of rheumatism, I shall have a blessed time with Dame Van Winkle." With some difficulty he got down into the glen; he found the gully up which he and his companion had ascended the preceding evening; but to his astonishment a mountain stream was now foaming down it, leaping from rock to rock, and filling the glen with babbling murmurs. He, however, made shift to scramble up its sides, working his toilsome way through thickets of birch, sassafras, and witch-hazel; and sometimes tripped up or entangled by the wild grape vines that twisted their coils and tendrils from tree to tree, and spread a kind of network in his path.

At length he reached to where the ravine had opened through the cliffs to the amphitheatre; but no traces of such opening remained. The rocks presented a high impenetrable wall, over which the torrent came tumbling in a sheet of feathery foam, and fell into a broad, deep basin, black from the shadows of the surrounding forest. Here, then, poor Rip was brought to a stand. He again called and whistled after his dog; he was only answered by the cawing of a flock of idle crows, sporting high in air about a dry tree that overhung a sunny precipice; and who, secure in their elevation, seemed to look down and scoff at the poor man's perplexities. What was to be done? The morning was passing away, and Rip felt famished for want of his breakfast. He grieved to give up his dog

and gun; he dreaded to meet his wife; but it would
not do to starve among the mountains. He shook his
head, shouldered the rusty firelock, and, with a heart
full of trouble and anxiety, turned his steps homeward.

As he approached the village he met a number of
people, but none whom he knew, which somewhat surprised him, for he had thought himself acquainted with
every one in the country round. Their dress, too,
was of a different fashion from that to which he was
accustomed. They all stared at him with equal marks
of surprise, and whenever they cast eyes upon him,
invariably stroked their chins. The constant recur-
rence of this gesture induced Rip, involuntarily, to do
the same, when, to his astonishment, he found his
beard had grown a foot long!

He had now entered the skirts of the village. A
troop of strange children ran at his heels, hooting
after him, and pointing at his gray beard. The dogs,
too, not one of which he recognized for an old acquaintance, barked at him as he passed. The very
village was altered: it was larger and more populous.
There were rows of houses which he had never seen
before, and those which had been his familiar haunts
had disappeared. Strange names were over the doors
—strange faces at the windows—everything was
strange. His mind now misgave him; he began to
doubt whether both he and the world around him
were not bewitched. Surely this was his native village, which he had left but a day before. There stood
the Kaatskill Mountains—there ran the silver Hudson

at a distance—there was every hill and dale precisely as it had always been—Rip was sorely perplexed— "That flagon last night," thought he, "has addled my poor head sadly!"

It was with some difficulty that he found the way to his own house, which he approached with silent awe, expecting every moment to hear the shrill voice of Dame Van Winkle. He found the house gone to decay—the roof fallen in, the windows shattered, and the doors off the hinges. A half-starved dog, that looked like Wolf, was skulking about it. Rip called him by name, but the cur snarled, showed his teeth, and passed on. This was an unkind cut indeed. "My very dog," sighed poor Rip, "has forgotten me!"

He entered the house, which, to tell the truth, Dame Van Winkle had always kept in neat order. It was empty, forlorn, and apparently abandoned. This desolateness overcame all his connubial fears—he called loudly for his wife and children—the lonely chambers rang for a moment with his voice, and then all again was silence.

He now hurried forth, and hastened to his old resort, the village inn—but it too was gone. A large rickety wooden building stood in its place, with great gaping windows, some of them broken, and mended with old hats and petticoats, and over the door was painted, "The Union Hotel, by Jonathan Doolittle." Instead of the great tree that used to shelter the quiet little Dutch inn of yore, there now was reared a tall naked pole, with something on the top that

looked like a red night-cap, and from it was fluttering
a flag, on which was a singular assemblage of stars
and stripes—all this was strange and incomprehensible. He recognized on the sign, however, the ruby
face of King George, under which he had smoked so
many a peaceful pipe, but even this was singularly
metamorphosed. The red coat was changed for one
of blue and buff, a sword was held in the hand instead of a sceptre, the head was decorated with a
cocked hat, and underneath was painted in large characters GENERAL WASHINGTON.

There was, as usual, a crowd of folk about the
door, but none that Rip recollected. The very character of the people seemed changed. There was a
busy, bustling, disputatious tone about it, instead of
the accustomed phlegm and drowsy tranquillity. He
looked in vain for the sage Nicholas Vedder, with his
broad face, double chin, and fair, long pipe, uttering
clouds of tobacco smoke, instead of idle speeches; or
Van Bummel, the schoolmaster, doling forth the contents of an ancient newspaper. In place of these, a
lean bilious-looking fellow, with his pockets full of
handbills, was haranguing vehemently about rights of
citizens—election—members of Congress—liberty—
Bunker   Hill—heroes   of   seventy-six—and   other
words, that were a perfect Babylonish jargon to the
bewildered Van Winkle.

The appearance of Rip, with his long, grizzled
beard, his rusty fowling-piece, his uncouth dress, and
the army of women and children that had gathered at
his heels, soon attracted the attention of the tavern

politicians. They crowded round him, eying him from head to foot, with great curiosity. The orator bustled up to him, and drawing him partly aside, inquired "on which side he voted?" Rip stared in vacant stupidity. Another short but busy little fellow pulled him by the arm, and rising on tiptoe, inquired in his ear, "whether he was Federal or Democrat." Rip was equally at a loss to comprehend the question; when a knowing, self-important old gentleman, in a sharp cocked hat, made his way through the crowd, putting them to the right and left with his elbows as he passed, and planting himself before Van Winkle, with one arm a-kimbo, the other resting on his cane, his keen eyes and sharp hat penetrating, as it were, into his very soul, demanded in an austere tone, "what brought him to the election with a gun on his shoulder, and a mob at his heels, and whether he meant to breed a riot in the village?"

"Alas! gentlemen," cried Rip, somewhat dismayed, "I am a poor, quiet man, a native of the place, and a loyal subject of the King, God bless him!"

Here a general shout burst forth from the bystanders:

"A tory! a tory! a spy! a refugee! hustle him! away with him!"

It was with great difficulty that the self-important man in the cocked hat restored order; and having assumed a tenfold austerity of brow, demanded again of the unknown culprit what he came there for, and whom he was seeking. The poor man humbly assured him that he meant no harm, but merely came there in search of some of his neighbors, who used to keep about the tavern.

"Well—who are they?—name them."

Rip bethought himself a moment and inquired, "Where's Nicholas Vedder?"

There was silence for a little while, when an old man replied, in a thin, piping voice, "Nicholas Vedder? why, he is dead and gone these eighteen years! There was a wooden tombstone in the churchyard that used to tell all about him, but that's rotten and gone too."

"Where's Brom Dutcher?"

"Oh, he went off to the army in the beginning of the war; some say he was killed at the storming of Stony Point—others say he was drowned in the squall, at the foot of Anthony's Nose. I don't know —he never came back again."

"Where's Van Bummel, the schoolmaster?"

"He went off to the wars, too; was a great militia general, and is now in Congress."

Rip's heart died away at hearing of these sad changes in his home and friends, and finding himself thus alone in the world. Every answer puzzled him, too, by treating of such enormous lapses of time, and of matters which he could not understand: war—Congress—Stony Point!—he had no courage to ask after any more friends, but cried out in despair, "Does nobody here know Rip Van Winkle?"

"Oh, Rip Van Winkle!" exclaimed two or three. "Oh, to be sure! that's Rip Van Winkle yonder, leaning against the tree."

Rip looked, and beheld a precise counterpart of himself as he went up the mountain; apparently as lazy, and certainly as ragged. The poor fellow was now completely confounded. He doubted his own identity, and whether he was himself or another man. In the midst of his bewilderment, the man in the cocked hat demanded who he was, and what was his name?

"God knows," exclaimed he at his wits' end; "I'm not myself—I'm somebody else—that's me yonder—no—that's somebody else, got into my shoes—I was myself last night, but I fell asleep on the mountain, and they've changed my gun, and everything's changed, and I'm changed, and I can't tell what's my name, or who I am!"

The bystanders began now to look at each other, nod, wink significantly, and tap their fingers against their foreheads. There was a whisper, also, about securing the gun, and keeping the old fellow from doing mischief; at the very suggestion of which the self-important man with the cocked hat retired with some precipitation. At this critical moment a fresh, comely woman passed through the throng to get a peep at the gray-bearded man. She had a chubby child in her arms, which, frightened at his looks, began to cry. "Hush, Rip," cried she, "hush, you little fool; the old man won't hurt you." The name of the child, the air of the mother, the tone of her voice, all awakened a train of recollections in his mind.

"What is your name, my good woman?" asked he.

"Judith Gardenier."

"And your father's name?"

"Ah, poor man, his name was Rip Van Winkle; it's twenty years since he went away from home with his gun, and never has been heard of since—his dog came home without him; but whether he shot himself, or was carried away by the Indians, nobody can tell. I was then but a little girl."

Rip had but one question more to ask; but he put it with a faltering voice:

"Where's your mother?"

Oh, she too had died but a short time since: she broke a blood-vessel in a fit of passion at a New England pedler.

There was a drop of comfort, at least, in this intelligence. The honest man could contain himself no longer. He caught his daughter and her child in his arms. "I am your father!" cried he—"Young Rip Van Winkle once—old Rip Van Winkle now!—Does nobody know poor Rip Van Winkle?"

All stood amazed, until an old woman, tottering out from among the crowd, put her hand to her brow, and peering under it in his face for a moment, exclaimed, "Sure enough! it is Rip Van Winkle—it is himself. Welcome home again, old neighbor! Why, where have you been these twenty long years?"

Rip's story was soon told, for the whole twenty years had been to him but as one night. The neighbors stared when they heard it; some were seen to wink at each other, and put their tongues in their cheeks; and the self-important man in the cocked hat, who, when the alarm was over, had returned to the field, screwed down the corners of his mouth, and shook his head—upon which there was a general shaking of the head throughout the assemblage.

It was determined, however, to take the opinion of old Peter Vanderdonk, who was seen slowly advancing up the road. He was a descendant of the historian of that name, who wrote one of the earliest accounts of the province. Peter was the most ancient inhabitant of the village, and well versed in all the wonderful events and traditions of the neighborhood. He recollected Rip at once, and corroborated his story in the most satisfactory manner. He assured the company that it was a fact, handed down from his ancestor, the historian, that the Kaatskill Mountains had always been haunted by strange beings. That it was affirmed that the great Hendrik Hudson, the first discoverer of the river and country, kept a kind of vigil there every twenty years, with his crew of the "Half-moon," being permitted in this way to revisit the scenes of his enterprise, and keep a guardian eye upon the river and the great city called by his name. That his father had once seen them in their old Dutch dresses playing at nine-pins in a hollow of the mountain; and that he himself had heard, one summer afternoon, the sound of their balls, like distant peals of thunder.

To make a long story short, the company broke up, and returned to the more important concerns of the election. Rip's daughter took him home to live with her; she had a snug, well-furnished house, and a stout, cheery farmer for a husband, whom Rip recol-

lected for one of the urchins that used to climb upon
his back.   As to Rip's son and heir, who was the
ditto of himself, seen leaning against the tree, he was
employed to work on the farm; but evinced a heredi-
tary disposition to attend to anything else but his
business.

Rip now resumed his old walks and habits; he soon
found many of his former cronies, though all rather
the worse for the wear and tear of time; and preferred making friends among the rising generation,
with whom he soon grew into great favor.

Having nothing to do at home, and being arrived
at that happy age when a man can do nothing with
impunity, he took his place once more on the bench,
at the inn door, and was reverenced as one of the
patriarchs of the village, and a chronicle of the old
times "before the war." It was some time before
he could get into the regular track of gossip, or could
be made to comprehend the strange events that had
taken place during his torpor. How that there had
been a revolutionary war—that the country had
thrown off the yoke of old England—and that, instead of being a subject of his majesty George the
Third, he was now a free citizen of the United States.
Rip, in fact, was no politician; the changes of states
and empires made but little impression on him; but
there was one species of despotism under which he
had long groaned, and that was—petticoat government.   Happily, that was at an end; he had got his
neck out of the yoke of matrimony, and could go in
and out whenever he pleased, without dreading the

Washington Irving

6

tyranny of Dame Van Winkle. Whenever her name was mentioned, however, he shook his head, shrugged his shoulders, and cast up his eyes; which might pass either for an expression of resignation to his fate, or joy at his deliverance.

He used to tell his story to every stranger that arrived at Mr. Doolittle's hotel. He was observed, at first, to vary on some points every time he told it, which was doubtless owing to his having so recently awaked. It at last settled down precisely to the tale I have related, and not a man, woman, or child in the neighborhood but knew it by heart. Some always pretended to doubt the reality of it, and insisted that Rip had been out of his head, and that this was one point on which he always remained flighty. The old Dutch inhabitants, however, almost universally gave it full credit. Even to this day, they never hear a thunderstorm of a summer afternoon about the Kaatskill but they say Hendrik Hudson and his crew are at their game of nine-pins; and it is a common wish of all henpecked husbands in the neighborhood, when life hangs heavy on their hands, that they might have a quieting draught out of Rip Van Winkle's flagon.

THE MURDERS IN THE RUE MORGUE

BY EDGAR ALLAN POE

Edgar Allan Poe (born January 19, 1809, in Boston, died October 3, 1849) is possibly the most shining illustration of that definition of genius which finds it to consist in "the capacity for taking infinite pains." This is especially noticeable in his tales of the discovery of treasure and detection of crime by close analysis of the surrounding circumstances. Of "The Murders in the Rue Morgue" in particular Brander Matthews writes: "It is indeed a story of the most marvelous skill. It was the first of its kind, and to this day it remains a model, not only unsurpassed, but unapproachable. It was the first of detective stories; and it has had thousands of imitations and no rival. The originality, the ingenuity, the verisimilitude of this tale and of its fellows are beyond all praise. Poe had a faculty which one may call imaginative ratiocination to a degree beyond all other writers of fiction."

THE MURDERS IN THE RUE MORGUE

BY EDGAR ALLAN POE

" What song the Syrens sang, or what name Achilles assumed when he hid him-self among women, although puzzling questions, are not beyond *all* conjecture."
—*Sir Thomas Browne.*

THE mental features discoursed of as the an-alytical are, in themselves, but little suscep-tible of analysis. We appreciate them only in their effects. We know of them, among other things, that they are always to their possessor, when inordinately possessed, a source of the liveliest enjoy-ment. As the strong man exults in his physical abil-ity, delighting in such exercises as call his muscles into action, so glories the analyst in that moral activ-ity which disentangles. He derives pleasure from even the most trivial occupations bringing his talent into play. He is fond of enigmas, of conundrums, hieroglyphics; exhibiting in his solutions of each a degree of acumen which appears to the ordinary ap-prehension preternatural. His results, brought about by the very soul and essence of method, have, in truth, the whole air of intuition.

The faculty of resolution is possibly much invig-orated by mathematical study, and especially by that highest branch of it which, unjustly, and merely on account of its retrograde operations, has been called, as

if par excellence, analysis. Yet to calculate is not in
itself to analyze. A chess-player, for example, does
the one, without effort at the other. It follows that
the game of chess, in its effects upon mental character, is greatly misunderstood. I am not now writing a treatise, but simply prefacing a somewhat peculiar narrative by observations very much at random;
I will, therefore, take occasion to assert that the
higher powers of the reflective intellect are more decidedly and more usefully tasked by the unosten-
tatious game of draughts than by all the elaborate
frivolity of chess. In this latter, where the pieces
have different and bizarre motions, with various and
variable values, what is only complex is mistaken (a
not unusual error) for what is profound. The attention is here called powerfully into play. If it flag
for an instant, an oversight is committed, resulting in
injury or defeat. The possible moves being not only
manifold, but involute, the chances of such oversights
are multiplied; and in nine cases out of ten, it is the
more concentrative rather than the more acute player
who conquers. In draughts, on the contrary, where
the moves are unique and have but little variation,
the probabilities of inadvertence are diminished, and
the mere attention being left comparatively unem-
ployed, what advantages are obtained by either party
are obtained by superior acumen. To be less abstract,
let us suppose a game of draughts where the pieces
are reduced to four kings, and where, of course, no
oversight is to be expected. It is obvious that here
the victory can be decided (the players being at all

équal) only by some recherché movement, the result of some strong exertion of the intellect. Deprived of ordinary resources the analyst throws himself into the spirit of his opponent, identifies himself therewith, and not infrequently sees thus, at a glance, the sole methods (sometimes indeed absurdly simple ones) by which he may seduce into error or hurry into miscalculation.

Whist has long been known for its influence upon what is termed the calculating power; and men of the highest order of intellect have been known to take an apparently unaccountable delight in it, while eschewing chess as frivolous. Beyond doubt there is nothing of a similar nature so greatly tasking the faculty of analysis. The best chess player in Christendom may be little more than the best player of chess; but proficiency in whist implies capacity for success in all those more important undertakings where mind struggles with mind. When I say proficiency, I mean that perfection in the game which includes a comprehension of all the sources whence legitimate advantage may be derived. These are not only manifold, but multiform, and lie frequently among recesses of thought altogether inaccessible to the ordinary understanding. To observe attentively is to remember distinctly; and, so far, the concentrative chess-player will do very well at whist; while the rules of Hoyle (themselves based upon the mere mechanism of the game) are sufficiently and generally comprehensible. Thus to have a retentive memory, and proceed by "the book," are points commonly regarded as the sum total of good playing. But it is in matters beyond the limits of mere rule that the skill of the analyst is evinced. He makes, in silence, a host of observations and inferences. So, perhaps, do his companions; and the difference in the extent of the information obtained lies not so much in the validity of the inference as in the quality of the observation. The necessary knowledge is that of what to observe. Our player confines himself not at all; nor, because the game is the object, does he reject deductions from things external to the game. He examines the countenance of his partner, comparing it carefully with that of each of his opponents. He considers the mode of assorting the cards in each hand; often counting trump by trump, and honor by honor, through the glances bestowed by their holders upon each. He notes every variation of face as the play progresses, gathering a fund of thought from the differences in the expression of certainty, of surprise, of triumph, or chagrin. From the manner of gathering up a trick he judges whether the person taking it can make another in the suit. He recognizes what is played through feint, by the manner with which it is thrown upon the table. A casual or inadvertent word; the accidental dropping or turning of a card, with the accompanying anxiety or carelessness in regard to its concealment; the counting of the tricks, with the order of their arrangement; embarrassment, hesitation, eagerness, or trepidation—all afford, to his apparently intuitive perception, indications of the true state of affairs. The first two or

three rounds having been played, he is in full posses-
sion of the contents of each hand, and thenceforward puts down his cards with as absolute a precision
of purpose as if the rest of the party had turned outward the faces of their own.

The analytical power should not be confounded
with simple ingenuity; for while the analyst is necessarily ingenious, the ingenious man is often remarkably incapable of analysis. The constructive
or combining power, by which ingenuity is usually
manifested, and to which the phrenologists (I believe erroneously) have assigned a separate organ, supposing it a primitive faculty, has been so frequently
seen in those whose intellect bordered otherwise upon
idiocy, as to have attracted general observation
among writers on morals. Between ingenuity and
the analytic ability there exists a difference far
greater, indeed, than that between the fancy and the
imagination, but of a character very strictly analogous. It will be found, in fact, that the ingenious are
always fanciful, and the truly imaginative never
otherwise than analytic.

The narrative which follows will appear to the
reader somewhat in the light of a commentary upon
the propositions just advanced.

Residing in Paris during the spring and part of the
summer of 18—, I there became acquainted with a
Monsieur C. Auguste Dupin. This young gentleman
was of an excellent, indeed of an illustrious family,
but, by a variety of untoward events, had been reduced to such poverty that the energy of his character

succumbed beneath it, and he ceased to bestir himself
in the world, or to care for the retrieval of his fortunes. By courtesy of his creditors, there still remained in his possession a small remnant of his patri-
mony; and, upon the income arising from this, he
managed, by means of a rigorous economy, to procure the necessaries of life, without troubling himself
about its superfluities. Books, indeed, were his sole
luxuries, and in Paris these are easily obtained.

Our first meeting was at an obscure library in the
Rue Montmartre, where the accident of our both being in search of the same very rare and very remarkable volume brought us into closer communion. We
saw each other again and again. I was deeply interested in the little family history which he detailed to
me with all the candor which a Frenchman indulges
whenever mere self is the theme. I was astonished,
too, at the vast extent of his reading; and, above all, I
felt my soul enkindled within me by the wild fervor
and the vivid freshness of his imagination. Seeking
in Paris the objects I then sought, I felt that the
society of such a man would be to me a treasure beyond price; and this feeling I frankly confided to him.
It was at length arranged that we should live together
during my stay in the city; and as my worldly circumstances were somewhat less embarrassed than his
own, I was permitted to be at the expense of renting,
and furnishing in a style which suited the rather fantastic gloom of our common temper, a time-eaten and
grotesque mansion, long deserted through superstitions into which we did not inquire, and tottering to

its fall in a retired and desolate portion of the Faubourg St. Germain.

Had the routine of our life at this place been known to the world, we should have been regarded as madmen—although, perhaps, as madmen of a harmless nature. Our seclusion was perfect. We admitted no visitors. Indeed, the locality of our retirement had been carefully kept a secret from my own former associates; and it had been many years since Dupin had ceased to know or be known in Paris. We existed within ourselves alone.

It was a freak of fancy in my friend (for what else shall I call it?) to be enamored of the night for her own sake; and into this bizarrerie, as into all his others, I quietly fell, giving myself up to his wild whims with a perfect abandon. The sable divinity would not herself dwell with us always; but we could counterfeit her presence. At the first dawn of the morning we closed all the massy shutters of our old building; lighted a couple of tapers which, strongly perfumed, threw out only the ghastliest and feeblest of rays. By the aid of these we then busied our souls in dreams—reading, writing, or conversing, until warned by the clock of the advent of the true Darkness. Then we sallied forth into the streets, arm in arm, continuing the topics of the day, or roaming far and wide until a late hour, seeking, amid the wild lights and shadows of the populous city, that infinity of mental excitement which quiet observation can afford.

At such times I could not help remarking and admiring (although from his rich ideality I had been prepared to expect it) a peculiar analytic ability in Dupin. He seemed, too, to take an eager delight in its exercise—if not exactly in its display—and did not hesitate to confess the pleasure thus derived. He boasted to me with a low, chuckling laugh, that most men, in respect to himself, wore windows in their bosoms, and was wont to follow up such assertions by direct and very startling proofs of his intimate knowledge of my own. His manner at these moments was frigid and abstract; his eyes were vacant in expression; while his voice, usually a rich tenor, rose into a treble which would have sounded petulant but for the deliberateness and entire distinctness of the enunciation. Observing him in these moods, I often dwelt meditatively upon the old philosophy of the Bi-Part Soul, and amused myself with the fancy of a double Dupin—the creative and the resolvent.

Let it not be supposed, from what I have just said, that I am detailing any mystery, or penning any romance. What I have described in the Frenchman was merely the result of an excited, or perhaps of a diseased intelligence. But of the character of his remarks at the periods in question an example will best convey the idea.

We were strolling one night down a long dirty street, in the vicinity of the Palais Royal. Being both, apparently, occupied with thought, neither of us had spoken a syllable for fifteen minutes at least. All at once Dupin broke forth with these words:

"He is a very little fellow, that's true, and would do better for the Théâtre des Variétés."

"There can be no doubt of that," I replied, unwittingly, and not at first observing (so much had I been absorbed in reflection) the extraordinary manner in which the speaker had chimed in with my meditations. In an instant afterward I recollected myself, and my astonishment was profound.

"Dupin," said I, gravely, "this is beyond my comprehension. I do not hesitate to say that I am amazed, and can scarcely credit my senses. How was it possible you should know I was thinking of—?" Here I paused, to ascertain beyond a doubt whether he really knew of whom I thought.

"—— of Chantilly," said he; "why do you pause? You were remarking to yourself that his diminutive figure unfitted him for tragedy."

That was precisely what had formed the subject of my reflections. Chantilly was a quondam cobbler of the Rue St. Dennis, who, becoming stage-mad, had attempted the rôle of Xerxes, in Crébillon's tragedy so called, and been notoriously pasquinaded for his pains.

"Tell me, for Heaven's sake," I exclaimed, "the method—if method there is—by which you have been enabled to fathom my soul in this matter." In fact, I was even more startled than I would have been willing to express.

"It was the fruiterer," replied my friend, "who brought you to the conclusion that the mender of soles was not of sufficient height for Xerxes *et id genus omne.*"

"The fruiterer!—you astonish me—I know no fruiterer whomsoever."

"The man who ran up against you as we entered the street—it may have been fifteen minutes ago."

I now remembered that, in fact, a fruiterer, carrying upon his head a large basket of apples, had nearly thrown me down, by accident, as we passed from the Rue C—— into the thoroughfare where we stood; but what this had to do with Chantilly I could not possibly understand.

There was not a particle of charlatânerie about Dupin. "I will explain," he said, "and that you may comprehend all clearly, we will first retrace the course of your meditations, from the moment in which I spoke to you until that of the rencontre with the fruiterer in question. The larger links of the chain run thus—Chantilly, Orion, Dr. Nichols, Epicurus, Stereotomy, the street stones, the fruiterer."

There are few persons who have not, at some period of their lives, amused themselves in retracing the steps by which particular conclusions of their own minds have been attained. The occupation is often full of interest; and he who attempts it for the first time is astonished by the apparently illimitable distance and incoherence between the starting-point and the goal. What, then, must have been my amazement when I heard the Frenchman speak what he had just spoken, and when I could not help acknowledging that he had spoken the truth. He continued:

"We had been talking of horses, if I remember aright, just before leaving the Rue C——. This was

the last subject we discussed. As we crossed into
this street, a fruiterer, with a large basket upon his
head, brushing quickly past us, thrust you upon a pile
of paving-stones collected at a spot where the cause-
way is undergoing repair. You stepped upon one of
the loose fragments, slipped, slightly strained your
ankle, appeared vexed or sulky, muttered a few
words, turned to look at the pile, and then proceeded
in silence. I was not particularly attentive to what
you did; but observation has become with me, of
late, a species of necessity.

"You kept your eyes upon the ground—glancing,
with a petulant expression, at the holes and ruts in
the pavement (so that I saw you were still thinking
of the stones), until we reached the little alley called
Lamartine, which has been paved, by way of experiment, with the overlapping and riveted blocks.
Here your countenance brightened up, and, perceiving
your lips move, I could not doubt that you murmured
the word 'stereotomy,' a term very affectedly applied
to this species of pavement. I knew that you could
not say to yourself 'stereotomy' without being
brought to think of atomies, and thus of the theories
of Epicurus; and since, when we discussed this subject not very long ago, I mentioned to you how singularly, yet with how little notice, the vague guesses
of that noble Greek had met with confirmation in
the late nebular cosmogony, I felt that you could not
avoid casting your eyes upward to the great nebula in
Orion, and I certainly expected that you would do so.
You did look up; and I was now assured that I had

correctly followed your steps. But in that bitter ti-
rade upon Chantilly, which appeared in yesterday's
'Musée,' the satirist, making some disgraceful allu-
sions to the cobbler's change of name upon assuming
the buskin, quoted a Latin line about which we have
often conversed. I mean the line

Perdidit antiquum litera prima sonum.

I had told you that this was in reference to Orion,
formerly written Urion; and, from certain pungen-
cies connected with this explanation, I was aware
that you could not have forgotten it. It was clear,
therefore, that you would not fail to combine the
two ideas of Orion and Chantilly. That you did
combine them I saw by the character of the smile
which passed over your lips. You thought of the
poor cobbler's immolation. So far, you had been
stooping in your gait; but now I saw you draw yourself up to your full height. I was then sure that you
reflected upon the diminutive figure of Chantilly. At
this point I interrupted your meditations to remark
that as, in fact, he was a very little fellow—that
Chantilly—he would do better at the Théâtre des
Variétés."

Not long after this, we were looking over an evening edition of the "Gazette des Tribunaux," when the
following paragraphs arrested our attention.

"*Extraordinary Murders.*—This morning, about
three o'clock, the inhabitants of the Quartier St. Roch
were roused from sleep by a succession of terrific
shrieks, issuing, apparently, from the fourth story of

a house in the Rue Morgue, known to be in the sole occupancy of one Madame L'Espanaye, and her daughter, Mademoiselle Camille L'Espanaye. After some delay, occasioned by a fruitless attempt to procure admission in the usual manner, the gateway was broken in with a crowbar, and eight or ten of the neighbors entered, accompanied by two gendarmes. By this time the cries had ceased; but, as the party rushed up the first flight of stairs, two or more rough voices, in angry contention, were distinguished, and seemed to proceed from the upper part of the house. As the second landing was reached, these sounds, also, had ceased, and everything remained perfectly quiet. The party spread themselves, and hurried from room to room. Upon arriving at a large back chamber in the fourth story (the door of which, being found locked, with the key inside, was forced open), a spectacle presented itself which struck every one present not less with horror than with astonishment.

"The apartment was in the wildest disorder—the furniture broken and thrown about in all directions. There was only one bedstead; and from this the bed had been removed, and thrown into the middle of the floor. On a chair lay a razor, besmeared with blood. On the hearth were two or three long and thick tresses of gray human hair, also dabbled with blood, and seeming to have been pulled out by the roots. Upon the floor were found four Napoleons, an earring of topaz, three large silver spoons, three smaller of métal d'Alger, and two bags, containing nearly four thousand francs in gold. The drawers of a bureau, which stood in one corner, were open, and had been, apparently, rifled, although many articles still remained in them. A small iron safe was discovered under the bed (not under the bedstead). It was open, with the key still in the door. It had no contents beyond a few old letters, and other papers of little consequence.

"Of Madame L'Espanaye no traces were here seen; but an unusual quantity of soot being observed in the fireplace, a search was made in the chimney, and (horrible to relate!) the corpse of the daughter, head downward, was dragged therefrom; it having been thus forced up the narrow aperture for a considerable distance. The body was quite warm. Upon examining it, many excoriations were perceived, no doubt occasioned by the violence with which it had been thrust up and disengaged. Upon the face were many severe scratches, and, upon the throat, dark bruises, and deep indentations of finger nails, as if the deceased had been throttled to death.

"After a thorough investigation of every portion of the house without further discovery, the party made its way into a small paved yard in the rear of the building, where lay the corpse of the old lady, with her throat so entirely cut that, upon an attempt to raise her, the head fell off. The body, as well as the head, was fearfully mutilated—the former so much so as scarcely to retain any semblance of humanity.

"To this horrible mystery there is not as yet, we believe, the slightest clew."

The next day's paper had these additional particulars:

"*The Tragedy in the Rue Morgue.*—Many individuals have been examined in relation to this most extraordinary and frightful affair" [the word 'affaire' has not yet, in France, that levity of import which it conveys with us], "but nothing whatever has transpired to throw light upon it. We give below all the material testimony elicited.

"*Pauline Dubourg,* laundress, deposes that she has known both the deceased for three years, having washed for them during that period. The old lady and her daughter seemed on good terms—very affectionate toward each other. They were excellent pay. Could not speak in regard to their mode or means of living. Believed that Madame L. told fortunes for a living. Was reputed to have money put by. Never met any person in the house when she called for the clothes or took them home. Was sure that they had no servant in employ. There appeared to be no furniture in any part of the building except in the fourth story.

"*Pierre Moreau,* tobacconist, deposes that he has been in the habit of selling small quantities of tobacco and snuff to Madame L'Espanaye for nearly four years. Was born in the neighborhood, and has always resided there. The deceased and her daughter had occupied the house in which the corpses were found, for more than six years. It was formerly occupied by a jeweler, who under-let the upper rooms to various persons. The house was the property of

Madame L. She became dissatisfied with the abuse of the premises by her tenant, and moved into them herself, refusing to let any portion. The old lady was childish. Witness had seen the daughter some five or six times during the six years. The two lived an exceedingly retired life—were reputed to have money. Had heard it said among the neighbors that Madame L. told fortunes—did not believe it. Had never seen any person enter the door except the old lady and her daughter, a porter once or twice, and a physician some eight or ten times.

"Many other persons, neighbors, gave evidence to the same effect. No one was spoken of as frequenting the house. It was not known whether there were any living connections of Madame L. and her daughter. The shutters of the front windows were seldom opened. Those in the rear were always closed, with the exception of the large back room, fourth story. The house was a good house—not very old.

"*Isidore Musèt*, gendarme, deposes that he was called to the house about three o'clock in the morning, and found some twenty or thirty persons at the gateway, endeavoring to gain admittance. Forced it open, at length, with a bayonet—not with a crow-bar. Had but little difficulty in getting it open, on account of its being a double or folding gate, and bolted neither at bottom nor top. The shrieks were contin-ued until the gate was forced—and then suddenly ceased. They seemed to be screams of some per-son (or persons) in great agony—were loud and drawn out, not short and quick. Witness led the way upstairs. Upon reaching the first landing, heard two voices in loud and angry contention—the one a gruff voice, the other much shriller—a very strange voice. Could distinguish some words of the former, which was that of a Frenchman. Was positive that it was not a woman's voice. Could distinguish the words '*sacré*' and '*diable*.' The shrill voice was that of a foreigner. Could not be sure whether it was the voice of a man or of a woman. Could not make out what was said, but believed the language to be Spanish. The state of the room and of the bodies was described by this witness as we described them yesterday.

"*Henri Duval,* a neighbor, and by trade a silversmith, deposes that he was one of the party who first entered the house. Corroborates the testimony of Musèt in general. As soon as they forced an entrance, they reclosed the door, to keep out the crowd, which collected very fast, notwithstanding the lateness of the hour. The shrill voice, this witness thinks, was that of an Italian. Was certain it was not French. Could not be sure that it was a man's voice. It might have been a woman's. Was not acquainted with the Italian language. Could not distinguish the words, but was convinced by the intonation that the speaker was an Italian. Knew Madame L. and her daughter. Had conversed with both frequently. Was sure that the shrill voice was not that of either of the deceased.

"—— *Odenheimer, restaurateur.*—This witness volunteered his testimony. Not speaking French,

was examined through an interpreter. Is a native
of Amsterdam. Was passing the house at the time
of the shrieks. They lasted for several minutes—
probably ten. They were long and loud—very awful and distressing. Was one of those who entered
the building. Corroborated the previous evidence in
every respect but one. Was sure that the shrill voice
was that of a man—of a Frenchman. Could not distinguish the words uttered. They were loud and
quick—unequal—spoken apparently in fear as well as
in anger. The voice was harsh—not so much shrill
as harsh. Could not call it a shrill voice. The gruff
voice said repeatedly, 'sacré,' 'diable,' and once 'mon
Dieu.'

"Jules Mignaud, banker, of the firm of Mignaud et
Fils, Rue Deloraine. Is the elder Mignaud. Madame
L'Espanaye had some property. Had opened an account with his banking house in the spring of the
year (eight years previously). Made frequent de-
posits in small sums. Had checked for nothing
until the third day before her death, when she took
out in person the sum of 4,000 francs. This sum
was paid in gold, and a clerk sent home with the
money.

"Adolphe Le Bon, clerk to Mignaud et Fils, deposes that on the day in question, about noon, he accompanied Madame L'Espanaye to her residence with
the 4,000 francs, put up in two bags. Upon the door
being opened, Mademoiselle L. appeared and took
from his hands one of the bags, while the old lady
relieved him of the other. He then bowed and de-

parted. Did not see any person in the street at the time. It is a by-street—very lonely.

"*William Bird,* tailor, deposes that he was one of the party who entered the house. Is an Englishman. Has lived in Paris two years. Was one of the first to ascend the stairs. Heard the voices in contention. The gruff voice was that of a Frenchman. Could make out several words, but can not now remember all. Heard distinctly '*sacré*' and '*mon Dieu.*' There was a sound at the moment as if of several persons struggling—a scraping and scuffling sound. The shrill voice was very loud—louder than the gruff one. Is sure that it was not the voice of an Englishman. Appeared to be that of a German. Might have been a woman's voice. Does not understand German.

"Four of the above-named witnesses being recalled, deposed that the door of the chamber in which was found the body of Mademoiselle L. was locked on the inside when the party reached it. Everything was perfectly silent—no groans or noises of any kind. Upon forcing the door no person was seen. The windows, both of the back and front room, were down and firmly fastened from within. A door between the two rooms was closed but not locked. The door leading from the front room into the passage was locked, with the key on the inside. A small room in the front of the house, on the fourth story, at the head of the passage, was open, the door being ajar. This room was crowded with old beds, boxes, and so forth. These were carefully removed and searched. There was not an inch of any portion of the house which was not carefully searched. Sweeps were sent up and down the chimneys. The house was a four-story one, with garrets (*mansardes*). A trap-door on the roof was nailed down very securely—did not appear to have been opened for years. The time elapsing between the hearing of the voices in contention and the breaking open of the room door was variously stated by the witnesses. Some made it as short as three minutes—some as long as five. The door was opened with difficulty.

"*Alfonzo Garco,* undertaker, deposes that he resides in the Rue Morgue. Is a native of Spain. Was one of the party who entered the house. Did not proceed upstairs. Is nervous, and was apprehensive of the consequences of agitation. Heard the voices in contention. The gruff voice was that of a Frenchman. Could not distinguish what was said. The shrill voice was that of an Englishman—is sure of this. Does not understand the English language, but judges by the intonation.

"*Alfonzo Garcio,* undertaker, deposes that he was among the first to ascend the stairs. Heard the voices in question. The gruff voice was that of a Frenchman. Distinguished several words. The speaker appeared to be expostulating. Could not make out the words of the shrill voice. Spoke quick and unevenly. Thinks it the voice of a Russian. Corroborates the general testimony. Is an Italian. Never conversed with a native of Russia.

"Several witnesses, recalled, here testified that the chimneys of all the rooms on the fourth story were

too narrow to admit the passage of a human being. By 'sweeps,' were meant cylindrical sweeping-
brushes, such as are employed by those who clean
chimneys. These brushes were passed up and down
every flue in the house. There is no back passage by
which any one could have descended while the party
proceeded upstairs. The body of Mademoiselle L'Espanaye was so firmly wedged in the chimney that it
could not be got down until four or five of the party
united their strength.

"*Paul Dumas*, physician, deposes that he was called
to view the bodies about daybreak. They were both
then lying on the sacking of the bedstead in the chamber where Mademoiselle L. was found. The corpse of
the young lady was much bruised and excoriated. The
fact that it had been thrust up the chimney would
sufficiently account for these appearances. The throat
was greatly chafed. There were several deep scratches
just below the chin, together with a series of livid spots
which were evidently the impression of fingers. The
face was fearfully discolored, and the eyeballs pro-
truded. The tongue had been partially bitten through.
A large bruise was discovered upon the pit of the stomach, produced, apparently, by the pressure of a knee.
In the opinion of M. Dumas, Mademoiselle L'Espanaye had been throttled to death by some person or
persons unknown. The corpse of the mother was horribly mutilated. All the bones of the right leg and
arm were more or less shattered. The left tibia much
splintered, as well as all the ribs of the left side. Whole
body dreadfully bruised and discolored. It was not pos-

sible to say how the injuries had been inflicted. A
heavy club of wood, or a broad bar of iron—a chair—
any large, heavy and obtuse weapon—would have produced such results, if wielded by the hands of a very
powerful man. No woman could have inflicted the
blows with any weapon. The head of the deceased,
when seen by witness, was entirely separated from the
body, and was also greatly shattered. The throat had
evidently been cut with some very sharp instrument—
probably with a razor.

"*Alexandre Étienne*, surgeon, was called with M.
Dumas to view the bodies. Corroborated the testimony and the opinions of M. Dumas.

"Nothing further of importance was elicited, although several other persons were examined. A murder so mysterious, and so perplexing in all its particulars, was never before committed in Paris—if indeed
a murder has been committed at all. The police are
entirely at fault—an unusual occurrence in affairs of
this nature. There is not, however, the shadow of a
clew apparent."

The evening edition of the paper stated that the
greatest excitement still continued in the Quartier St.
Roch—that the premises in question had been carefully
researched, and fresh examinations of witnesses insti-
tuted, but all to no purpose. A postscript, however,
mentioned that Adolphe Le Bon had been arrested and
imprisoned—although nothing appeared to criminate
him beyond the facts already detailed.

Dupin seemed singularly interested in the progress
of this affair—at least so I judged from his manner,

for he made no comments. It was only after the announcement that Le Bon had been imprisoned that he asked me my opinion respecting the murders.

I could merely agree with all Paris in considering them an insoluble mystery. I saw no means by which it would be possible to trace the murderer.

"We must not judge of the means," said Dupin, "by this shell of an examination. The Parisian police, so much extolled for acumen, are cunning, but no more. There is no method in their proceedings, beyond the method of the moment. They make a vast parade of measures; but, not unfrequently, these are so ill-adapted to the objects proposed, as to put us in mind of Monsieur Jourdain's calling for his robe-de-chambre —*pour mieux entendre la musique*. The results attained by them are not unfrequently surprising, but, for the most part, are brought about by simple diligence and activity. When these qualities are unavailing, their schemes fail. Vidocq, for example, was a good guesser, and a persevering man. But, without educated thought, he erred continually by the very intensity of his investigations. He impaired his vision by holding the object too close. He might see, perhaps, one or two points with unusual clearness, but in so doing he, necessarily, lost sight of the matter as a whole. Thus there is such a thing as being too profound. Truth is not always in a well. In fact, as regards the more important knowledge, I do believe that she is invariably superficial. The depth lies in the valleys where we seek her, and not upon the mountain-tops where she is found. The modes and sources of this kind of error are well typified in the contemplation of the heavenly bodies. To look at a star by glances— to view it in a sidelong way, by turning toward it the exterior portions of the retina (more susceptible of feeble impressions of light than the interior), is to behold the star distinctly—is to have the best appreciation of its lustre—a lustre which grows dim just in proportion as we turn our vision fully upon it. A greater number of rays actually fall upon the eye in the latter case, but in the former there is the more refined capacity for comprehension. By undue profundity we perplex and enfeeble thought; and it is possible to make even Venus herself vanish from the firmament by a scrutiny too sustained, too concentrated, or too direct.

"As for these murders, let us enter into some examinations for ourselves, before we make up an opinion respecting them. An inquiry will afford us amusement" [I thought this an odd term, so applied, but said nothing], "and besides, Le Bon once rendered me a service for which I am not ungrateful. We will go and see the premises with our own eyes. I know G——, the Prefect of Police, and shall have no difficulty in obtaining the necessary permission."

The permission was obtained, and we proceeded at once to the Rue Morgue. This is one of those miserable thoroughfares which intervene between the Rue Richelieu and the Rue St. Roch. It was late in the afternoon when we reached it, as this quarter is at a great distance from that in which we resided. The house was readily found; for there were still many

persons gazing up at the closed shutters, with an ob-
jectless curiosity, from the opposite side of the way.
It was an ordinary Parisian house, with a gateway,
on one side of which was a glazed watch-box, with a
sliding panel in the window, indicating a *loge de con-
cierge*. Before going in we walked up the street,
turned down an alley, and then, again turning, passed
in the rear of the building—Dupin, meanwhile, examining the whole neighborhood, as well as the house,
with a minuteness of attention for which I could see
no possible object.

Retracing our steps we came again to the front of
the dwelling, rang, and, having shown our creden-
tials, were admitted by the agents in charge. We went
upstairs—into the chamber where the body of Mademoiselle L'Espanaye had been found, and where both
the deceased still lay. The disorders of the room had,
as usual, been suffered to exist. I saw nothing beyond what had been stated in the "Gazette des Tribunaux." Dupin scrutinized everything—not excepting
the bodies of the victims. We then went into the other
rooms, and into the yard; a gendarme accompanying
us throughout. The examination occupied us until
dark, when we took our departure. On our way home
my companion stepped in for a moment at the office of
one of the daily papers.

I have said that the whims of my friend were manifold, and that *Je les ménagais:*—for this phrase there
is no English equivalent. It was his humor, now, to
decline all conversation on the subject of the murder,
until about noon the next day. He then asked me,

suddenly, if I had observed anything peculiar at the scene of the atrocity.

There was something in his manner of emphasizing the word "peculiar" which caused me to shudder without knowing why.

"No, nothing peculiar," I said; "nothing more, at least, than we both saw stated in the paper."

"The 'Gazette,'" he replied, "has not entered, I fear, into the unusual horror of the thing. But dismiss the idle opinions of this print. It appears to me that this mystery is considered insoluble, for the very reason which should cause it to be regarded as easy of solution—I mean for the *outré* character of its features. The police are confounded by the seeming absence of motive—not for the murder itself—but for the atrocity of the murder. They are puzzled, too, by the seeming impossibility of reconciling the voices heard in contention, with the facts that no one was discovered upstairs but the assassinated Mademoiselle L'Espanaye, and that there were no means of egress without the notice of the party ascending. The wild disorder of the room; the corpse thrust, with the head downward, up the chimney; the frightful mutilation of the body of the old lady; these considerations, with those just mentioned, and others which I need not mention, have sufficed to paralyze the powers, by putting completely at fault the boasted acumen, of the government agents. They have fallen into the gross but common error of confounding the unusual with the abstruse. But it is by these deviations from the plane of the ordinary that reason feels its way, if at all, in its search for the true. In investigations such as we are now pursuing, it should not be so much asked 'what has occurred?' as 'what has occurred that has never occurred before?' In fact, the facility with which I shall arrive, or have arrived, at the solution of this mystery, is in the direct ratio of its apparent insolubility in the eyes of the police."

I stared at the speaker in mute astonishment.

"I am now awaiting," continued he, looking toward the door of our apartment—"I am now awaiting a person who, although perhaps not the perpetrator of these butcheries, must have been in some measure implicated in their perpetration. Of the worst portion of the crimes committed, it is probable that he is innocent. I hope that I am right in this supposition; for upon it I build my expectation of reading the entire riddle. I look for the man here—in this room—every moment. It is true that he may not arrive; but the probability is that he will. Should he come, it will be necessary to detain him. Here are pistols; and we both know how to use them when occasion demands their use."

I took the pistols, scarcely knowing what I did, or believing what I heard, while Dupin went on, very much as if in a soliloquy. I have already spoken of his abstract manner at such times. His discourse was addressed to myself; but his voice, although by no means loud, had that intonation which is commonly employed in speaking to some one at a great distance. His eyes, vacant in expression, regarded only the wall.

"That the voices heard in contention," he said, "by

the party upon the stairs, were not the voices of the women themselves, was fully proved by the evidence. This relieves us of all doubt upon the question whether the old lady could have first destroyed the daughter, and afterward have committed suicide. I speak of this point chiefly for the sake of method; for the strength of Madame L'Espanaye would have been utterly unequal to the task of thrusting her daughter's corpse up the chimney as it was found; and the nature of the wounds upon her own person entirely precludes the idea of self-destruction. Murder, then, has been committed by some third party; and the voices of this third party were those heard in contention. Let me now advert—not to the whole testimony respecting these voices—but to what was peculiar in that testimony. Did you observe anything peculiar about it?"

I remarked that, while all the witnesses agreed in supposing the gruff voice to be that of a Frenchman, there was much disagreement in regard to the shrill, or, as one individual termed it, the harsh voice.

"That was the evidence itself," said Dupin, "but it was not the peculiarity of the evidence. You have observed nothing distinctive. Yet there was something to be observed. The witnesses, as you remark, agreed about the gruff voice; they were here unanimous. But in regard to the shrill voice, the peculiarity is—not that they disagreed—but that, while an Italian, an Englishman, a Spaniard, a Hollander, and a Frenchman attempted to describe it, each one spoke of it as that of a foreigner. Each is sure that it was not the voice of one of his own countrymen. Each likens it—

not to the voice of an individual of any nation with
whose language he is conversant—but the converse.
The Frenchman supposes it the voice of a Spaniard,
and 'might have distinguished some words had he been
acquainted with the Spanish.' The Dutchman main-
tains it to have been that of a Frenchman; but we find
it stated that 'not understanding French this witness
was examined through an interpreter.' The Englishman thinks it the voice of a German, and 'does not
understand German.' The Spaniard 'is sure' that it
was that of an Englishman, but 'judges by the intonation' altogether, 'as he has no knowledge of the
English.' The Italian believes it the voice of a Russian, but 'has never conversed with a native of Russia.'
A second Frenchman differs, moreover, with the first,
and is positive that the voice was that of an Italian;
but, not being cognizant of that tongue, is, like the
Spaniard, 'convinced by the intonation.' Now, how
strangely unusual must that voice have really been,
about which such testimony as this could have been
elicited!—in whose tones, even, denizens of the five
great divisions of Europe could recognize nothing
familiar! You will say that it might have been the
voice of an Asiatic—of an African. Neither Asiatics
nor Africans abound in Paris; but, without denying
the inference, I will now merely call your attention to
three points. The voice is termed by one witness
'harsh rather than shrill.' It is represented by two
others to have been 'quick and unequal.' No words—
no sounds resembling words—were by any witness
mentioned as distinguishable.

"I know not," continued Dupin, "what impression I may have made, so far, upon your own understanding; but I do not hesitate to say that legitimate deductions even from this portion of the testimony—the portion respecting the gruff and shrill voices—are in themselves sufficient to engender a suspicion which should give direction to all further progress in the investigation of the mystery. I said 'legitimate deductions'; but my meaning is not thus fully expressed. I designed to imply that the deductions are the sole proper ones, and that the suspicion arises inevitably from them as the single result. What the suspicion is, however, I will not say just yet. I merely wish you to bear in mind that, with myself, it was sufficiently forcible to give a definite form—a certain tendency—to my inquiries in the chamber.

"Let us now transport ourselves, in fancy, to this chamber. What shall we first seek here? The means of egress employed by the murderers. It is not too much to say that neither of us believes in preternatural events. Madame and Mademoiselle L'Espanaye were not destroyed by spirits. The doers of the deed were material and escaped materially. Then how? Fortunately there is but one mode of reasoning upon the point, and that mode must lead us to a definite decision. Let us examine, each by each, the possible means of egress. It is clear that the assassins were in the room where Mademoiselle L'Espanaye was found, or at least in the room adjoining, when the party ascended the stairs. It is then only from these two apartments that we have to seek issues. The police

have laid bare the floors, the ceiling, and the masonry
of the walls, in every direction. No secret issues
could have escaped their vigilance. But, not trusting
to their eyes, I examined with my own. There were,
then, no secret issues. Both doors leading from the
rooms into the passage were securely locked, with the
keys inside. Let us turn to the chimneys. These,
although of ordinary width for some eight or ten feet
above the hearths, will not admit, throughout their
extent, the body of a large cat. The impossibility of
egress, by means already stated, being thus absolute,
we are reduced to the windows. Through those of
the front room no one could have escaped without
notice from the crowd in the street. The murderers
must have passed, then, through those of the back
room. Now, brought to this conclusion in so un-
equivocal a manner as we are, it is not our part, as
reasoners, to reject it on account of apparent impossibilities. It is only left for us to prove that these
apparent 'impossibilities' are, in reality, not such.

"There are two windows in the chamber. One of
them is unobstructed by furniture, and is wholly visible.
The lower portion of the other is hidden from view by
the head of the unwieldy bedstead which is thrust close
up against it. The former was found securely fastened
from within. It resisted the utmost force of those who
endeavored to raise it. A large gimlet-hole had been
pierced in its frame to the left, and a very stout nail
was found fitted therein, nearly to the head. Upon
examining the other window, a similar nail was seen
similarly fitted in it; and a vigorous attempt to raise

this sash failed also. The police were now entirely satisfied that egress had not been in these directions. And, therefore, it was thought a matter of supererogation to withdraw the nails and open the windows.

"My own examination was somewhat more particular, and was so for the reason I have just given—because here it was, I knew, that all apparent impossibilities must be proved to be not such in reality.

"I proceeded to think thus—*a posteriori*. The murderers did escape from one of these windows. This being so, they could not have refastened the sashes from the inside, as they were found fastened; the consideration which put a stop, through its obviousness, to the scrutiny of the police in this quarter. Yet the sashes were fastened. They must then have the power of fastening themselves. There was no escape from this conclusion. I stepped to the unobstructed casement, withdrew the nail with some difficulty, and attempted to raise the sash. It resisted all my efforts, as I had anticipated. A concealed spring must, I now knew, exist; and this corroboration of my idea convinced me that my premises, at least, were correct, however mysterious still appeared the circumstances attending the nails. A careful search soon brought to light the hidden spring. I pressed it, and, satisfied with the discovery, forbore to upraise the sash.

"I now replaced the nail and regarded it attentively. A person passing out through this window might have reclosed it, and the spring would have caught—but the nail could not have been replaced. The conclusion was plain, and again narrowed in the field of my investigations. The assassins must have escaped through the other window. Supposing, then, the springs upon each sash to be the same, as was probable, there must be found a difference between the nails, or at least between the modes of their fixture. Getting upon the sacking of the bedstead, I looked over the head-board minutely at the second casement. Passing my hand down behind the board, I readily discovered and pressed the spring, which was, as I had supposed, identical in character with its neighbor. I now looked at the nail. It was as stout as the other, and apparently fitted in the same manner—driven in nearly up to the head.

"You will say that I was puzzled; but, if you think so, you must have misunderstood the nature of the inductions. To use a sporting phrase, I had not been once 'at fault.' The scent had never for an instant been lost. There was no flaw in any link of the chain. I had traced the secret to its ultimate result—and that result was the nail. It had, I say, in every respect, the appearance of its fellow in the other window; but this fact was an absolute nullity (conclusive as it might seem to be) when compared with the consideration that here, at this point, terminated the clew. 'There must be something wrong,' I said, 'about the nail.' I touched it; and the head, with about a quarter of an inch of the shank, came off in my fingers. The rest of the shank was in the gimlet-hole where it had been broken off. The fracture was an old one (for its edges were incrusted with rust), and had apparently

been accomplished by the blow of a hammer, which had
partially imbedded, in the top of the bottom sash, the
head portion of the nail. I now carefully replaced
this head portion in the indentation whence I had
taken it, and the resemblance to a perfect nail was
complete—the fissure was invisible. Pressing the
spring, I gently raised the sash for a few inches; the
head went up with it, remaining firm in its bed. I
closed the window, and the semblance of the whole
nail was again perfect.

"This riddle,' so far, was now unriddled. The
assassin had escaped through the window which looked
upon the bed. Dropping of its own accord upon his
exit (or perhaps purposely closed), it had become fastened by the spring, and it was the retention of this
spring which had been mistaken by the police for that
of the nail—further inquiry being thus considered un-
necessary.

"The next question is that of the mode of descent.
Upon this point I had been satisfied in my walk with
you around the building. About five feet and a half
from the casement in question there runs a lightning-
rod. From this rod it would have been impossible for
any one to reach the window itself, to say nothing of
entering it. I observed, however, that the shutters of
the fourth story were of the peculiar kind called
by Parisian carpenters *ferrades*—a kind rarely employed at the present day, but frequently seen upon
very old mansions at Lyons and Bordeaux. They are
in the form of an ordinary door (a single, not a folding door), except that the lower half is latticed or

worked in open trellis—thus affording an excellent
hold for the hands.   In the present instance these
shutters are fully three feet and a half broad.   When
we saw them from the rear of the house, they were
both about half open—that is to say, they stood off at
right angles from the wall.   It is probable that the
police, as well as myself, examined the back of the
tenement; but, if so, in looking at these *ferrades* in
the line of their breadth (as they must have done),
they did not perceive this great breadth itself, or, at
all events, failed to take it into due consideration.   In
fact, having once satisfied themselves that no egress
could have been made in this quarter, they would naturally bestow here a very cursory examination.   It
was clear to me, however, that the shutter belonging
to the window at the head of the bed, would, if swung
fully back to the wall, reach to within two feet of
the lightning-rod.   It was also evident that, by exertion of a very unusual degree of activity and courage,
an entrance into the window, from the rod, might
have been thus effected.   By reaching to the distance
of two feet and a half (we now suppose the shutter
open to its whole extent) a robber might have taken
a firm grasp upon the trellis-work.   Letting go, then,
his hold upon the rod, placing his feet securely against
the wall, and springing boldly from it, he might have
swung the shutter so as to close it, and, if we imagine
the window open at the time, might even have swung
himself into the room.

"I wish you to bear especially in mind that I have
spoken of a very unusual degree of activity as requi-

site to success in so hazardous and so difficult a feat.
It is my design to show you first, that the thing might
possibly have been accomplished; but, secondly and
chiefly, I wish to impress upon your understanding the very extraordinary, the almost preternatural
character of that agility which could have accomplished it.

"You will say, no doubt, using the language of the
law, that 'to make out my case,' I should rather under-
value than insist upon a full estimation of the activity required in this matter. This may be the practice
in law, but it is not the usage of reason. My ultimate
object is only the truth. My immediate purpose is to
lead you to place in juxtaposition that very unusual
activity of which I have just spoken, with that very
peculiar shrill (or harsh) and unequal voice, about
whose nationality no two persons could be found to
agree, and in whose utterance no syllabification could
be detected."

At these words a vague and half-formed conception
of the meaning of Dupin flitted over my mind. I
seemed to be upon the verge of comprehension, without power to comprehend—as men, at times, find themselves upon the brink of remembrance, without being
able, in the end, to remember. My friend went on with
his discourse.

"You will see," he said, "that I have shifted the
question from the mode of egress to that of ingress.
It was my design to convey the idea that both were
effected in the same manner, at the same point. Let
us now revert to the interior of the room. Let us

survey the appearances here.   The drawers of the bureau, it is said, have been rifled, although many articles of apparel still remained within them.   The conclusion here is absurd.   It is a mere guess—a very silly one—and no more.   How are we to know that the articles found in the drawers were not all these drawers had originally contained?   Madame L'Espanaye and her daughter lived an exceedingly retired life—saw no company—seldom went out—had little use for numerous changes of habiliment.   Those found were at least of as good quality as any likely to be possessed by these ladies.   If a thief had taken any, why did he not take the best—why did he not take all? In a word, why did he abandon four thousand francs in gold to incumber himself with a bundle of linen? The gold was abandoned.   Nearly the whole sum mentioned by Monsieur Mignaud, the banker, was discovered, in bags, upon the floor.   I wish you, therefore, to discard from your thoughts the blundering idea of motive, engendered in the brains of the police by that portion of the evidence which speaks of money delivered at the door of the house.   Coincidences ten times as remarkable as this (the delivery of the money, and murder committed within three days upon the party receiving it), happen to all of us every hour of our lives, without attracting even momentary notice.   Coincidences, in general, are great stumbling-blocks in the way of that class of thinkers who have been educated to know nothing of the theory of probabilities—that theory to which the most glorious objects of human research are indebted for the most glorious of illustrations. In the present instance, had the gold been gone, the fact of its delivery three days before would have formed something more than a coincidence. It would have been corroborative of this idea of motive. But, under the real circumstances of the case, if we are to suppose gold the motive of this outrage, we must also imagine the perpetrator so vacillating an idiot as to have abandoned his gold and his motive together.

"Keeping now steadily in mind the points to which I have drawn your attention—that peculiar voice, that unusual agility, and that startling absence of motive in a murder so singularly atrocious as this—let us glance at the butchery itself. Here is a woman strangled to death by manual strength, and thrust up a chimney head downward. Ordinary assassins employ no such mode of murder as this. Least of all do they thus dispose of the murdered. In the manner of thrusting the corpse up the chimney, you will admit that there was something excessively *outré*—something altogether irreconcilable with our common notions of human action, even when we suppose the actors the most depraved of men. Think, too, how great must have been that strength which could have thrust the body up such an aperture so forcibly that the united vigor of several persons was found barely sufficient to drag it down!

"Turn, now, to other indications of the employment of a vigor most marvelous. On the hearth were thick tresses—very thick tresses—of gray human hair. These had been torn out by the roots. You are aware of the great force necessary in tearing thus from the head

even twenty or thirty hairs together. You saw the
locks in question as well as myself. Their roots (a
hideous sight!) were clotted with fragments of the
flesh of the scalp—sure token of the prodigious power
which had been exerted in uprooting perhaps half a
million of hairs at a time. The throat of the old
lady was not merely cut, but the head absolutely severed from the body: the instrument was a mere razor.
I wish you also to look at the brutal ferocity of these
deeds. Of the bruises upon the body of Madame
L'Espanaye I do not speak. Monsieur Dumas, and
his worthy coadjutor Monsieur Étienne, have pro-
nounced that they were inflicted by some obtuse instrument; and so far these gentlemen are very correct. The
obtuse instrument was clearly the stone pavement in
the yard, upon which the victim had fallen from the
window which looked in upon the bed. This idea,
however simple it may now seem, escaped the police
for the same reason that the breadth of the shutters
escaped them—because, by the affair of the nails, their
perceptions had been hermetically sealed against the
possibility of the windows having ever been opened
at all.

"If now, in addition to all these things, you have
properly reflected upon the odd disorder of the chamber, we have gone so far as to combine the ideas of
an agility astounding, a strength superhuman, a ferocity brutal, a butchery without motive, a grotesquerie
in horror absolutely alien from humanity, and a voice
foreign in tone to the ears of men of many nations,
and devoid of all distinct or intelligible syllabification.

What result, then, has ensued? What impression
have I made upon your fancy?"

I felt a creeping of the flesh as Dupin asked me the
question. "A madman," I said, "has done this deed
—some raving maniac, escaped from a neighboring
Maison de Santé."

"In some respects," he replied, "your idea is not
irrelevant. But the voices of madmen, even in their
wildest paroxysms, are never found to tally with that
peculiar voice heard upon the stairs. Madmen are of
some nation, and their language, however incoherent
in its words, has always the coherence of syllabification. Besides, the hair of a madman is not such as I
now hold in my hand. I disentangled this little tuft
from the rigidly clutched fingers of Madame L'Espanaye. Tell me what you can make of it."

"Dupin!" I said, completely unnerved; "this hair
is most unusual—this is no human hair."

"I have not asserted that it is," said he; "but, before we decide this point, I wish you to glance at the
little sketch I have here traced upon this paper. It is
a fac-simile drawing of what has been described in
one portion of the testimony as 'dark bruises and deep
indentations of finger nails' upon the throat of Mademoiselle L'Espanaye, and in another (by Messrs. Dumas and Étienne) as a 'series of livid spots, evidently
the impression of fingers.'

"You will perceive," continued my friend, spreading
out the paper upon the table before us, "that this drawing gives the idea of a firm and fixed hold. There is
no *slipping* apparent. Each finger has retained—pos-

sibly until the death of the victim—the fearful grasp by which it originally imbedded itself. Attempt, now, to place all your fingers, at the same time, in the respective impressions as you see them."

I made the attempt in vain.

"We are possibly not giving this matter a fair trial," he said. "The paper is spread out upon a plane surface; but the human throat is cylindrical. Here is a billet of wood, the circumference of which is about that of the throat. Wrap the drawing around it, and try the experiment again."

I did so; but the difficulty was even more obvious than before. "This," I said, "is the mark of no human hand."

"Read now," replied Dupin, "this passage from Cuvier."

It was a minute anatomical and generally descriptive account of the large fulvous Orang-Outang of the East Indian Islands. The gigantic stature, the prodigious strength and activity, the wild ferocity, and the imitative propensities of these mammalia are sufficiently well known to all. I understood the full horrors of the murder at once.

"The description of the digits," said I, as I made an end of the reading, "is in exact accordance with this drawing. I see that no animal but an Orang-Outang, of the species here mentioned, could have impressed the indentations as you have traced them. This tuft of tawny hair, too, is identical in character with that of the beast of Cuvier. But I can not possibly comprehend the particulars of this frightful mystery. Besides, there were two voices heard in contention, and one of them was unquestionably the voice of a Frenchman."

"True; and you will remember an expression attributed almost unanimously, by the evidence, to this voice —the expression, 'mon Dieu!' This, under the circumstances, has been justly characterized by one of the witnesses (Montani, the confectioner) as an expression of remonstrance or expostulation. Upon these two words, therefore, I have mainly built my hopes of a full solution of the riddle. A Frenchman was cognizant of the murder. It is possible—indeed it is far more than probable—that he was innocent of all participation in the bloody transactions which took place. The Orang-Outang may have escaped from him. He may have traced it to the chamber; but, under the agitating circumstances which ensued, he could never have recaptured it. It is still at large. I will not pursue these guesses—for I have no right to call them more—since the shades of reflection upon which they are based are scarcely of sufficient depth to be appreciable by my own intellect, and since I could not pretend to make them intelligible to the understanding of another. We will call them guesses, then, and speak of them as such. If the Frenchman in question is indeed, as I suppose, innocent of this atrocity, this advertisement, which I left last night, upon our return home, at the office of 'Le Monde' (a paper devoted to the shipping interest, and much sought by sailors), will bring him to our residence."

He handed me a paper, and I read thus:

CAUGHT—*In the Bois de Boulogne, early in the morning of the — inst.* (morning of the murder), *a very large, tawny Orang-Outang of the Bornese species. The owner (who is ascertained to be a sailor, belonging to a Maltese vessel) may have the animal again, upon identifying it satisfactorily, and paying a few charges arising from its capture and keeping. . Call at No. — Rue ——, Faubourg St. Germain—au troisième."*

"How was it possible," I asked, "that you should know the man to be a sailor, and belonging to a Maltese vessel?"

"I do not know it," said Dupin. "I am not sure of it. Here, however, is a small piece of ribbon, which from its form, and from its greasy appearance, has evidently been used in tying the hair in one of those long queues of which sailors are so fond. Moreover, this knot is one which few besides sailors can tie, and it is peculiar to the Maltese. I picked the ribbon up at the foot of the lightning-rod. It could not have belonged to either of the deceased. Now if, after all, I am wrong in my induction from this ribbon, that the Frenchman was a sailor belonging to a Maltese vessel, still I can have done no harm in saying what I did in the advertisement. If I am in error, he will merely suppose that I have been misled by some circumstance into which he will not take the trouble to inquire. But if I am right, a great point is gained. Cognizant although innocent of the murder, the Frenchman will naturally hesitate about replying to the advertisement

—about demanding the Orang-Outang. He will reason
thus:—'I am innocent; I am poor; my Orang-Outang
is of great value—to one in my circumstances a fortune of itself—why should I lose it through idle ap-
prehensions of danger? Here it is, within my grasp.
It was found in the Bois de Boulogne—at a vast distance from the scene of that butchery. How can it
ever be suspected that a brute beast should have done
the deed? The police are at fault—they have failed to
procure the slightest clew. Should they even trace
the animal, it would be impossible to prove me cognizant of the murder, or to implicate me in guilt on
account of that cognizance. Above all, I am known.
The advertiser designates me as the possessor of the
beast. I am not sure to what limit his knowledge may
extend. Should I avoid claiming a property of so
great value, which it is known that I possess, I will
render the animal at least liable to suspicion. It is
not my policy to attract attention either to myself or
to the beast. I will answer the advertisement, get the
Orang-Outang, and keep it close until this matter has
blown over.' "

At this moment we heard a step upon the stairs.

"Be ready," said Dupin, "with your pistols, but
neither use them nor show them until at a signal from
myself."

The front door of the house had been left open,
and the visitor had entered, without ringing, and advanced several steps upon the staircase. Now, however, he seemed to hesitate. Presently we heard him
descending. Dupin was moving quickly to the door,

when we again heard him coming up. He did not turn back a second time, but stepped up with decision, and rapped at the door of our chamber.

"Come in," said Dupin, in a cheerful and hearty tone.

A man entered. He was a sailor, evidently—a tall, stout, and muscular-looking person, with a certain dare-devil expression of countenance, not altogether unprepossessing. His face, greatly sunburned, was more than half hidden by whisker and mustachio. He had with him a huge oaken cudgel, but appeared to be otherwise unarmed. He bowed awkwardly, and bade us "good-evening," in French accents, which, although somewhat Neufchatelish, were still sufficiently indicative of a Parisian origin.

"Sit down, my friend," said Dupin. "I suppose you have called about the Orang-Outang. Upon my word, I almost envy you the possession of him; a remarkably fine, and no doubt a very valuable, animal. How old do you suppose him to be?"

The sailor drew a long breath, with the air of a man relieved of some intolerable burden, and then replied, in an assured tone:

"I have no way of telling—but he can't be more than four or five years old. Have you got him here?"

"Oh, no; we had no conveniences for keeping him here. He is at a livery stable in the Rue Dubourg, just by. You can get him in the morning. Of course you are prepared to identify the property?"

"To be sure I am, sir."

"I shall be sorry to part with him," said Dupin.

"I don't mean that you should be at all this trouble for nothing, sir," said the man. "Couldn't expect it. Am very willing to pay a reward for the finding of the animal—that is to say, anything in reason."

"Well," replied my friend, "that is all very fair, to be sure. Let me think!—what should I have? Oh! I will tell you. My reward shall be this. You shall give me all the information in your power about these murders in the Rue Morgue."

Dupin said the last words in a very low tone, and very quietly. Just as quietly, too, he walked toward the door, locked it, and put the key in his pocket. He then drew a pistol from his bosom and placed it, without the least flurry, upon the table.

The sailor's face flushed up as if he were struggling with suffocation. He started to his feet and grasped his cudgel; but the next moment he fell back into his seat, trembling violently, and with the countenance of death itself. He spoke not a word. I pitied him from the bottom of my heart.

"My friend," said Dupin, in a kind tone, "you are alarming yourself unnecessarily—you are indeed. We mean you no harm whatever. I pledge you the honor of a gentleman, and of a Frenchman, that we intend you no injury. I perfectly well know that you are innocent of the atrocities in the Rue Morgue. It will not do, however, to deny that you are in some measure implicated in them. From what I have already said, you must know that I have had means of information about this matter—means of which you could never have dreamed. Now, the thing stands thus. You have done nothing which you could have avoided—nothing, certainly, which renders you culpable. You were not even guilty of robbery, when you might have robbed with impunity. You have nothing to conceal. You have no reason for concealment. On the other hand, you are bound by every principle of honor to confess all you know. An innocent man is now imprisoned, charged with that crime of which you can point out the perpetrator."

The sailor had recovered his presence of mind, in a great measure, while Dupin uttered these words; but his original boldness of bearing was all gone.

"So help me God!" said he, after a brief pause, "I *will* tell you all I know about this affair;—but I do not expect you to believe one half I say—I would be a fool indeed if I did. Still, I *am* innocent, and I will make a clean breast, if I die for it."

What he stated was, in substance, this. He had lately made a voyage to the Indian Archipelago. A party, of which he formed one, landed at Borneo, and passed into the interior on an excursion of pleasure. Himself and a companion had captured the Orang-Outang. This companion dying, the animal fell into his own exclusive possession. After great trouble, occasioned by the intractable ferocity of his captive during the home voyage, he at length succeeded in lodging it safely at his own residence in Paris, where, not to attract toward himself the unpleasant curiosity of his neighbors, he kept it carefully secluded, until such time as it should recover from a wound in the foot, received from a splinter on board ship. His ultimate design was to sell it.

Returning home from some sailor's frolic on the night, or rather in the morning, of the murder, he found the beast occupying his own bedroom, into which it had broken from a closet adjoining, where it had been, as was thought, securely confined. Razor in hand, and fully lathered, it was sitting before a looking-glass, attempting the operation of shaving, in which it had no doubt previously watched its master through the keyhole of the closet. Terrified at the sight of so dangerous a weapon in the possession of an animal so ferocious, and so well able to use it, the man, for some moments, was at a loss what to do. He had been accustomed, however, to quiet the creature, even in its fiercest moods, by the use of a whip, and to this he now resorted. Upon sight of it, the Orang-Outang sprang at once through the door of the chamber, down the stairs, and thence, through a window, unfortunately open, into the street.

The Frenchman followed in despair; the ape, razor still in hand, occasionally stopping to look back and gesticulate at his pursuer, until the latter had nearly come up with it. It then again made off. In this manner the chase continued for a long time. The streets were profoundly quiet, as it was nearly three o'clock in the morning. In passing down an alley in the rear of the Rue Morgue, the fugitive's attention was arrested by a light gleaming from the open window of Madame L'Espanaye's chamber, in the fourth story of her house. Rushing to the building, it perceived the lightning-rod, clambered up with inconceivable agility, grasped the shutter, which was thrown fully back against the wall, and, by its means, swung itself directly upon the headboard of the bed. The whole feat did not occupy a minute. The shutter was kicked open again by the Orang-Outang as it entered the room.

The sailor, in the meantime, was both rejoiced and perplexed. He had strong hopes of now recapturing the brute, as it could scarcely escape from the trap into which it had ventured, except by the rod, where it might be intercepted as it came down. On the other hand, there was much cause for anxiety as to what it might do in the house. This latter reflection urged the man still to follow the fugitive. A lightning-rod is ascended without difficulty, especially by a sailor; but, when he had arrived as high as the window, which lay far to his left, his career was stopped; the most that he could accomplish was to reach over so as to obtain a glimpse of the interior of the room. At this glimpse he nearly fell from his hold through excess of horror. Now it was that those hideous shrieks arose upon the night, which had startled from slumber the inmates of the Rue Morgue. Madame L'Espanaye and her daughter, habited in their night clothes, had apparently been occupied in arranging some papers in the iron chest already mentioned, which had been wheeled into the middle of the room. It was open, and its contents lay beside it on the floor. The victims must have been sitting with their backs toward the window; and, from the time elapsing between the ingress of the beast and the screams, it seems probable that it was not immediately perceived. The flapping to of the shutter would naturally have been attributed to the wind.

As the sailor looked in, the gigantic animal had seized Madame L'Espanaye by the hair (which was loose, as she had been combing it), and was flourishing the razor about her face, in imitation of the motions of a barber. The daughter lay prostrate and motionless; she had swooned. The screams and struggles of the old lady (during which the hair was torn from her head) had the effect of changing the probably pacific purposes of the Orang-Outang into those of wrath. With one determined sweep of its muscular arm it nearly severed her head from her body. The sight of blood inflamed its anger into frenzy. Gnashing its teeth, and flashing fire from its eyes, it flew upon the body of the girl and imbedded its fearful talons in her throat, retaining its grasp until she expired. Its wandering and wild glances fell at this moment upon the head of the bed, over which the face of its master, rigid with horror, was just discernible. The fury of the beast, who no doubt bore still in mind the dreaded whip, was instantly converted into fear. Conscious of having deserved punishment, it seemed desirous of concealing its bloody deeds, and skipped about the chamber in an agony of nervous agitation; throwing down and breaking the furniture as it moved, and dragging the bed from the bedstead. In conclusion, it seized first the corpse of the daughter, and thrust it up the chimney, as it was found; then that of the old lady, which it immediately hurled through the window headlong.

As the ape approached the casement with its muti-lated burden, the sailor shrank aghast to the rod, and, rather gliding than clambering down it, hurried at once home—dreading the consequences of the butch-ery, and gladly abandoning, in his terror, all so-licitude about the fate of the Orang-Outang. The words heard by the party upon the staircase were the Frenchman's exclamations of horror and affright, commingled with the fiendish jabberings of the brute.

I have scarcely anything to add. The Orang-Outang must have escaped from the chamber, by the rod, just before the breaking of the door. It must have closed the window as it passed through it. It was subsequently caught by the owner himself, who obtained for it a very large sum at the Jardin des Plantes. Le Bon was instantly released, upon our nar-ration of the circumstances (with some comments from Dupin) at the bureau of the Prefect of Police. This functionary, however well disposed to my friend, could not altogether conceal his chagrin at the turn which affairs had taken, and was fain to indulge in a sarcasm or two about the propriety of every person minding his own business.

"Let him talk," said Dupin, who had not thought it necessary to reply. "Let him discourse; it will ease his conscience. I am satisfied with having de-feated him in his own castle. Nevertheless, that he failed in the solution of this mystery is by no means that matter for wonder which he supposes it; for, in truth, our friend the Prefect is somewhat too cunning to be profound. In his wisdom is no *stamen.* It is all head and no body, like the pictures of the Goddess Laverna—or, at best, all head and shoulders, like a codfish. But he is a good creature after all. I like him especially for one masterstroke of cant, by which he has attained his reputation for ingenuity; I mean the way he has '*de nier ce qui est, et d'expliquer ce qui n'est pas.*' " *

---

* Rousseau—"Nouvelle Heloïse."

THE GREAT STONE FACE

BY NATHANIEL HAWTHORNE

Nathaniel Hawthorne (born at Salem, Massachusetts, July 4, 1804, died May 18, 1864) has thus been described by the severest and most competent critic of literary style whom America has yet produced—Edgar Allan Poe: "He has the purest style, the finest taste, the most available scholarship, the most touching pathos, the most radiant imagination, the most consummate ingenuity." "The Great Stone Face" appeared in 1842 in the second series of "Twice-Told Tales." It has that perfection of form which belongs in common to every supreme literary production, whether a story, a poem or a parable, to all of which its spirit is akin. Indeed it has been compared to a sermon— one, however, delivered in the open fields, for, as James T. Fields wrote of Hawthorne, "His religion was deep and broad, but it was irksome for him to be fastened in by a pew door."

THE GREAT STONE FACE

BY NATHANIEL HAWTHORNE

ONE afternoon, when the sun was going down, a mother and her little boy sat at the door of their cottage, talking about the Great Stone Face. They had but to lift their eyes, and there it was plainly to be seen, though miles away, with the sunshine brightening all its features.

And what was the Great Stone Face?

Embosomed among a family of lofty mountains, there was a valley so spacious that it contained many thousand inhabitants. Some of these good people dwelt in log-huts, with the black forests all around them on the steep and difficult hillsides. Others had their homes in comfortable farmhouses, and cultivated the rich soil on the gentle slopes or level surfaces of the valley. Others, again, were congregated into populous villages, where some wild, highland rivulet, tumbling down from its birthplace in the upper mountain region, had been caught and tamed by human cunning, and compelled to turn the machinery of cotton factories. The inhabitants of this valley, in short, were numerous, and of many modes of life. But all of them, grown people and children, had a kind of familiarity with the Great Stone Face, although some possessed the gift of distinguishing this grand natural

Published by arrangement with Messrs. Houghton, Mifflin & Co., authorized publishers of Hawthorne's works.

phenomenon more perfectly than many of their neighbors.

The Great Stone Face, then, was a work of Nature
in her mood of majestic playfulness, formed on the
perpendicular side of a mountain by some immense
rocks, which had been thrown together in such a position as, when viewed at a proper distance, precisely
to resemble the features of the human countenance.
It seemed as if an enormous giant, or a Titan, had
sculptured his own likeness on the precipice. There
was the broad arch of the forehead, a hundred feet
in height; the nose, with its long bridge; and the vast
lips, which, if they could have spoken, would have
rolled their thunder accents from one end of the valley to the other. True it is, that if the spectator approached too near he lost the outline of the gigantic
visage, and could discern only a heap of ponderous and
gigantic rocks, piled in chaotic ruin one upon another.
Retracing his steps, however, the wondrous features
would again be seen; and the further he withdrew
from them, the more like a human face, with all its
original divinity intact, did they appear; until, as it
grew dim in the distance, with the clouds and glorified
vapor of the mountains clustering about it, the Great
Stone Face seemed positively to be alive.

It was a happy lot for children to grow up to manhood or womanhood with the Great Stone Face before
their eyes, for all the features were noble, and the expression was at once grand and sweet, as if it were
the glow of a vast, warm heart, that embraced all
mankind in its affections, and had room for more. It

was an education only to look at it. According to the
belief of many people, the valley owed much of its
fertility to this benign aspect that was continually
beaming over it, illuminating the clouds, and infusing
its tenderness into the sunshine.

As we began with saying, a mother and her little
boy sat at their cottage door, gazing at the Great
Stone Face, and talking about it. The child's name
was Ernest.

"Mother," said he, while the Titanic visage smiled
on him, "I wish that it could speak, for it looks so
very kindly that its voice must needs be pleasant. If
I were to see a man with such a face, I should love
him dearly."

"If an old prophecy should come to pass," answered
his mother, "we may see a man, some time or other,
with exactly such a face as that."

"What prophecy do you mean, dear mother?"
eagerly inquired Ernest. "Pray tell me all about it!"

So his mother told him a story that her own mother
had told to her, when she herself was younger than
little Ernest; a story, not of things that were past,
but of what was yet to come; a story, nevertheless, so
very old that even the Indians, who formerly inhabited this valley, had heard it from their forefathers, to
whom, as they affirmed, it had been murmured by the
mountain streams, and whispered by the wind among
the tree-tops. The purport was that, at some future
day, a child should be born hereabouts who was destined to become the greatest and noblest personage of
his time, and whose countenance, in manhood, should

bear an exact resemblance to the Great Stone Face. Not a few old-fashioned people, and young ones likewise, in the ardor of their hopes, still cherished an enduring faith in this old prophecy. But others, who had seen more of the world, had watched and waited till they were weary, and had beheld no man with such a face, nor any man that proved to be much greater or nobler than his neighbors, concluded it to be nothing but an idle tale. At all events, the great man of the prophecy had not yet appeared.

"Oh, mother, dear mother!" cried Ernest, clapping his hands above his head, "I do hope that I shall live to see him!"

His mother was an affectionate and thoughtful woman, and felt that it was wisest not to discourage the generous hopes of her little boy. So she only said to him, "Perhaps you may."

And Ernest never forgot the story that his mother told him. It was always in his mind, whenever he looked upon the Great Stone Face. He spent his childhood in the log-cottage where he was born, and was dutiful to his mother, and helpful to her in many things, assisting her much with his little hands, and more with his loving heart. In this manner, from a happy yet often pensive child, he grew up to be a mild, quiet, unobtrusive boy, and sun-browned with labor in the fields, but with more intelligence brightening his aspect than is seen in many lads who have been taught at famous schools. Yet Ernest had had no teacher, save only that the Great Stone Face became one to him. When the toil of the day was over, he would

gaze at it for hours, until he began to imagine that
those vast features recognized him and gave him a
smile of kindness and encouragement, responsive to
his own look of veneration. We must not take upon
us to affirm that this was a mistake, although the Face
may have looked no more kindly at Ernest than at all
the world besides. But the secret was that the boy's
tender and confiding simplicity discerned what other
people could not see; and thus the love, which was
meant for all, became his peculiar portion.

About this time there went a rumor throughout the
valley that the great man, foretold from ages long ago,
who was to bear a resemblance to the Great Stone
Face had appeared at last. It seems that, many years
before, a young man had migrated from the valley and
settled at a distant seaport, where, after getting together a little money, he had set up as a shopkeeper.
His name—but I could never learn whether it was
his real one, or a nickname that had grown out of his
habits and success in life—was Gathergold. Being
shrewd and active, and endowed by Providence with
that inscrutable faculty which develops itself in what
the world calls luck, he became an exceedingly rich
merchant, and owner of a whole fleet of bulky-bot-
tomed ships. All the countries of the globe appeared
to join hands for the mere purpose of adding heap
after heap to the mountainous accumulation of this
one man's wealth. The cold regions of the north, almost within the gloom and shadow of the Arctic
Circle, sent him their tribute in the shape of furs; hot
Africa sifted for him the golden sands of her rivers,

and gathered up the ivory tusks of her great elephants out of the forests; the East came bringing him the rich shawls, and spices, and teas, and the effulgence of diamonds, and the gleaming purity of large pearls. The ocean, not to be behindhand with the earth, yielded up her mighty whales, that Mr. Gathergold might sell their oil, and make a profit on it. Be the original commodity what it might, it was gold within his grasp. It might be said of him, as of Midas in the fable, that whatever he touched with his finger immediately glistened, and grew yellow, and was changed at once into sterling metal, or, which suited him still better, into piles of coin. And when Mr. Gathergold had become so very rich that it would have taken him a hundred years only to count his wealth, he bethought himself of his native valley, and resolved to go back thither, and end his days where he was born. With this purpose in view, he sent a skilful architect to build him such a palace as should be fit for a man of his vast wealth to live in.

As I have said above, it had already been rumored in the valley that Mr. Gathergold had turned out to be the prophetic personage so long and vainly looked for, and that his visage was the perfect and undeniable similitude of the Great Stone Face. People were the more ready to believe that this must needs be the fact when they beheld the splendid edifice that rose, as if by enchantment, on the site of his father's old weather-beaten farmhouse. The exterior was of marble, so dazzlingly white that it seemed as though the whole structure might melt away in the sunshine, like those humbler ones which Mr. Gathergold, in his young play-days, before his fingers were gifted with the touch of transmutation, had been accustomed to build of snow. It had a richly ornamental portico, supported by tall pillars, beneath which was a lofty door, studded with silver knobs, and made of a kind of variegated wood that had been brought from beyond the sea. The windows, from the floor to the ceiling of each stately apartment, were composed, respectively, of but one enormous pane of glass, so transparently pure that it was said to be a finer medium than even the vacant atmosphere. Hardly anybody had been permitted to see the interior of this palace; but it was reported, and with good semblance of truth, to be far more gorgeous than the outside, insomuch that whatever was iron or brass in other houses was silver or gold in this; and Mr. Gathergold's bedchamber, especially, made such a glittering appearance that no ordinary man would have been able to close his eyes there. But, on the other hand, Mr. Gathergold was now so inured to wealth that perhaps he could not have closed his eyes unless where the gleam of it was certain to find its way beneath his eyelids.

In due time, the mansion was finished; next came the upholsterers, with magnificent furniture; then, a whole troop of black and white servants, the harbingers of Mr. Gathergold, who, in his own majestic person, was expected to arrive at sunset. Our friend Ernest, meanwhile, had been deeply stirred by the idea that the great man, the noble man, the man of prophecy, after so many ages of delay, was at length to be made manifest to his native valley. He knew, boy as he was, that there were a thousand ways in which Mr. Gathergold, with his vast wealth, might transform himself into an angel of beneficence, and assume a control over human affairs as wide and benignant as the smile of the Great Stone Face. Full of faith and hope, Ernest doubted not that what the people said was true, and that now he was to behold the living likeness of those wondrous features on the mountain-side. While the boy was still gazing up the valley, and fancying, as he always did, that the Great Stone Face returned his gaze and looked kindly at him, the rumbling of wheels was heard, approaching swiftly along the winding road.

"Here he comes!" cried a group of people who were assembled to witness the arrival. "Here comes the great Mr. Gathergold!"

A carriage, drawn by four horses, dashed round the turn of the road. Within it, thrust partly out of the window, appeared the physiognomy of the old man, with a skin as yellow as if his own Midas hand had transmuted it. He had a low forehead, small, sharp eyes, puckered about with innumerable wrinkles, and very thin lips, which he made still thinner by pressing them forcibly together.

"The very image of the Great Stone Face!" shouted the people. "Sure enough, the old prophecy is true; and here we have the great man come at last!"

And, what greatly perplexed Ernest, they seemed actually to believe that here was the likeness which they spoke of. By the roadside there chanced to be an old beggar-woman and two little beggar-children, stragglers from some far-off region, who, as the carriage rolled onward, held out their hands and lifted up their doleful voices, most piteously beseeching charity. A yellow claw—the very same that had clawed together so much wealth—poked itself out of the coach-window, and dropped some copper coins upon the ground; so that, though the great man's name seems to have been Gathergold, he might just as suitably have been nicknamed Scattercopper. Still, nevertheless, with an earnest shout, and evidently with as much good faith as ever, the people bellowed:

"He is the very image of the Great Stone Face!"

But Ernest turned sadly from the wrinkled shrewdness of that sordid visage, and gazed up the valley, where, amid a gathering mist, gilded by the last sunbeams, he could still distinguish those glorious features which had impressed themselves into his soul. Their aspect cheered him. What did the benign lips seem to say?

"He will come! Fear not, Ernest; the man will come!"

The years went on, and Ernest ceased to be a boy. He had grown to be a young man now. He attracted little notice from the other inhabitants of the valley; for they saw nothing remarkable in his way of life, save that, when the labor of the day was over, he still loved to go apart and gaze and meditate upon the Great Stone Face. According to their idea of the matter, it was a folly, indeed, but pardonable, inasmuch as Ernest was industrious, kind, and neighborly, and neglected no duty for the sake of indulging this idle habit. They knew not that the Great Stone Face had become a teacher to him and that the sentiment which was expressed in it would enlarge the young man's heart, and fill it with wider and deeper sympathies than other hearts. They knew not that thence would come a better wisdom than could be learned from books, and a better life than could be molded on the defaced example of other human lives. Neither did Ernest know that the thoughts and affections which came to him so naturally, in the fields and at the fireside, and wherever he communed with himself, were of a higher tone than those which all men shared with him. A simple soul—simple as when his mother first taught him the old prophecy—he beheld the marvelous features beaming adown the valley, and still wondered that their human counterpart was so long in making his appearance.

By this time poor Mr. Gathergold was dead and buried; and the oddest part of the matter was, that his wealth, which was the body and spirit of his existence, had disappeared before his death, leaving nothing of him but a living skeleton, covered over with a wrinkled, yellow skin. Since the melting away of his gold, it had been very generally conceded that there was no such striking resemblance, after all, betwixt the ignoble features of the ruined merchant and that majestic face upon the mountain-side. So the people ceased to honor him during his lifetime, and quietly consigned him to forgetfulness after his decease. Once in a while, it is true, his memory was

brought up in connection with the magnificent palace
which he had built, and which had long ago been
turned into a hotel for the accommodation of strangers, multitudes of whom came, every summer, to visit
that famous natural curiosity, the Great Stone Face.
Thus, Mr. Gathergold being discredited and thrown
into the shade, the man of prophecy was yet to come.

It so happened that a native born son of the valley,
many years before, had enlisted as a soldier, and,
after a great deal of hard fighting, had now become
an illustrious commander. Whatever he may be called
in history, he was known in camps and on the battlefield under the nickname of Old Blood-and-Thunder.
This war-worn veteran, being now infirm with age
and wounds, and weary of the turmoil of a military
life, and of the roll of the drum and the clangor of
the trumpet, that had so long been ringing in his
ears, had lately signified a purpose of returning to his
native valley, hoping to find repose where he remembered to have left it. The inhabitants, his old neighbors and their grown-up children, were resolved to
welcome the renowned warrior with a salute of cannon
and a public dinner; and all the more enthusiastically,
it being affirmed that now, at last, the likeness of the
Great Stone Face had actually appeared. An aid-
de-camp of Old Blood-and-Thunder, traveling through
the valley, was said to have been struck with the resemblance. Moreover, the schoolmates and early acquaintances of the general were ready to testify, on
oath, that, to the best of their recollection, the afore-
said general had been exceedingly like the majestic

image, even when a boy, only that the idea had never
occurred to them at that period. Great, therefore, was
the excitement throughout the valley; and many people,
who had never once thought of glancing at the
Great Stone Face for years before, now spent their
time in gazing at it, for the sake of knowing exactly
how General Blood-and-Thunder looked.

On the day of the great festival, Ernest, with all
the other people of the valley, left their work, and
proceeded to the spot where the sylvan banquet was
prepared. As he approached, the loud voice of the
Rev. Dr. Battleblast was heard, beseeching a blessing
on the good things set before them, and on the distinguished friend of peace in whose honor they were
assembled. The tables were arranged in a cleared
space of the woods, shut in by the surrounding trees,
except where a vista opened eastward, and afforded a
distant view of the Great Stone Face. Over the general's chair, which was a relic from the home of Washington, there was an arch of verdant boughs, with the
laurel profusely intermixed, and surmounted by his
country's banner, beneath which he had won his victo-
ries. Our friend Ernest raised himself on his tiptoes,
in hopes to get a glimpse of the celebrated guest; but
there was a mighty crowd about the tables anxious
to hear the toasts and speeches, and to catch any word
that might fall from the general in reply; and a vol-
unteer company, doing duty as a guard, pricked ruthlessly with their bayonets at any particularly quiet person among the throng. So Ernest, being of an unobtrusive character, was thrust quite into the background,

where he could see no more of Old Blood-and-Thunder's physiognomy than if it had been still blazing on the battlefield. To console himself, he turned toward the Great Stone Face, which, like a faithful and long-remembered friend, looked back and smiled upon him through the vista of the forest. Meantime, however, he could overhear the remarks of various individuals, who were comparing the features of the hero with the face on the distant mountain-side.

" 'Tis the same face, to a hair!" cried one man, cutting a caper for joy.

"Wonderfully like, that's a fact!" responded another.

"Like! why, I call it Old Blood-and-Thunder himself, in a monstrous looking-glass!" cried a third. "And why not? He's the greatest man of this or any other age, beyond a doubt."

And then all three of the speakers gave a great shout, which communicated electricity to the crowd, and called forth a roar from a thousand voices that went reverberating for miles among the mountains, until you might have supposed that the Great Stone Face had poured its thunder-breath into the cry. All these comments, and this vast enthusiasm, served the more to interest our friend; nor did he think of questioning that now, at length, the mountain-visage had found its human counterpart. It is true, Ernest had imagined that this long-looked-for personage would appear in the character of a man of peace, uttering wisdom, and doing good, and making people happy. But, taking an habitual breadth of view, with all his simplicity, he contended that Providence should choose its own method of blessing mankind, and could conceive that this great end might be effected even by a warrior and a bloody sword, should inscrutable wisdom see fit to order matters so.

"The general! the general!" was now the cry. "Hush! silence! Old Blood-and-Thunder's going to make a speech."

Even so; for, the cloth being removed, the general's health had been drunk amid shouts of applause, and he now stood upon his feet to thank the company. Ernest saw him. There he was, over the shoulders of the crowd, from the two glittering epaulets and embroidered collar upward, beneath the arch of green boughs with intertwined laurel, and the banner drooping as if to shade his brow! And there, too, visible in the same glance, through the vista of the forest, appeared the Great Stone Face! And was there, indeed, such a resemblance as the crowd had testified? Alas, Ernest could not recognize it! He beheld a war-worn and weather-beaten countenance, full of energy, and expressive of an iron will; but the gentle wisdom, the deep, broad, tender sympathies, were altogether wanting in Old Blood-and-Thunder's visage; and even if the Great Stone Face had assumed his look of stern command, the milder traits would still have tempered it.

"This is not the man of prophecy," sighed Ernest to himself, as he made his way out of the throng. "And must the world wait longer yet?"

The mists had congregated about the distant moun-

Nathaniel Hawthorne.

tain-side, and there were seen the grand and awful features of the Great Stone Face, awful but benignant, as if a mighty angel were sitting among the hills, and enrobing himself in a cloud-vesture of gold and purple. As he looked, Ernest could hardly believe but that a smile beamed over the whole visage, with a radiance still brightening, although without motion of the lips. It was probably the effect of the western sunshine, melting through the thinly diffused vapors that had swept between him and the object that he gazed at. But—as it always did—the aspect of his marvelous friend made Ernest as hopeful as if he had never hoped in vain.

"Fear not, Ernest," said his heart, even as if the Great Face were whispering to him—"fear not, Ernest; he will come."

More years sped swiftly and tranquilly away. Ernest still dwelt in his native valley, and was now a man of middle age. By imperceptible degrees, he had become known among the people. Now, as heretofore, he labored for his bread, and was the same simple-hearted man that he had always been. But he had thought and felt so much, he had given so many of the best hours of his life to unworldly hopes for some great good to mankind, that it seemed as though he had been talking with the angels, and had imbibed a portion of their wisdom unawares. It was visible in the calm and well-considered beneficence of his daily life, the quiet stream of which had made a wide green margin all along its course. Not a day passed by that the world was not the better because this man, humble as he was, had lived. He never stepped aside from his own path, yet would always reach a blessing to his neighbor. Almost involuntarily, too, he had become a preacher. The pure and high simplicity of his thought, which, as one of its manifestations, took shape in the good deeds that dropped silently from his hand, flowed also forth in speech. He uttered truths that wrought upon and molded the lives of those who heard him. His auditors, it may be, never suspected that Ernest, their own neighbor and familiar friend, was more than an ordinary man; least of all did Ernest himself suspect it; but, inevitably as the murmur of a rivulet, came thoughts out of his mouth that no other human lips had spoken.

When the people's minds had had a little time to cool, they were ready enough to acknowledge their mistake in imagining a similarity between General Blood-and-Thunder's truculent physiognomy and the benign visage on the mountain-side. But now, again, there were reports and many paragraphs in the newspapers, affirming that the likeness of the Great Stone Face had appeared upon the broad shoulders of a certain eminent statesman. He, like Mr. Gathergold and Old Blood-and-Thunder, was a native of the valley, but had left it in his early days, and taken up the trades of law and politics. Instead of the rich man's wealth and the warrior's sword, he had but a tongue, and it was mightier than both together. So wonderfully eloquent was he that whatever he might choose to say, his auditors had no choice but to believe him; wrong looked like right and right like wrong; for when it pleased him he could make a kind of illuminated fog with his mere breath and obscure the natural daylight with it. His tongue, indeed, was a magic instrument: sometimes it rumbled like the thunder; sometimes it warbled like the sweetest music. It was the blast of war—the song of peace; and it seemed to have a heart in it, when there was no such matter. In good truth, he was a wondrous man; and when his tongue had acquired him all other imaginable success—when it had been heard in halls of state, and in the courts of princes and potentates—after it had made him known all over the world, even as a voice crying from shore to shore—it finally persuaded his countrymen to select him for the Presidency. Before this time—indeed, as soon as he began to grow celebrated—his admirers had found out the resemblance between him and the Great Stone Face; and so much were they struck by it that throughout the country this distinguished gentleman was known by the name of Old Stony Phiz. The phrase was considered as giving a highly favorable aspect to his political prospects; for, as is likewise the case with the Popedom, nobody ever becomes President without taking a name other than his own.

While his friends were doing their best to make him President, Old Stony Phiz, as he was called, set out on a visit to the valley where he was born. Of course, he had no other object than to shake hands with his fellow-citizens, and neither thought nor cared about any effect which his progress through the country might have upon the election. Magnificent preparations were made to receive the illustrious statesman; a cavalcade of horsemen set forth to meet him at the boundary line of the State, and all the people left their business and gathered along the wayside to see him pass. Among these was Ernest. Though more than once disappointed, as we have seen, he had such a hopeful and confiding nature that he was always ready to believe in whatever seemed beautiful and good. He kept his heart continually open, and thus was sure to catch the blessing from on high when it should come. So now again, as buoyantly as ever, he went forth to behold the likeness of the Great Stone Face.

The cavalcade came prancing along the road, with a great clattering of hoofs and a mighty cloud of dust, which rose up so dense and high that the visage of the mountain-side was completely hidden from Ernest's eyes. All the great men of the neighborhood were there on horseback; militia officers in uniform; the member of Congress; the sheriff of the county; the editors of newspapers; and many a farmer, too, had mounted his patient steed, with his Sunday coat upon his back. It really was a very brilliant spectacle, especially as there were numerous banners flaunting over the cavalcade, on some of which were gorgeous portraits of the illustrious statesman and the Great Stone Face, smiling familiarly at one another, like two brothers. If the pictures were to be trusted, the mutual resemblance, it must be confessed, was marvelous. We must not forget to mention that there was a band of music, which made the echoes of the mountains ring and reverberate with the loud triumph of its strains;

so that airy and soul-thrilling melodies broke out
among all the heights and hollows, as if every nook
of his native valley had found a voice to welcome
the distinguished guest. But the grandest effect was
when the far-off mountain precipice flung back the
music; for then the Great Stone Face itself seemed
to be swelling the triumphant chorus, in acknowledg-
ment that, at length, the man of prophecy was come.

All this while the people were throwing up their
hats and shouting, with enthusiasm so contagious that
the heart of Ernest kindled up, and he likewise threw
up his hat, and shouted, as loudly as the loudest,
"Huzza for the great man! Huzza for Old Stony
Phiz!" But as yet he had not seen him.

"Here he is, now!" cried those who stood near Ernest. "There! There! Look at Old Stony Phiz and
then at the Old Man of the Mountain, and see if they
are not as like as two twin-brothers!"

In the midst of all this gallant array came an open
barouche, drawn by four white horses; and in the barouche, with his massive head uncovered, sat the illustrious statesman, Old Stony Phiz himself.

"Confess it," said one of Ernest's neighbors to him,
"the Great Stone Face has met its match at last!"

Now, it must be owned that, at his first glimpse of
the countenance which was bowing and smiling from
the barouche, Ernest did fancy that there was a resemblance between it and the old familiar face upon
the mountain-side. The brow, with its massive depth
and loftiness, and all the other features, indeed, were
boldly and strongly hewn as if in emulation of a more

than heroic, of a Titanic, model. But the sublimity and stateliness, the grand expression of a divine sympathy, that illuminated the mountain visage and etherealized its ponderous granite substance into spirit, might here be sought in vain. Something had been originally left out, or had departed. And therefore the marvelously gifted statesman had always a weary gloom in the deep caverns of his eyes, as of a child that has outgrown its playthings or a man of mighty faculties and little aims, whose life, with all its high performances, was vague and empty, because no high purpose had endowed it with reality.

Still Ernest's neighbor was thrusting his elbow into his side, and pressing him for an answer.

"Confess! confess! Is not he the very picture of your Old Man of the Mountain?"

"No!" said Ernest, bluntly, "I see little or no likeness."

"Then so much the worse for the Great Stone Face!" answered his neighbor; and again he set up a shout for Old Stony Phiz.

But Ernest turned away, melancholy, and almost despondent: for this was the saddest of his disappointments, to behold a man who might have fulfilled the prophecy and had not willed to do so. Meantime, the cavalcade, the banners, the music, and the barouches swept past him, with the vociferous crowd in the rear, leaving the dust to settle down, and the Great Stone Face to be revealed again, with the grandeur that it had worn for untold centuries.

"Lo, here I am, Ernest!" the benign lips seemed to

say. "I have waited longer than thou, and am not yet weary. Fear not; the man will come."

The years hurried onward, treading in their haste on one another's heels. And now they began to bring white hairs, and scatter them over the head of Ernest; they made reverend wrinkles across his forehead and furrows in his cheeks. He was an aged man. But not in vain had he grown old: more than the white hairs on his head were the sage thoughts in his mind; his wrinkles and furrows were inscriptions that Time had graved, and in which he had written legends of wisdom that had been tested by the tenor of a life. And Ernest had ceased to be obscure. Unsought for, undesired, had come the fame which so many seek, and made him known in the great world, beyond the limits of the valley in which he had dwelt so quietly. College professors, and even the active men of cities, came from far to see and converse with Ernest; for the report had gone abroad that this simple husbandman had ideas unlike those of other men, not gained from books, but of a higher tone—a tranquil and familiar majesty, as if he had been talking with the angels as his daily friends. Whether it were sage, statesman, or philanthropist, Ernest received these visitors with the gentle sincerity that had characterized him from boyhood, and spoke freely with them of whatever came uppermost, or lay deepest in his heart or their own. While they talked together, his face would kindle, unawares, and shine upon them, as with a mild evening light. Pensive with the fulness of such discourse, his guests took leave and went their way; and passing up the valley, paused to look at the Great Stone Face, imagining that they had seen its likeness in a human countenance, but could not remember where.

While Ernest had been growing up and growing old, a bountiful Providence had granted a new poet to this earth. He, likewise, was a native of the valley, but had spent the greater part of his life at a distance from that romantic region, pouring out his sweet music amid the bustle and din of cities. Often, however, did the mountains which had been familiar to him in his childhood lift their snowy peaks into the clear atmosphere of his poetry. Neither was the Great Stone Face forgotten, for the poet had celebrated it in an ode, which was grand enough to have been uttered by its own majestic lips. This man of genius, we may say, had come down from heaven with wonderful endowments. If he sang of a mountain, the eyes of all mankind beheld a mightier grandeur reposing on its breast, or soaring to its summit, than had before been seen there. If his theme were a lovely lake, a celestial smile had now been thrown over it, to gleam forever on its surface. If it were the vast old sea, even the deep immensity of its dread bosom seemed to swell the higher, as if moved by the emotions of the song. Thus the world assumed another and a better aspect from the hour that the poet blessed it with his happy eyes. The Creator had bestowed him, as the last best touch to his own handiwork. Creation was not finished till the poet came to interpret, and so complete it.

The effect was no less high and beautiful when his

human brethren were the subject of his verse. The
man or woman, sordid with the common dust of life,
who crossed his daily path, and the little child who
played in it, were glorified if he beheld them in his
mood of poetic faith. He showed the golden links of
the great chain that intertwined them with an angelic
kindred; he brought out the hidden traits of a celestial
birth that made them worthy of such kin. Some, indeed, there were who thought to show the soundness
of their judgment by affirming that all the beauty and
dignity of the natural world existed only in the poet's
fancy. Let such men speak for themselves, who undoubtedly appear to have been spawned forth by Nature with a contemptuous bitterness; she having plas-
tered them up out of her refuse stuff, after all the
swine were made. As respects all things else, the
poet's ideal was the truest truth.

The songs of this poet found their way to Ernest.
He read them after his customary toil, seated on the
bench before his cottage door, where for such a length
of time he had filled his repose with thought by gazing at the Great Stone Face. And now as he read
stanzas that caused the soul to thrill within him, he
lifted his eyes to the vast countenance beaming on him
so benignantly.

"Oh, majestic friend," he murmured, addressing
the Great Stone Face, "is not this man worthy to resemble thee?"

The Face seemed to smile, but answered not a word.

Now it happened that the poet, though he dwelt
so far away, had not only heard of Ernest, but had

meditated much upon his character, until he deemed
nothing so desirable as to meet this man, whose un-
taught wisdom walked hand in hand with the noble
simplicity of his life. One summer morning, therefore, he took passage by the railroad, and, in the decline of the afternoon, alighted from the cars at no
great distance from Ernest's cottage. The great hotel,
which had formerly been the palace of Mr. Gathergold, was close at hand, but the poet, with his carpet-
bag on his arm, inquired at once where Ernest dwelt,
and was resolved to be accepted as his guest.

Approaching the door, he there found the good old
man, holding a volume in his hand, which alternately
he read, and then, with a finger between the leaves,
looked lovingly at the Great Stone Face.

"Good-evening," said the poet. "Can you give a
traveler a night's lodging?"

"Willingly," answered Ernest; and then he added,
smiling, "Methinks I never saw the Great Stone Face
look so hospitably at a stranger."

The poet sat down on the bench beside him, and he
and Ernest talked together. Often had the poet held
intercourse with the wittiest and the wisest, but never
before with a man like Ernest, whose thoughts and
feelings gushed up with such a natural freedom, and
who made great truths so familiar by his simple utterance of them. Angels, as had been so often said,
seemed to have wrought with him at his labor in the
fields; angels seemed to have sat with him by the fireside; and, dwelling with angels as friend with friends,
he had imbibed the sublimity of their ideas, and im-

bued it with the sweet and lowly charm of household
words.   So thought the poet.   And Ernest, on the
other hand, was moved and agitated by the living images which the poet flung out of his mind, and which
peopled all the air about the cottage door with shapes
of beauty, both gay and pensive.   The sympathies of
these two men instructed them with a profounder
sense than either could have attained alone.   Their
minds accorded into one strain, and made delightful
music which neither of them could have claimed as all
his own, nor distinguished his own share from the
other's.   They led one another, as it were, into a high
pavilion of their thoughts, so remote, and hitherto so
dim, that they had never entered it before, and so
beautiful that they desired to be there always.

As Ernest listened to the poet, he imagined that
the Great Stone Face was bending forward to listen
too.   He gazed earnestly into the poet's glowing eyes.

"Who are you, my strangely gifted guest?" he
said.

The poet laid his finger on the volume that Ernest
had been reading.

"You have read these poems," said he.   "You know
me, then—for I wrote them."

Again, and still more earnestly than before, Ernest
examined the poet's features; then turned toward the
Great Stone Face; then back, with an uncertain aspect, to his guest.   But his countenance fell; he shook
his head and sighed.

"Wherefore are you sad?" inquired the poet.

"Because," replied Ernest, "all through life I have

awaited the fulfilment of a prophecy; and, when I read
these poems, I hoped that it might be fulfilled in you."

"You hoped," answered the poet, faintly smiling,
"to find in me the likeness of the Great Stone Face.
And you are disappointed, as formerly with Mr. Gathergold, and Old Blood-and-Thunder, and Old Stony
Phiz. Yes, Ernest, it is my doom. You must add my
name to the illustrious three, and record another failure of your hopes. For—in shame and sadness do I
speak it, Ernest—I am not worthy to be typified by
yonder benign and majestic image."

"And why?" asked Ernest. He pointed to the volume. "Are not those thoughts divine?"

"They have a strain of the Divinity," replied the
poet. "You can hear in them the far-off echo of a
heavenly song. But my life, dear Ernest, has not
corresponded with my thought. I have had grand
dreams, but they have been only dreams, because I
have lived—and that, too, by my own choice—among
poor and mean realities. Sometimes even—shall I
dare to say it?—I lack faith in the grandeur, the beauty,
and the goodness, which my own works are said to
have made more evident in nature and in human life.
Why, then, pure seeker of the good and true, shouldst
thou hope to find me in yonder image of the divine?"

The poet spoke sadly, and his eyes were dim with
tears. So, likewise, were those of Ernest.

At the hour of sunset, as had long been his frequent
custom, Ernest was to discourse to an assemblage of the
neighboring inhabitants in the open air. He and the
poet, arm in arm, still talking together as they went

along, proceeded to the spot. It was a small nook among the hills, with a gray precipice behind, the stern front of which was relieved by the pleasant foliage of many creeping plants that made a tapestry for the naked rock, by hanging their festoons from all its rugged angles. At a small elevation above the ground, set in a rich framework of verdure, there appeared a niche, spacious enough to admit a human figure, with freedom for such gestures as spontaneously accompany earnest thought and genuine emotion. Into this natural pulpit Ernest ascended, and threw a look of familiar kindness around upon his audience. They stood, or sat, or reclined upon the grass, as seemed good to each, with the departing sunshine falling obliquely over them, and mingling its subdued cheerfulness with the solemnity of a grove of ancient trees, beneath and amid the boughs of which the golden rays were constrained to pass. In another direction was seen the Great Stone Face, with the same cheer, combined with the same solemnity, in its benignant aspect.

Ernest began to speak, giving to the people of what was in his heart and mind. His words had power, because they accorded with his thoughts; and his thoughts had reality and depth, because they harmonized with the life which he had always lived. It was not mere breath that this preacher uttered; they were the words of life, because a life of good deeds and holy love was melted into them. Pearls, pure and rich, had been dissolved into this precious draught. The poet, as he listened, felt that the being and character of Ernest were a nobler strain of poetry than he had ever written. His eyes glistening with tears, he gazed reverentially at the venerable man, and said within himself that never was there an aspect so worthy of a prophet and a sage as that mild, sweet, thoughtful countenance, with the glory of white hair diffused about it. At a distance, but distinctly to be seen, high up in the golden light of the setting sun, appeared the Great Stone Face, with hoary mists around it, like the white hairs around the brow of Ernest. Its look of grand beneficence seemed to embrace the world.

At that moment, in sympathy with a thought which he was about to utter, the face of Ernest assumed a grandeur of expression so imbued with benevolence that the poet, by an irresistible impulse, threw his arms aloft, and shouted:

"Behold! Behold! Ernest is himself the likeness of the Great Stone Face!"

Then all the people looked, and saw that what the deep-sighted poet said was true. The prophecy was fulfilled. But Ernest, having finished what he had to say, took the poet's arm, and walked slowly homeward, still hoping that some wiser and better man than himself would by and by appear, bearing a resemblance to the GREAT STONE FACE.

THE MAN IN THE RESERVOIR

BY CHARLES FENNO HOFFMAN

Charles Fenno Hoffman (born in New York in 1806, died June 7, 1884) was a literary lion of his day, with all the polite accomplishments. He roared gently as a sucking dove in poetry—"No American," says R. W. Griswold, "is comparable to him as a song writer." He rivaled N. P. Willis as an editor, establishing "The Knickerbocker Magazine," and conducting at various times "The American Monthly," "The Mirror," and "The Literary World." He wrote one of the best novels of the period, "Greyslaer." His short stories, however, have proved the most enduring of his works. "The Man in the Reservoir" is a fine specimen of the ready journalism that rises by its cleverness to the rank of genuine literature, and receives general acceptance as classic. For the last thirty-five years of his life Hoffman suffered from mental derangement.

THE MAN IN THE RESERVOIR

BY CHARLES FENNO HOFFMAN

YOU may see some of the best society in New York on the top of the Distributing Reservoir, any of these fine October mornings. There were two or three carriages in waiting, and half a dozen senatorial-looking mothers with young children, pacing the parapet, as we basked there the other day in the sunshine—now watching the pickerel that glide along the lucid edges of the black pool within, and now looking off upon the scene of rich and wondrous variety that spreads along the two rivers on either side.

"They may talk of Alpheus and Arethusa," murmured an idling sophomore, who had found his way thither during recitation hours, "but the Croton in passing over an arm of the sea at Spuyten Duyvil, and bursting to sight again in this truncated pyramid, beats it all hollow. By George, too, the bay yonder looks as blue as ever the Ægean Sea to Byron's eye, gazing from the Acropolis! But the painted foliage on these crags!—the Greeks must have dreamed of such a vegetable phenomenon in the midst of their grayish olive groves, or they never would have supplied the want of it in their landscape by embroidering their marble temples with gay colors. Did you see that pike break, sir?"

"I did not."

"Zounds! his silver fin flashed upon the black Acheron, like a restless soul that hoped yet to mount from the pool."

"The place seems suggestive of fancies to you?" we observed in reply to the rattlepate.

"It is, indeed, for I have done up a good deal of anxious thinking within a circle of a few yards where that fish broke just now."

"A singular place for meditation—the middle of the Reservoir!"

"You look incredulous, sir; but it's a fact. A fellow can never tell, until he is tried, in what situation his most earnest meditations may be concentrated. I am boring you, though?"

"Not at all. But you seem so familiar with the spot, I wish you could tell me why that ladder leading down to the water is lashed against the stonework in yonder corner."

"That ladder," said the young man, brightening at the question—"why, the position, perhaps the very existence, of that ladder resulted from my meditations in the Reservoir, at which you smiled just now. Shall I tell you all about them?"

"Pray do."

"Well, you have seen the notice forbidding any one to fish in the Reservoir. Now, when I read that warning, the spirit of the thing struck me at once as inferring nothing more than that one should not sully the temperance potations of our citizens by steeping bait in it, of any kind; but you probably know the common way of taking pike with a slip noose of delicate wire. I was determined to have a touch at the fellows with this kind of tackle.

"I chose a moonlight night; and an hour before the edifice was closed to visitors, I secreted myself within the walls, determined to pass the night on the top. All went as I could wish it. The night proved cloudy, but it was only a variable drift of broken clouds which obscured the moon. I had a walking cane-rod with me which would reach to the margin of the water, and several feet beyond if necessary. To this was attached the wire, about fifteen inches in length.

"I prowled along the parapet for a considerable time, but not a single fish could I see. The clouds made a flickering light and shade, that wholly foiled my steadfast gaze. I was convinced that should they come up thicker, my whole night's venture would be thrown away. 'Why should I not descend the sloping wall and get nearer on a level with the fish, for thus alone can I hope to see one?' The question had hardly shaped itself in my mind before I had one leg over the iron railing.

"If you look around you will see now that there are some half-dozen weeds growing here and there, amid the fissures of the solid masonry. In one of the fissures from whence these spring, I planted a foot and began my descent. The Reservoir was fuller than it is now, and a few strides would have carried me to the margin of the water. Holding on to the cleft above, I felt round with one foot for a place to plant it below me.

"In that moment the flap of a pound pike made me look round, and the roots of the weed upon which I partially depended gave way as I was in the act of turning. Sir, one's senses are sharpened in deadly peril; as I live now, I distinctly heard the bells of Trinity chiming midnight, as I rose to the surface the next instant, immersed in the stone caldron, where I must swim for my life Heaven only could tell how long!

"I am a capital swimmer; and this naturally gave me a degree of self-possession. Falling as I had, I of course had pitched out some distance from the sloping parapet. A few strokes brought me to the edge. I really was not yet certain but that I could clamber up the face of the wall anywhere. I hoped that I could. I felt certain at least there was some spot where I might get hold with my hands, even if I did not ultimately ascend it.

"I tried the nearest spot. The inclination of the wall was so vertical that it did not even rest me to lean against it. I felt with my hands and with my feet. Surely, I thought, there must be some fissure like those in which that ill-omened weed had found a place for its root!

"There was none. My fingers became sore in busying themselves with the harsh and inhospitable stones. My feet slipped from the smooth and slimy masonry beneath the water; and several times my face came in rude contact with the wall, when my foothold gave way on the instant that I seemed to have found some diminutive rocky cleat upon which I could stay myself.

"Sir, did you ever see a rat drowned in a half-filled hogshead—how he swims round, and round, and round; and after vainly trying the sides again and again with his paws, fixes his eyes upon the upper rim as if he would *look himself* out of his watery prison?

"I thought of the miserable vermin, thought of him as I had often watched thus his dying agonies, when a cruel urchin of eight or ten. Boys are horribly cruel, sir; boys, women, and savages. All child-like things are cruel; cruel from a want of thought and from perverse ingenuity, although by instinct each of these is so tender. You may not have observed it, but a savage is as tender to his own young as a boy is to a favorite puppy—the same boy that will torture a kitten out of existence. I thought then, I say, of the rat drowning in a half-filled cask of water, and lifting his gaze out of the vessel as he grew more and more desperate, and I flung myself on my back, and, floating thus, fixed my eyes upon the face of the moon.

"The moon is well enough in her way, however you may look at her; but her appearance is, to say the least of it, peculiar to a man floating on his back in the centre of a stone tank, with a dead wall of some fifteen or twenty feet rising squarely on every side of him!" (The young man smiled bitterly as he said this, and shuddered once or twice before he went on musingly.) "The last time I had noted the planet with any emotion she was on the wane. Mary was with me; I had brought her out here one morning to look at the

view from the top of the Reservoir. She said little
of the scene, but as we talked of our old childish loves,
I saw that its fresh features were incorporating themselves with tender memories of the past, and I was
content.

"There was a rich golden haze upon the landscape,
and as my own spirits rose amid the voluptuous atmosphere, she pointed to the waning planet, discernible like a faint gash in the welkin, and wondered how
long it would be before the leaves would fall. Strange
girl! did she mean to rebuke my joyous mood, as if
we had no right to be happy while Nature, withering
in her pomp, and the sickly moon, wasting in the blaze
of noontide, were there to remind us of 'the-gone-for-
ever'? 'They will all renew themselves, dear Mary,'
said I, encouragingly, 'and there is one that will ever
keep tryst alike with thee and nature through all sea-
sons, if thou wilt but be true to one of us, and remain
as now a child of nature.'

"A tear sprang to her eye, and then searching her
pocket for her card-case, she remembered an engagement to be present at Miss Lawson's opening of fall
bonnets at two o'clock!

"And yet, dear, wild, wayward Mary, I thought of
her now. You have probably outlived this sort of
thing, sir; but I, looking at the moon, as I floated
there upturned to her yellow light, thought of the
loved being whose tears I knew would flow when she
heard of my singular fate, at once so grotesque, yet
melancholy to awfulness.

"And how often we have talked, too, of that Carian

shepherd who spent his damp nights upon the hills,
gazing as I do on the lustrous planet! Who will
revel with her amid those old superstitions? Who,
from our own unlegended woods, will evoke their yet
undetected, haunting spirits? Who peer with her in
prying scrutiny into nature's laws, and challenge the
whispers of poetry from the voiceless throat of matter? Who laugh merrily over the stupid guesswork
of pedants, that never mingled with the infinitude of
nature, through love exhaustless and all-embracing,
as we have? Poor girl! she will be companionless.

"Alas! companionless forever—save in the exciting stages of some brisk flirtation. She will live here-
after by feeding other hearts with love's lore she has
learned from me, and then, Pygmalion-like, grow
fond of the images she has herself endowed with
semblance of divinity, until they seem to breathe
back the mystery the soul can truly catch from only
one.

"How anxious she will be lest the coroner shall
have discovered any of her notes in my pocket!

"I felt chilly as this last reflection crossed my mind,
partly at thought of the coroner, partly at the idea
of Mary being unwillingly compelled to wear mourning for me, in case of such a disclosure of our engagement. It is a provoking thing for a girl of
nineteen to have to go into mourning for a deceased
lover at the beginning of her second winter in the
metropolis.

"The water, though, with my motionless position,
must have had something to do with my chilliness. I

see, sir, you think that I tell my story with great
levity; but indeed, indeed I should grow delirious did
I venture to hold steadily to the awfulness of my feelings the greater part of that night. I think, indeed,
I must have been most of the time hysterical with horror, for the vibrating emotions I have recapitulated
did pass through my brain even as I have detailed
them.

"But as I now became calm in thought, I sum-
moned up again some resolution of action.

"I will begin at that corner (said I), and swim
around the whole inclosure. I will swim slowly and
again feel the sides of the tank with my feet. If die
I must, let me perish at least from well-directed
though exhausting effort, not sink from mere boot-
less weariness in sustaining myself till the morning
shall bring relief.

"The sides of the place seemed to grow higher as I
now kept my watery course beneath them. It was not
altogether a dead pull. I had some variety of emotion in making my circuit. When I swam in the
shadow, it looked to me more cheerful beyond in the
moonlight. When I swam in the moonlight, I had
the hope of making some discovery when I should
again reach the shadow. I turned several times on
my back to rest just where those wavy lines would
meet. The stars looked viciously bright to me from
the bottom of that well; there was such a company of
them; they were so glad in their lustrous revelry; and
they had such space to move in! I was alone, sad to
despair, in a strange element, prisoned, and a solitary

gazer upon their mocking chorus. And yet there was
nothing else with which I could hold communion!

"I turned upon my breast and struck out almost
frantically once more. The stars were forgotten; the
moon, the very world of which I as yet formed a part,
my poor Mary herself, were forgotten. I thought only
of the strong man there perishing; of me in my lusty
manhood, in the sharp vigor of my dawning prime,
with faculties illimitable, with senses all alert, battling
there with physical obstacles which men like myself
had brought together for my undoing. The Eternal
could never have willed this thing! I could not and
I would not perish thus. And I grew strong in in-
solence of self-trust; and I laughed aloud as I dashed
the sluggish water from side to side.

"Then came an emotion of pity for myself—of
wild regret; of sorrow, O, infinite for a fate so desolate, a doom so dreary, so heart-sickening! You may
laugh at the contradiction if you will, sir, but I felt
that I could sacrifice my own life on the instant, to
redeem another fellow-creature from such a place of
horror, from an end so piteous. My soul and my vital
spirit seemed in that desperate moment to be sepa-
rating; while one in parting grieved over the deplor-
able fate of the other.

"And then I prayed! I prayed, why or wherefore
I know not. It was not from fear. It could not have
been in hope. The days of miracles are past, and
there was no natural law by whose providential inter-
position I could be saved. *I* did not pray; it prayed of
itself, my soul within me.

6

"Was the calmness that I now felt torpidity—the torpidity that precedes dissolution to the strong swimmer who, sinking from exhaustion, must at last add a bubble to the wave as he suffocates beneath the element which now denied his mastery? If it were so, how fortunate was it that my floating rod at that moment attracted my attention as it dashed through the water by me. I saw on the instant that a fish had entangled itself in the wire noose. The rod quivered, plunged, came again to the surface, and rippled the water as it shot in arrowy flight from side to side of the tank. At last, driven toward the southeast corner of the Reservoir, the small end seemed to have got foul somewhere. The brazen butt, which, every time the fish sounded, was thrown up to the moon, now sank by its own weight, showing that the other end must be fast. But the cornered fish, evidently anchored somewhere by that short wire, floundered several times to the surface before I thought of striking out to the spot.

"The water is low now, and tolerably clear. You may see the very ledge there, sir, in yonder corner, on which the small end of my rod rested when I secured that pike with my hands. I did not take him from the slip-noose, however; but, standing upon the ledge, handled the rod in a workmanlike manner, as I flung that pound pickerel over the iron railing upon the top of the parapet. The rod, as I have told you, barely reached from the railing to the water. It was a heavy, strong bass rod which I had borrowed in the 'Spirit of the Times' office; and when I discovered

that the fish at the end of the wire made a strong
enough knot to prevent me from drawing my tackle
away from the railing around which it twined itself as
I threw, why, as you can at once see, I had but little
difficulty in making my way up the face of the wall
with such assistance. The ladder which attracted
your notice is, as you see, lashed to the iron railing in
the identical spot where I thus made my escape; and,
for fear of similar accidents, they have placed another
one in the corresponding corner of the other compart-
ment of the tank ever since my remarkable night's
adventure in the Reservoir."

THE DIAMOND LENS

BY FITZ-JAMES O'BRIEN

Fitz-James O'Brien (born in Limerick, Ireland, in 1828, died of wounds received as a Union soldier, 1862) may be claimed as an American author, since his work of enduring literary quality was all produced in this country, to which he removed in 1852. "He was a distinguished figure in the Bohemian New York of his day," says the "International Encyclopædia," "and witness to the impression that he made in that sprightly circle is preserved in a sheaf of personal recollections prefixed to 'The Poems and Stories of Fitz-James O'Brien,' edited by his friend, William Winter (1881)." His stories in particular display striking originality, marvelous ingenuity, and rare imagination. "The Diamond Lens" is acknowledged to be his masterpiece, although "The Wondersmith," a story of manikins animated by all the diabolic passions of life, presses hard upon it for imaginative quality.

THE DIAMOND LENS

BY FITZ-JAMES O'BRIEN

I

FROM a very early period of my life the entire bent of my inclinations had been toward microscopic investigations. When I was not more than ten years old, a distant relative of our family, hoping to astonish my inexperience, constructed a simple microscope for me by drilling in a disk of copper a small hole in which a drop of pure water was sustained by capillary attraction. This very primitive apparatus, magnifying some fifty diameters, presented, it is true, only indistinct and imperfect forms, but still sufficiently wonderful to work up my imagination to a preternatural state of excitement.

Seeing me so interested in this rude instrument, my cousin explained to me all that he knew about the principles of the miscroscope, related to me a few of the wonders which had been accomplished through its agency, and ended by promising to send me one regularly constructed, immediately on his return to the city. I counted the days, the hours, the minutes that intervened between that promise and his departure.

Meantime, I was not idle. Every transparent substance that bore the remotest resemblance to a lens I eagerly seized upon, and employed in vain attempts to realize that instrument the theory of whose construction I as yet only vaguely comprehended. All panes of glass containing those oblate spheroidal knots familiarly known as "bull's-eyes" were ruthlessly destroyed in the hope of obtaining lenses of marvelous power. I even went so far as to extract the crystalline humor from the eyes of fishes and animals, and endeavored to press it into the microscopic service. I plead guilty to having stolen the glasses from my Aunt Agatha's spectacles, with a dim idea of grinding them into lenses of wondrous magnifying properties—in which attempt it is scarcely necessary to say that I totally failed.

At last the promised instrument came. It was of that order known as Field's simple microscope, and had cost perhaps about fifteen dollars. As far as educational purposes went, a better apparatus could not have been selected. Accompanying it was a small treatise on the microscope—its history, uses, and discoveries. I comprehended then for the first time the "Arabian Nights' Entertainments." The dull veil of ordinary existence that hung across the world seemed suddenly to roll away, and to lay bare a land of enchantments. I felt toward my companions as the seer might feel toward the ordinary masses of men. I held conversations with nature in a tongue which they could not understand. I was in daily communication with living wonders such as they never imagined in their wildest visions. I penetrated beyond the external portal of things, and roamed through the sanctuaries. Where they beheld only a drop of rain slowly rolling down the window-glass, I saw a uni-

verse of beings animated with all the passions common
to physical life, and convulsing their minute sphere
with struggles as fierce and protracted as those of
men. In the common spots of mould, which my
mother, good housekeeper that she was, fiercely
scooped away from her jam-pots, there abode for me,
under the name of mildew, enchanted gardens, filled
with dells and avenues of the densest foliage and most
astonishing verdure, while from the fantastic boughs
of these microscopic forests hung strange fruits glittering with green and silver and gold.

It was no scientific thirst that at this time filled my
mind. It was the pure enjoyment of a poet to whom
a world of wonders has been disclosed. I talked of my
solitary pleasures to none. Alone with my microscope, I dimmed my sight, day after day and night
after night, poring over the marvels which it unfolded to me. I was like one who, having discovered
the ancient Eden still existing in all its primitive
glory, should resolve to enjoy it in solitude, and never
betray to mortal the secret of its locality. The rod
of my life was bent at this moment. I destined myself to be a microscopist.

Of course, like every novice, I fancied myself a discoverer. I was ignorant at the time of the thousands
of acute intellects engaged in the same pursuit as
myself, and with the advantage of instruments a thousand times more powerful than mine. The names
of Leeuwenhoek, Williamson, Spencer, Ehrenberg,
Schultz, Dujardin, Schact, and Schleiden were then
entirely unknown to me, or, if known, I was ignorant

of their patient and wonderful researches. In every fresh specimen of cryptogamia which I placed beneath my instrument I believed that I discovered wonders of which the world was as yet ignorant. I remember well the thrill of delight and admiration that shot through me the first time that I discovered the common wheel animalcule (*Rotifera vulgaris*) expanding and contracting its flexible spokes and seemingly rotating through the water. Alas! as I grew older, and obtained some works treating of my favorite study, I found that I was only on the threshold of a science to the investigation of which some of the greatest men of the age were devoting their lives and intellects.

As I grew up, my parents, who saw but little likelihood of anything practical resulting from the examination of bits of moss and drops of water through a brass tube and a piece of glass, were anxious that I should choose a profession. It was their desire that I should enter the counting-house of my uncle, Ethan Blake, a prosperous merchant, who carried on business in New York. This suggestion I decisively combated. I had no taste for trade; I should only make a failure; in short, I refused to become a merchant.

But it was necessary for me to select some pursuit. My parents were staid New England people, who insisted on the necessity of labor, and therefore, although, thanks to the bequest of my poor Aunt Agatha, I should, on coming of age, inherit a small fortune sufficient to place me above want, it was decided that, instead of waiting for this, I should act the nobler part, and employ the intervening years in rendering myself independent.

After much cogitation, I complied with the wishes of my family, and selected a profession. I determined to study medicine at the New York Academy. This disposition of my future suited me. A removal from my relatives would enable me to dispose of my time as I pleased without fear of detection. As long as I paid my Academy fees, I might shirk attending the lectures if I chose; and, as I never had the remotest intention of standing an examination, there was no danger of my being "plucked." Besides, a metropolis was the place for me. There I could obtain excellent instruments, the newest publications, intimacy with men of pursuits kindred with my own—in short, all things necessary to ensure a profitable devotion of my life to my beloved science. I had an abundance of money, few desires that were not bounded by my illuminating mirror on one side and my object-glass on the other; what, therefore, was to prevent my becoming an illustrious investigator of the veiled worlds? It was with the most buoyant hope that I left my New England home and established myself in New York.

II

My first step, of course, was to find suitable apartments. These I obtained, after a couple of days' search, in Fourth Avenue; a very pretty second floor, unfurnished, containing sitting-room, bedroom, and a smaller apartment which I intended to fit up as a laboratory. I furnished my lodgings simply, but rather elegantly, and then devoted all my energies to the adornment of the temple of my worship. I visited Pike, the celebrated optician, and passed in review his splendid collection of microscopes—Field's Compound, Hingham's, Spencer's, Nachet's Binocular (that founded on the principles of the stereoscope), and at length fixed upon that form known as Spencer's Trunnion Microscope, as combining the greatest number of improvements with an almost perfect freedom from tremor. Along with this I purchased every possible accessory—draw-tubes, micrometers, a *camera lucida,* lever-stage, achromatic condensers, white cloud illuminators, prisms, parabolic condensers, polarizing apparatus, forceps, aquatic boxes, fishing-tubes, with a host of other articles, all of which would have been useful in the hands of an experienced microscopist, but, as I afterward discovered, were not of the slightest present value to me. It takes years of practice to know how to use a complicated microscope. The optician looked suspiciously at me as I made these valuable purchases. He evidently was uncertain whether to set me down as some scientific celebrity or a madman. I think he was inclined to the latter belief. I suppose I was mad. Every great genius is mad upon the subject in which he is greatest. The unsuccessful madman is disgraced and called a lunatic.

Mad or not, I set myself to work with a zeal which few scientific students have ever equaled. I had everything to learn relative to the delicate study upon which I had embarked—a study involving the most earnest patience, the most rigid analytic powers, the steadiest hand, the most untiring eye, the most refined and subtle manipulation.

For a long time half my apparatus lay inactively on the shelves of my laboratory, which was now most amply furnished with every possible contrivance for facilitating my investigations. The fact was that I did not know how to use some of my scientific implements—never having been taught microscopics—and those whose use I understood theoretically were of little avail until by practice I could attain the necessary delicacy of handling. Still, such was the fury of my ambition, such the untiring perseverance of my experiments, that, difficult of credit as it may be, in the course of one year I became theoretically and practically an accomplished microscopist.

During this period of my labors, in which I submitted specimens of every substance that came under my observation to the action of my lenses, I became a discoverer—in a small way, it is true, for I was very young, but still a discoverer. It was I who destroyed Ehrenberg's theory that the *Volvox globator* was an animal, and proved that his "monads" with stomachs and eyes were merely phases of the formation of a vegetable cell, and were, when they reached their mature state, incapable of the act of conjugation, or any true generative act, without which no organism rising to any stage of life higher than vegetable can be said to be complete. It was I who resolved the singular problem of rotation in the cells and hairs of plants into ciliary attraction, in spite of the assertions of Wen-

ham and others that my explanation was the result
of an optical illusion.

But notwithstanding these discoveries, laboriously
and painfully made as they were, I felt horribly dissatisfied. At every step I found myself stopped by
the imperfections of my instruments. Like all active
microscopists, I gave my imagination full play. Indeed, it is a common complaint against many such that
they supply the defects of their instruments with the
creations of their brains. I imagined depths beyond
depths in nature which the limited power of my lenses
prohibited me from exploring. I lay awake at night
constructing imaginary microscopes of immeasurable
power, with which I seemed to pierce through all the
envelopes of matter down to its original atom. How
I cursed those imperfect mediums which necessity
through ignorance compelled me to use! How I
longed to discover the secret of some perfect lens,
whose magnifying power should be limited only by
the resolvability of the object, and which at the same
time should be free from spherical and chromatic aber-
rations—in short, from all the obstacles over which the
poor microscopist finds himself continually stumbling!
I felt convinced that the simple microscope, composed
of a single lens of such vast yet perfect power, was
possible of construction. To attempt to bring the compound microscope up to such a pitch would have been
commencing at the wrong end; this latter being simply a partially successful endeavor to remedy those
very defects of the simplest instrument which, if con-
quered, would leave nothing to be desired.

It was in this mood of mind that I became a constructive microscopist. After another year passed in this new pursuit, experimenting on every imaginable substance—glass, gems, flints, crystals, artificial crystals formed of the alloy of various vitreous materials —in short, having constructed as many varieties of lenses as Argus had eyes—I found myself precisely where I started, with nothing gained save an extensive knowledge of glass-making. I was almost dead with despair. My parents were surprised at my apparent want of progress in my medical studies (I had not attended one lecture since my arrival in the city), and the expenses of my mad pursuit had been so great as to embarrass me very seriously.

I was in this frame of mind one day, experimenting in my laboratory on a small diamond—that stone, from its great refracting power, having always occupied my attention more than any other—when a young Frenchman who lived on the floor above me, and who was in the habit of occasionally visiting me, entered the room.

I think that Jules Simon was a Jew. He had many traits of the Hebrew character: a love of jewelry, of dress, and of good living. There was something mysterious about him. He always had something to sell, and yet went into excellent society. When I say sell, I should perhaps have said peddle; for his operations were generally confined to the disposal of single articles—a picture, for instance, or a rare carving in ivory, or a pair of duelling-pistols, or the dress of a Mexican *caballero*. When I was first furnishing my rooms, he paid me a visit, which ended in **my pur-chasing** an antique silver lamp, which he assured **me** was a Cellini—it was handsome enough even for that —and some other knick-knacks for my sitting-room. Why Simon should pursue this petty trade I never could imagine. He apparently had plenty of money, and had the *entrée* of the best houses in the city— taking care, however, I suppose, to drive no bargains within the enchanted circle of the Upper Ten. I came at length to the conclusion that this peddling was but a mask to cover some greater object, and even went so far as to believe my young acquaintance to be im-plicated in the slave-trade. That, however, was none of my affair.

On the present occasion, Simon entered my room in a state of considerable excitement.

"Ah! mon ami!" he cried, before I could even offer him the ordinary salutation, "it has occurred to me to be the witness of the most astonishing things in the world. I promenade myself to the house of Ma-dame—— How does the little animal—*le renard*— name himself in the Latin?"

"Vulpes," I answered.

"Ah! yes—Vulpes. I promenade myself to the house of Madame Vulpes."

"The spirit medium?"

"Yes, the great medium. Great heavens! what a woman! I write on a slip of paper many of questions concerning affairs of the most secret—affairs that conceal themselves in the abysses of my heart the most profound; and behold, by example, what occurs? This devil of a woman makes me replies the most truthful to all of them. She talks to me of things that I do not love to talk of to myself. What am I to think? I am fixed to the earth!"

"Am I to understand you, M. Simon, that this Mrs. Vulpes replied to questions secretly written by you, which questions related to events known only to yourself?"

"Ah! more than that, more than that," he answered, with an air of some alarm. "She related to me things— But," he added after a pause, and suddenly changing his manner, "why occupy ourselves with these follies? It was all the biology, without doubt. It goes without saying that it has not my credence. But why are we here, *mon ami?* It has occurred to me to discover the most beautiful thing as you can imagine— a vase with green lizards on it, composed by the great Bernard Palissy. It is in my apartment; let us mount. I go to show it to you."

I followed Simon mechanically; but my thoughts were far from Palissy and his enameled ware, although I, like him, was seeking in the dark a great discovery. This casual mention of the spiritualist, Madame Vulpes, set me on a new track. What if, through communication with more subtle organisms than my own, I could reach at a single bound the goal which perhaps a life of agonizing mental toil would never enable me to attain?

While purchasing the Palissy vase from my friend Simon, I was mentally arranging a visit to Madame Vulpes.

III

Two evenings after this, thanks to an arrangement
by letter and the promise of an ample fee, I found Madame Vulpes awaiting me at her residence alone.   She
was a coarse-featured woman, with keen and rather
cruel dark eyes, and an exceedingly sensual expression about her mouth and under jaw.   She received
me in perfect silence, in an apartment on the ground
floor, very sparely furnished.   In the centre of the
room, close to where Mrs. Vulpes sat, there was a
common round mahogany table.   If I had come for
the purpose of sweeping her chimney, the woman could
not have looked more indifferent to my appearance.
There was no attempt to inspire the visitor with awe.
Everything bore a simple and practical aspect.   This
intercourse with the spiritual world was evidently as
familiar an occupation with Mrs. Vulpes as eating her
dinner or riding in an omnibus.

"You come for a communication, Mr. Linley?" said
the medium, in a dry, businesslike tone of voice.

"By appointment—yes."

"What sort of communication do you want—a written one?"

"Yes, I wish for a written one."

"From any particular spirit?"

"Yes."

"Have you ever known this spirit on this earth?"

"Never.   He died long before I was born.   I
wish merely to obtain from him some information

which he ought to be able to give better than any other."

"Will you seat yourself at the table, Mr. Linley," said the medium, "and place your hands upon it?"

I obeyed, Mrs. Vulpes being seated opposite to me, with her hands also on the table. We remained thus for about a minute and a half, when a violent succession of raps came on the table, on the back of my chair, on the floor immediately under my feet, and even on the window-panes. Mrs. Vulpes smiled composedly.

"They are very strong to-night," she remarked. "You are fortunate." She then continued, "Will the spirits communicate with this gentleman?"

Vigorous affirmative.

"Will the particular spirit he desires to speak with communicate?"

A very confused rapping followed this question.

"I know what they mean," said Mrs. Vulpes, addressing herself to me; "they wish you to write down the name of the particular spirit that you desire to converse with. Is that so?" she added, speaking to her invisible guests.

That it was so was evident from the numerous affirmatory responses. While this was going on, I tore a slip from my pocket-book and scribbled a name under the table.

"Will this spirit communicate in writing with this gentleman?" asked the medium once more.

After a moment's pause, her hand seemed to be seized with a violent tremor, shaking so forcibly that the table vibrated. She said that a spirit had seized her hand and would write. I handed her some sheets of paper that were on the table and a pencil. The latter she held loosely in her hand, which presently began to move over the paper with a singular and seemingly involuntary motion. After a few moments had elapsed, she handed me the paper, on which I found written, in a large, uncultivated hand, the words, "He is not here, but has been sent for." A pause of a minute or so ensued, during which Mrs. Vulpes remained perfectly silent, but the raps continued at regular intervals. When the short period I mention had elapsed, the hand of the medium was again seized with its convulsive tremor, and she wrote, under this strange influence, a few words on the paper, which she handed to me. They were as follows:

"I am here. Question me.
                    "LEEUWENHOEK."

I was astounded. The name was identical with that I had written beneath the table, and carefully kept concealed. Neither was it at all probable that an uncultivated woman like Mrs. Vulpes should know even the name of the great father of microscopics. It may have been biology; but this theory was soon doomed to be destroyed. I wrote on my slip—still concealing it from Mrs. Vulpes—a series of questions which, to avoid tediousness, I shall place with the responses, in the order in which they occurred:

I.—Can the microscope be brought to perfection?
Spirit.—Yes.
I.—Am I destined to accomplish this great task?

Spirit.—You are.

I.—I wish to know how to proceed to attain this end. For the love which you bear to science, help me!

Spirit.—A diamond of one hundred and forty carats, submitted to electro-magnetic currents for a long period, will experience a rearrangement of its atoms *inter se,* and from that stone you will form the universal lens.

I.—Will great discoveries result from the use of such a lens?

Spirit.—So great that all that has gone before is as nothing.

I.—But the refractive power of the diamond is so immense that the image will be formed within the lens. How is that difficulty to be surmounted?

Spirit.—Pierce the lens through its axis, and the difficulty is obviated. The image will be formed in the pierced space, which will itself serve as a tube to look through. Now I am called. Good-night.

I can not at all describe the effect that these extraordinary communications had upon me. I felt completely bewildered. No biological theory could account for the *discovery* of the lens. The medium might, by means of biological *rapport* with my mind, have gone so far as to read my questions and reply to them coherently. But biology could not enable her to discover that magnetic currents would so alter the crystals of the diamond as to remedy its previous defects and admit of its being polished into a perfect lens. Some such theory may have passed through my head,

it is true; but if so, I had forgotten it. In my
excited condition of mind there was no course
left but to become a convert, and it was in a
state of the most painful nervous exaltation that I
left the medium's house that evening. She accompanied me to the door, hoping that I was satisfied. The raps followed us as we went through
the hall, sounding on the balusters, the flooring, and
even the lintels of the door. I hastily expressed my
satisfaction, and escaped hurriedly into the cool night
air. I walked home with but one thought possessing
me—how to obtain a diamond of the immense size
required. My entire means multiplied a hundred times
over would have been inadequate to its purchase. Besides, such stones are rare, and become historical. I
could find such only in the regalia of Eastern or Euro-
pean monarchs.

IV

There was a light in Simon's room as I entered
my house. A vague impulse urged me to visit him.
As I opened the door of his sitting-room unannounced,
he was bending, with his back toward me, over a Carcel
lamp, apparently engaged in minutely examining some
object which he held in his hands. As I entered, he
started suddenly, thrust his hand into his breast pocket,
and turned to me with a face crimson with confusion.

"What!" I cried, "poring over the miniature of
some fair lady? Well, don't blush so much; I won't
ask to see it."

Simon laughed awkwardly enough, but made none

of the negative protestations usual on such occasions.
He asked me to take a seat.

"Simon," said I, "I have just come from Madame
Vulpes."

This time Simon turned as white as a sheet, and
seemed stupefied, as if a sudden electric shock had
smitten him. He babbled some incoherent words, and
went hastily to a small closet where he usually kept
his liquors. Although astonished at his emotion, I
was too preoccupied with my own idea to pay much
attention to anything else.

"You say truly when you call Madame Vulpes a
devil of a woman," I continued. "Simon, she told me
wonderful things to-night, or rather was the means of
telling me wonderful things. Ah! if I could only get
a diamond that weighed one hundred and forty carats!"

Scarcely had the sigh with which I uttered this
desire died upon my lips when Simon, with the aspect
of a wild beast, glared at me savagely, and, rushing to
the mantelpiece, where some foreign weapons hung
on the wall, caught up a Malay creese, and brandished
it furiously before him.

"No!" he cried in French, into which he always
broke when excited. "No! you shall not have it!
You are perfidious! You have consulted with
that demon, and desire my treasure! But I will
die first! Me, I am brave! You can not make
me fear!"

All this, uttered in a loud voice, trembling with
excitement, astounded me. I saw at a glance that
I had accidentally trodden upon the edges of Simon's

secret, whatever it was. It was necessary to reassure him.

"My dear Simon," I said, "I am entirely at a loss to know what you mean. I went to Madame Vulpes to consult with her on a scientific problem, to the solution of which I discovered that a diamond of the size I just mentioned was necessary. You were never alluded to during the evening, nor, so far as I was concerned, even thought of. What can be the meaning of this outburst? If you happen to have a set of valuable diamonds in your possession, you need fear nothing from me. The diamond which I require you could not possess; or, if you did possess it, you would not be living here."

Something in my tone must have completely reassured him, for his expression immediately changed to a sort of constrained merriment, combined, however, with a certain suspicious attention to my movements. He laughed, and said that I must bear with him; that he was at certain moments subject to a species of vertigo, which betrayed itself in incoherent speeches, and that the attacks passed off as rapidly as they came. He put his weapon aside while making this explanation, and endeavored, with some success, to assume a more cheerful air.

All this did not impose on me in the least. I was too much accustomed to analytical labors to be baffled by so flimsy a veil. I determined to probe the mystery to the bottom.

"Simon," I said gayly, "let us forget all this over a bottle of Burgundy. I have a case of Lausseure's

Clos Vougeot downstairs, fragrant with the odors and ruddy with the sunlight of the Côte d'Or. Let us have up a couple of bottles. What say you?"

"With all my heart," answered Simon smilingly.

I produced the wine and we seated ourselves to drink. It was of a famous vintage, that of 1848, a year when war and wine throve together, and its pure but powerful juice seemed to impart renewed vitality to the system. By the time we had half finished the second bottle, Simon's head, which I knew was a weak one, had begun to yield, while I remained calm as ever, only that every draught seemed to send a flush of vigor through my limbs. Simon's utterance became more and more indistinct. He took to singing French *chansons* of a not very moral tendency. I rose suddenly from the table just at the conclusion of one of those incoherent verses, and, fixing my eyes on him with a quiet smile, said, "Simon, I have deceived you. I learned your secret this evening. You may as well be frank with me. Mrs. Vulpes—or rather, one of her spirits—told me all."

He started with horror. His intoxication seemed for the moment to fade away, and he made a movement toward the weapon that he had a short time before laid down. I stopped him with my hand.

"Monster!" he cried passionately, "I am ruined! What shall I do? You shall never have it! I swear by my mother!"

"I don't want it," I said; "rest secure, but be frank with me. Tell me all about it."

The drunkenness began to return. He protested

with maudlin earnestness that I was entirely mistaken
—that I was intoxicated; then asked me to swear eternal secrecy, and promised to disclose the mystery to
me. I pledged myself, of course, to all. With an uneasy look in his eyes, and hands unsteady with drink
and nervousness, he drew a small case from his breast
and opened it. Heavens! How the mild lamplight
was shivered into a thousand prismatic arrows as it
fell upon a vast rose-diamond that glittered in the case!
I was no judge of diamonds, but I saw at a glance
that this was a gem of rare size and purity. I looked
at Simon with wonder and—must I confess it?—with
envy. How could he have obtained this treasure?
In reply to my questions, I could just gather from his
drunken statements (of which, I fancy, half the incoherence was affected) that he had been superintend-
ing a gang of slaves engaged in diamond-washing in
Brazil; that he had seen one of them secrete a diamond,
but, instead of informing his employers, had quietly
watched the negro until he saw him bury his treasure;
that he had dug it up and fled with it, but that as yet
he was afraid to attempt to dispose of it publicly—so
valuable a gem being almost certain to attract too
much attention to its owner's antecedents—and he
had not been able to discover any of those obscure
channels by which such matters are conveyed away
safely. He added that, in accordance with oriental
practice, he had named his diamond with the fanciful title of "The Eye of Morning."

While Simon was relating this to me, I regarded
the great diamond attentively. Never had I beheld

anything so beautiful. All the glories of light ever imagined or described seemed to pulsate in its crystalline chambers. Its weight, as I learned from Simon, was exactly one hundred and forty carats. Here was an amazing coincidence. The hand of destiny seemed in it. On the very evening when the spirit of Leeuwenhoek communicates to me the great secret of the microscope, the priceless means which he directs me to employ start up within my easy reach! I determined, with the most perfect deliberation, to possess myself of Simon's diamond.

I sat opposite to him while he nodded over his glass, and calmly revolved the whole affair. I did not for an instant contemplate so foolish an act as a common theft, which would of course be discovered, or at least necessitate flight and concealment, all of which must interfere with my scientific plans. There was but one step to be taken—to kill Simon. After all, what was the life of a little peddling Jew in comparison with the interests of science? Human beings are taken every day from the condemned prisons to be experimented on by surgeons. This man, Simon, was by his own confession a criminal, a robber, and I believed on my soul a murderer. He deserved death quite as much as any felon condemned by the laws: why should I not, like government, contrive that his punishment should contribute to the progress of human knowledge?

The means for accomplishing everything I desired lay within my reach. There stood upon the mantelpiece a bottle half full of French laudanum. Simon was so occupied with his diamond, which I had just restored to him, that it was an affair of no difficulty to drug his glass. In a quarter of an hour he was in a profound sleep.

I now opened his waistcoat, took the diamond from the inner pocket in which he had placed it, and removed him to the bed, on which I laid him so that his feet hung down over the edge. I had possessed myself of the Malay creese, which I held in my right hand, while with the other I discovered as accurately as I could by pulsation the exact locality of the heart. It was essential that all the aspects of his death should lead to the surmise of self-murder. I calculated the exact angle at which it was probable that the weapon, if leveled by Simon's own hand, would enter his breast; then with one powerful blow I thrust it up to the hilt in the very spot which I desired to penetrate. A convulsive thrill ran through Simon's limbs. I heard a smothered sound issue from his throat, precisely like the bursting of a large air-bubble sent up by a diver when it reaches the surface of the water; he turned half round on his side, and, as if to assist my plans more effectually, his right hand, moved by some mere spasmodic impulse, clasped the handle of the creese, which it remained holding with extraordinary muscular tenacity. Beyond this there was no apparent struggle. The laudanum, I presume, paralyzed the usual nervous action. He must have died instantly.

There was yet something to be done. To make it certain that all suspicion of the act should be diverted from any inhabitant of the house to Simon himself, it was necessary that the door should be found in the morning *locked on the inside*. How to do this, and afterward escape myself? Not by the window; that was a physical impossibility. Besides, I was determined that the windows *also* should be found bolted. The solution was simple enough. I descended softly to my own room for a peculiar instrument which I had used for holding small slippery substances, such as minute spheres of glass, etc. This instrument was nothing more than a long, slender hand-vise, with a very powerful grip and a considerable leverage, which last was accidentally owing to the shape of the handle. Nothing was simpler than, when the key was in the lock, to seize the end of its stem in this vise, through the keyhole, from the outside, and so lock the door. Previously, however, to doing this, I burned a number of papers on Simon's hearth. Suicides almost always burn papers before they destroy themselves. I also emptied some more laudanum into Simon's glass—having first removed from it all traces of wine —cleaned the other wine-glass, and brought the bottles away with me. If traces of two persons drinking had been found in the room, the question naturally would have arisen, Who was the second? Besides, the wine-bottles might have been identified as belonging to me. The laudanum I poured out to account for its presence in his stomach, in case of a *post-mortem* examination. The theory naturally would be that he first intended to poison himself, but, after swallowing a little of the drug, was either disgusted with its taste, or changed his mind from other motives, and chose the dagger. These arrangements made, I walked out, leaving the gas burning, locked the door with my vise, and went to bed.

Simon's death was not discovered until nearly three in the afternoon. The servant, astonished at seeing the gas burning—the light streaming on the dark landing from under the door—peeped through the keyhole and saw Simon on the bed. She gave the alarm. The door was burst open, and the neighborhood was in a fever of excitement.

Every one in the house was arrested, myself included. There was an inquest; but no clew to his death beyond that of suicide could be obtained. Curiously enough, he had made several speeches to his friends the preceding week that seemed to point to self-destruction. One gentleman swore that Simon had said in his presence that "he was tired of life." His landlord affirmed that Simon, when paying him his last month's rent, remarked that "he should not pay him rent much longer." All the other evidence corresponded—the door locked inside, the position of the corpse, the burned papers. As I anticipated, no one knew of the possession of the diamond by Simon, so that no motive was suggested for his murder. The jury, after a prolonged examination, brought in the usual verdict, and the neighborhood once more settled down to its accustomed quiet.

V

The three months succeeding Simon's catastrophe I devoted night and day to my diamond lens. I had constructed a vast galvanic battery, composed of nearly two thousand pairs of plates: a higher power I dared not use, lest the diamond should be calcined. By means of this enormous engine I was enabled to send a powerful current of electricity continually through my great diamond, which it seemed to me gained in lustre every day. At the expiration of a month I commenced the grinding and polishing of the lens, a work of intense toil and exquisite delicacy. The great density of the stone, and the care required to be taken with the curvatures of the surfaces of the lens, rendered the labor the severest and most harassing that I had yet undergone.

At last the eventful moment came; the lens was completed. I stood trembling on the threshold of new worlds. I had the realization of Alexander's famous wish before me. The lens lay on the table, ready to be placed upon its platform. My hand fairly shook as I enveloped a drop of water with a thin coating of oil of turpentine, preparatory to its examination, a process necessary in order to prevent the rapid evaporation of the water. I now placed the drop on a thin slip of glass under the lens, and throwing upon it, by the combined aid of a prism and a mirror, a powerful stream of light, I approached my eye to the minute hole drilled through the axis of the lens. For an instant I saw nothing save what seemed to be an illuminated chaos, a vast, luminous abyss. A pure white light, cloudless and serene, and seemingly limitless as space itself, was my first impression. Gently, and with the greatest care, I depressed the lens a few hairbreadths. The wondrous illumination still continued, but as the lens approached the object a scene of indescribable beauty was unfolded to my view.

I seemed to gaze upon a vast space, the limits of which extended far beyond my vision. An atmosphere of magical luminousness permeated the entire field of view. I was amazed to see no trace of animalculous life. Not a living thing, apparently, inhabited that dazzling expanse. I comprehended instantly that, by the wondrous power of my lens, I had penetrated beyond the grosser particles of aqueous matter, beyond the realms of infusoria and protozoa, down to the original gaseous globule, into whose luminous interior I was gazing as into an almost boundless dome filled with a supernatural radiance.

It was, however, no brilliant void into which I looked. On every side I beheld beautiful inorganic forms, of unknown texture, and colored with the most enchanting hues. These forms presented the appearance of what might be called, for want of a more specific definition, foliated clouds of the highest rarity —that is, they undulated and broke into vegetable formations, and were tinged with splendors compared with which the gilding of our autumn woodlands is as dross compared with gold. Far away into the illimitable distance stretched long avenues of these gaseous forests, dimly transparent, and painted with prismatic hues of unimaginable brilliancy. The pendent branches waved along the fluid glades until every vista seemed to break through half-lucent ranks of many-colored drooping silken pennons. What seemed to be either fruits or flowers, pied with a thousand hues, lustrous and ever-varying, bubbled from the crowns of this fairy foliage. No hills, no lakes, no rivers, no forms animate or inanimate, were to be seen, save those vast auroral copses that floated serenely in the luminous stillness, with leaves and fruits and flowers gleaming with unknown fires, unrealizable by mere imagination.

How strange, I thought, that this sphere should be thus condemned to solitude! I had hoped, at least, to discover some new form of animal life, perhaps of a lower class than any with which we are at present acquainted, but still some living organism. I found my newly discovered world, if I may so speak, a beautiful chromatic desert.

While I was speculating on the singular arrangements of the internal economy of Nature, with which she so frequently splinters into atoms our most compact theories, I thought I beheld a form moving slowly through the glades of one of the prismatic forests. I looked more attentively, and found that I was not mistaken. Words can not depict the anxiety with which I awaited the nearer approach of this mysterious object. Was it merely some inanimate substance, held in suspense in the attenuated atmosphere of the globule, or was it an animal endowed with vitality and motion? It approached, flitting behind the gauzy, colored veils of cloud-foliage, for seconds dimly revealed, then vanishing. At last the violet pennons that trailed nearest to me vibrated; they

were gently pushed aside, and the form floated out
into the broad light.

It was a female human shape. When I say human,
I mean it possessed the outlines of humanity; but there
the analogy ends. Its adorable beauty lifted it illimitable heights beyond the loveliest daughter of Adam.

I can not, I dare not, attempt to inventory the
charms of this divine revelation of perfect beauty.
Those eyes of mystic violet, dewy and serene, evade
my words. Her long, lustrous hair following her
glorious head in a golden wake, like the track sown
in heaven by a falling star, seems to quench my most
burning phrases with its splendors. If all the bees of
Hybla nestled upon my lips, they would still sing but
hoarsely the wondrous harmonies of outline that inclosed her form.

She swept out from between the rainbow-curtains
of the cloud-trees into the broad sea of light that lay
beyond. Her motions were those of some graceful
naiad, cleaving, by a mere effort of her will, the clear,
unruffled waters that fill the chambers of the sea. She
floated forth with the serene grace of a frail bubble
ascending through the still atmosphere of a June day.
The perfect roundness of her limbs formed suave and
enchanting curves. It was like listening to the most
spiritual symphony of Beethoven the divine, to watch
the harmonious flow of lines. This, indeed, was a
pleasure cheaply purchased at any price. What cared
I if I had waded to the portal of this wonder through
another's blood. I would have given my own to enjoy
one such moment of intoxication and delight.

Breathless with gazing on this lovely wonder, and forgetful for an instant of everything save her presence, I withdrew my eye from the microscope eagerly. Alas! as my gaze fell on the thin slide that lay beneath my instrument, the bright light from mirror and from prism sparkled on a colorless drop of water! There, in that tiny bead of dew, this beautiful being was forever imprisoned. The planet Neptune was not more distant from me than she. I hastened once more to apply my eye to the microscope.

Animula (let me now call her by that dear name which I subsequently bestowed on her) had changed her position. She had again approached the wondrous forest, and was gazing earnestly upward. Presently one of the trees—as I must call them—unfolded a long ciliary process, with which it seized one of the gleaming fruits that glittered on its summit, and, sweeping slowly down, held it within reach of Animula. The sylph took it in her delicate hand and began to eat. My attention was so entirely absorbed by her that I could not apply myself to the task of determining whether this singular plant was or was not instinct with volition.

I watched her, as she made her repast, with the most profound attention. The suppleness of her motions sent a thrill of delight through my frame; my heart beat madly as she turned her beautiful eyes in the direction of the spot in which I stood. What would I not have given to have had the power to precipitate myself into that luminous ocean and float with her through those grooves of purple and gold!

While I was thus breathlessly following her every movement, she suddenly started, seemed to listen foɪ a moment, and then cleaving the brilliant ether in which she was floating, like a flash of light, pierced through the opaline forest and disappeared.

Instantly a series of the most singular sensations attacked me. It seemed as if I had suddenly gone blind. The luminous sphere was still before me, but my daylight had vanished. What caused this sudden disappearance? Had she a lover or a husband? Yes, that was the solution! Some signal from a happy fellow-being had vibrated through the avenues of the forest, and she had obeyed the summons.

The agony of my sensations, as I arrived at this conclusion, startled me. I tried to reject the conviction that my reason forced upon me. I battled against the fatal conclusion—but in vain. It was so. I had no escape from it. I loved an animalcule.

It is true that, thanks to the marvelous power of my microscope, she appeared of human proportions. Instead of presenting the revolting aspect of the coarser creatures, that live and struggle and die, in the more easily resolvable portions of the water-drop, she was fair and delicate and of surpassing beauty. But of what account was all that? Every time that my eye was withdrawn from the instrument it fell on a miserable drop of water, within which, I must be content to know, dwelt all that could make my life lovely.

Could she but see me once! Could I for one moment pierce the mystical walls that so inexorably rose to separate us, and whisper all that filled my soul, I might consent to be satisfied for the rest of my life with the knowledge of her remote sympathy. It would be something to have established even the faintest personal link to bind us together—to know that at times, when roaming through these enchanted glades, she might think of the wonderful stranger who had broken the monotony of her life with his presence and left a gentle memory in her heart!

But it could not be. No invention of which human intellect was capable could break down the barriers that nature had erected. I might feast my soul upon her wondrous beauty, yet she must always remain ignorant of the adoring eyes that day and night gazed upon her, and, even when closed, beheld her in dreams. With a bitter cry of anguish I fled from the room, and, flinging myself on my bed, sobbed myself to sleep like a child.

VI

I arose the next morning almost at daybreak, and rushed to my microscope. I trembled as I sought the luminous world in miniature that contained my all. Animula was there. I had left the gas-lamp, surrounded by its moderators, burning when I went to bed the night before. I found the sylph bathing, as it were, with an expression of pleasure animating her features, in the brilliant light which surrounded her. She tossed her lustrous golden hair over her shoulders with innocent coquetry. She lay at full length in the transparent medium, in which she supported herself

with ease, and gamboled with the enchanting grace
that the nymph Salmacis might have exhibited when
she sought to conquer the modest Hermaphroditus.
I tried an experiment to satisfy myself if her powers
of reflection were developed. I lessened the lamplight
considerably. By the dim light that remained, I could
see an expression of pain flit across her face. She
looked upward suddenly, and her brows contracted.
I flooded the stage of the microscope again with a
full stream of light, and her whole expression
changed. She sprang forward like some substance
deprived of all weight. Her eyes sparkled and her
lips moved. Ah! if science had only the means of
conducting and reduplicating sounds, as it does rays
of light, what carols of happiness would then have
entranced my ears! what jubilant hymns to Adonais
would have thrilled the illumined air!

I now comprehended how it was that the Count de
Cabalis peopled his mystic world with sylphs—beautiful beings whose breath of life was lambent fire, and
who sported forever in regions of purest ether and
purest light. The Rosicrucian had anticipated the
wonder that I had practically realized.

How long this worship of my strange divinity went
on thus I scarcely know. I lost all note of time. All
day from early dawn, and far into the night, I was
to be found peering through that wonderful lens. I
saw no one, went nowhere, and scarce allowed myself sufficient time for my meals. My whole life was
absorbed in contemplation as rapt as that of any of
the Romish saints. Every hour that I gazed upon the

divine form strengthened my passion—a passion that was always overshadowed by the maddening conviction that, although I could gaze on her at will, she never, never could behold me!

At length I grew so pale and emaciated, from want of rest and continual brooding over my insane love and its cruel conditions, that I determined to make some effort to wean myself from it. "Come," I said, "this is at best but a fantasy. Your imagination has bestowed on Animula charms which in reality she does not possess. Seclusion from female society has produced this morbid condition of mind. Compare her with the beautiful women of your own world, and this false enchantment will vanish."

I looked over the newspapers by chance. There I beheld the advertisement of a celebrated *danseuse* who appeared nightly at Niblo's. The Signorina Caradolce had the reputation of being the most beautiful as well as the most graceful woman in the world. I instantly dressed and went to the theatre.

The curtain drew up. The usual semicircle of fairies in white muslin were standing on the right toe around the enameled flower-bank of green canvas, on which the belated prince was sleeping. Suddenly a flute is heard. The fairies start. The trees open, the fairies all stand on the left toe, and the queen enters. It was the Signorina. She bounded forward amid thunders of applause, and, lighting on one foot, remained poised in the air. Heavens! was this the great enchantress that had drawn monarchs at her chariot-wheels? Those heavy, muscular limbs, those thick ankles, those cavernous eyes, that stereotyped smile, those crudely painted cheeks! Where were the vermeil blooms, the liquid, expressive eyes, the harmonious limbs of Animula?

The Signorina danced. What gross, discordant movements! The play of her limbs was all false and artificial. Her bounds were painful athletic efforts; her poses were angular and distressed the eye. I could bear it no longer; with an exclamation of disgust that drew every eye upon me, I rose from my seat in the very middle of the Signorina's *pas-de-fascination* and abruptly quitted the house.

I hastened home to feast my eyes once more on the lovely form of my sylph. I felt that henceforth to combat this passion would be impossible. I applied my eyes to the lens. Animula was there—but what could have happened? Some terrible change seemed to have taken place during my absence. Some secret grief seemed to cloud the lovely features of her I gazed upon. Her face had grown thin and haggard; her limbs trailed heavily; the wondrous lustre of her golden hair had faded. She was ill—ill, and I could not assist her! I believe at that moment I would have forfeited all claims to my human birthright if I could only have been dwarfed to the size of an animalcule, and permitted to console her from whom fate had forever divided me.

I racked my brain for the solution of this mystery. What was it that afflicted the sylph? She seemed to suffer intense pain. Her features contracted, and she even writhed, as if with some internal agony. The

wondrous forests appeared also to have lost half their
beauty. Their hues were dim and in some places
faded away altogether. I watched Animula for hours
with a breaking heart, and she seemed absolutely to
wither away under my very eye. Suddenly I remembered that I had not looked at the water-drop for
several days. In fact, I hated to see it; for it reminded me of the natural barrier between Animula
and myself. I hurriedly looked down on the stage of
the microscope. The slide was still there—but, great
heavens, the water drop had vanished! The awful
truth burst upon me; it had evaporated, until it had
become so minute as to be invisible to the naked eye;
I had been gazing on its last atom, the one that contained Animula—and she was dying!

I rushed again to the front of the lens and looked
through. Alas! the last agony had seized her. The
rainbow-hued forests had all melted away, and Animula lay struggling feebly in what seemed to be a
spot of dim light. Ah! the sight was horrible: the
limbs once so round and lovely shriveling up into
nothings; the eyes—those eyes that shone like heaven
—being quenched into black dust; the lustrous golden
hair now lank and discolored. The last throe came.
I beheld that final struggle of the blackening form—
and I fainted.

When I awoke out of a trance of many hours, I
found myself lying amid the wreck of my instrument,
myself as shattered in mind and body as it. I crawled
feebly to my bed, from which I did not rise for many
months.

They say now that I am mad; but they are mistaken. I am poor, for I have neither the heart nor the will to work; all my money is spent, and I live on charity. Young men's associations that love a joke invite me to lecture on optics before them, for which they pay me, and laugh at me while I lecture. "Linley, the mad microscopist," is the name I go by. I suppose that I talk incoherently while I lecture. Who could talk sense when his brain is haunted by such ghastly memories, while ever and anon among the shapes of death I behold the radiant form of my lost Animula!

THE MAN WITHOUT A COUNTRY

BY EDWARD EVERETT HALE

Edward Everett Hale (born in Boston, April 3, 1822) has given in an article entitled "The Story of a Story," appearing in "The Writer" for June, 1897, a most interesting and valuable account of how he conceived, planned, and builded his masterpiece, "The Man Without a Country." He says in part: "At that time (1863) a Western politician of some notoriety (Clement L. Vallandigham) had said that he did not wish to belong to the United States. General Burnside, who was in command of the district where he lived, arrested him and sent him over the border. ... I had determined to show that it is a very bad thing to have no country. I had to show this for a whole lifetime. So I invented a man who expressed this wish when a young man, and who died as an old man, after he had tried his experiment."

THE MAN WITHOUT A COUNTRY

BY EDWARD EVERETT HALE

I SUPPOSE that very few casual readers of the "New York Herald" of August 13, 1863, observed, in an obscure corner, among the "Deaths," the announcement:

> "NOLAN. Died, on board U. S. Corvette "Levant," Lat. 2° 11′ S., Long. 131° W., on the 11th of May, PHILIP NOLAN."

I happened to observe it, because I was stranded at the old Mission House in Mackinaw, waiting for a Lake Superior steamer which did not choose to come, and I was devouring to the very stubble all the current literature I could get hold of, even down to the deaths and marriages in the "Herald." My memory for names and people is good, and the reader will see, as he goes on, that I had reason enough to remember Philip Nolan. There are hundreds of readers who would have paused at that announcement, if the officer of the "Levant" who reported it had chosen to make it thus: "Died, May 11, THE MAN WITHOUT A COUNTRY." For it was as "The Man Without a Country" that poor Philip Nolan had generally been known by the officers who had him in charge during some fifty years, as, indeed, by all the men who sailed under them. I dare say there is many a man who has taken wine with him once a fortnight, in a three years' cruise, who never knew that his name was "Nolan," or whether the poor wretch had any name at all.

There can now be no possible harm in telling this poor creature's story. Reason enough there has been till now, ever since Madison's administration went out in 1817, for very strict secrecy, the secrecy of honor itself, among the gentlemen of the navy who have had Nolan in successive charge. And certainly it speaks well for the *esprit de corps* of the profession, and the personal honor of its members, that to the press this man's story has been wholly unknown— and, I think, to the country at large also. I have reason to think, from some investigations I made in the Naval Archives when I was attached to the Bureau of Construction, that every official report relating to him was burned when Ross burned the public buildings at Washington. One of the Tuckers, or possibly one of the Watsons, had Nolan in charge at the end of the war; and when, on returning from his cruise, he reported at Washington to one of the Crowninshields— who was in the Navy Department when he came home —he found that the Department ignored the whole business. Whether they really knew nothing about it, or whether it was a "Non mi ricordo," determined on as a piece of policy, I do not know. But this I do know, that since 1817, and possibly before, no naval officer has mentioned Nolan in his report of a cruise.

But, as I say, there is no need for secrecy any longer. And now the poor creature is dead, it seems to me worth while to tell a little of his story, by way

of showing young Americans of to-day what it is to
be A Man Without a Country.

.   .   .   .

Philip Nolan was as fine a young officer as there was
in the "Legion of the West," as the Western division
of our army was then called. When Aaron Burr made
his first dashing expedition down to New Orleans in
1805, at Fort Massac, or somewhere above on the
river, he met, as the Devil would have it, this gay,
dashing, bright young fellow; at some dinner-party,
I think. Burr marked him, talked to him, walked with
him, took him a day or two's voyage in his flatboat,
and, in short, fascinated him. For the next year, bar-
rack-life was very tame to poor Nolan. He occasionally availed himself of the permission the great man
had given him to write to him. Long, high-worded,
stilted letters the poor boy wrote and rewrote and
copied. But never a line did he have in reply from the
gay deceiver. The other boys in the garrison sneered
at him, because he sacrificed in this unrequited affection for a politician the time which they devoted to
Monongahela, hazard, and high-low-jack. • Bourbon,
euchre, and poker were still unknown. But one day
Nolan had his revenge. This time Burr came down
the river not as an attorney seeking a place for his
office, but as a disguised conqueror. He had defeated
I know not how many district attorneys; he had dined
at I know not how many public dinners; he had been
heralded in I know not how many "Weekly Arguses,"
and it was rumored that he had an army behind him
and an empire before him. It was a great day—his

arrival—to poor Nolan. Burr had not been at the fort an hour before he sent for him. That evening he asked Nolan to take him out in his skiff, to show him a canebrake or a cottonwood tree, as he said—really to seduce him; and by the time the sail was over, Nolan was enlisted body and soul. From that time, though he did not yet know it, he lived as A MAN WITHOUT A COUNTRY.

What Burr meant to do I know no more than you, dear reader. It is none of our business just now. Only, when the grand catastrophe came, and Jefferson and the House of Virginia of that day undertook to break on the wheel all the possible Clarences of the then House of York, by the great treason trial at Richmond, some of the lesser fry in that distant Mississippi Valley, which was further from us than Puget's Sound is to-day, introduced the like novelty on their provincial stage; and, to while away the monotony of the summer at Fort Adams, got up, for *spectacles,* a string of court-martials on the officers there. One and another of the colonels and majors were tried, and, to fill out the list, little Nolan, against whom, Heaven knows, there was evidence enough—that he was sick of the service, had been willing to be false to it, and would have obeyed any order to march anywhither with any one who would follow him had the order been signed "By command of His Exc. A. Burr." The courts dragged on. The big flies escaped—rightly, for all I know. Nolan was proved guilty enough, as I say. Yet you and I would never have heard of him, reader, but that, when the president of the court

asked him at the close whether he wished to say anything to show that he had always been faithful to the
United States, he cried out in a fit of frenzy:

"Damn the United States! I wish I may never
hear of the United States again!"

I suppose he did not know how the words shocked
old Colonel Morgan, who was holding the court.
Half the officers who sat in it had served through the
Revolution, and their lives, not to say their necks, had
been risked for the very idea which he so cavalierly
cursed in his madness. He, on his part, had grown up
in the West of those days, in the midst of "Spanish
plot," "Orleans plot," and all the rest. He had been educated on a plantation where the finest company was a
Spanish officer or a French merchant from Orleans. His
education, such as it was, had been perfected in com-
mercial expeditions to Vera Cruz, and I think he told
me his father once hired an Englishman to be a private
tutor for a winter on the plantation. He had spent
half his youth with an older brother, hunting horses
in Texas, and, in a word, to him "United States" was
scarcely a reality. Yet he had been fed by "United
States" for all the years since he had been in the
army. He had sworn on his faith as a Christian to be
true to "United States." It was "United States" which
gave him the uniform he wore, and the sword by his
side. Nay, my poor Nolan, it was only because
"United States" had picked you out first as one of her
own confidential men of honor that "A. Burr" cared
for you a straw more than for the flat-boat men who
sailed his ark for him. I do not excuse Nolan; I only

explain to the reader why he damned his country, and wished he might never hear her name again.

He heard her name but once again. From that moment, September 23, 1807, till the day he died, May 11, 1863, he never heard her name again. For that half-century and more he was a man without a country.

Old Morgan, as I said, was terribly shocked. If Nolan had compared George Washington to Benedict Arnold, or had cried "God save King George," Morgan would not have felt worse. He called the court into his private room, and returned in fifteen minutes, with a face like a sheet, to say:

"Prisoner, hear the sentence of the Court! The Court decides, subject to the approval of the President, that you never hear the name of the United States again."

Nolan laughed. But nobody else laughed. Old Morgan was too solemn, and the whole room was hushed dead as night for a minute. Even Nolan lost his swagger in a moment. Then Morgan added:

"Mr. Marshal, take the prisoner to Orleans in an armed boat, and deliver him to the naval commander there."

The marshal gave his orders and the prisoner was taken out of court.

"Mr. Marshal," continued old Morgan, "see that no one mentions the United States to the prisoner. Mr. Marshal, make my respects to Lieutenant Mitchell at Orleans, and request him to order that no one shall mention the United States to the prisoner while he is on board ship. You will receive your written orders

from the officer on duty here this evening. The court
is adjourned without day."

I have always supposed that Colonel Morgan himself
took the proceedings of the court to Washington city
and explained them to Mr. Jefferson. Certain it is
that the President approved them—certain, that is, if
I may believe the men who say they have seen his
signature. Before the "Nautilus" got round from
New Orleans to the northern Atlantic coast with the
prisoner on board, the sentence had been approved,
and he was a man without a country.

The plan then adopted was substantially the same
which was necessarily followed ever after. Perhaps it
was suggested by the necessity of sending him by water from Fort Adams and Orleans. The Secretary of
the Navy—it must have been the first Crowninshield,
though he is a man I do not remember—was requested
to put Nolan on board a government vessel bound on
a long cruise, and to direct that he should be only so
far confined there as to make it certain that he never
saw or heard of the country. We had few long
cruises then, and the navy was very much out of favor;
and as almost all of this story is traditional, as I have
explained, I do not know certainly what his first cruise
was. But the commander to whom he was intrusted—
perhaps it was Tingey or Shaw, though I think it was
one of the younger men (we are all old enough now)
—regulated the etiquette and the precautions of the
affair, and according to his scheme they were carried
out, I suppose, till Nolan died.

When I was second officer of the "Intrepid," some

thirty years after, I saw the original paper of instructions. I have been sorry ever since that I did not copy the whole of it. It ran, however, much in this way:

"WASHINGTON (with a date which must have been late in 1807).

"*Sir*—You will receive from Lieutenant Neale the person of Philip Nolan, late a lieutenant in the United States Army.

"This person on his trial by court-martial expressed, with an oath, the wish that he might 'never hear of the United States again.'

"The Court sentenced him to have his wish fulfilled.

"For the present, the execution of the order is intrusted by the President to this Department.

"You will take the prisoner on board your ship, and keep him there with such precautions as shall prevent his escape.

"You will provide him with such quarters, rations, and clothing as would be proper for an officer of his late rank if he were a passenger on your vessel on the business of his Government.

"The gentlemen on board will make any arrangements agreeable to themselves regarding his society. He is to be exposed to no indignity of any kind, nor is he ever unnecessarily to be reminded that he is a prisoner.

"But under no circumstances is he ever to hear of his country or to see any information regarding it; and you will especially caution all the officers under your command to take care that, in the various indulgences which may be granted, this rule, in which his punishment is involved, shall not be broken.

"It is the intention of the Government that he shall never again see the country which he has disowned. Before the end of your cruise you will receive orders which will give effect to this intention.

"Respectfully yours,
"W. SOUTHARD, for the
"Secretary of the Navy."

If I had only preserved the whole of this paper, there would be no break in the beginning of my sketch of this story. For Captain Shaw, if it were he, handed it to his successor in the charge, and he to his, and I suppose the commander of the "Levant" has it to-day as his authority for keeping this man in this mild custody.

The rule adopted on board the ships on which I have met "the man without a country" was, I think, transmitted from the beginning.   No mess liked to have him permanently, because his presence cut off all talk of home or of the prospect of return, of politics or letters, of peace or of war—cut off more than half the talk men like to have at sea.   But it was always thought too hard that he should never meet the rest of us, except to touch hats, and we finally sank into one system.   He was not permitted to talk with the men unless an officer was by.   With officers he had unrestrained intercourse, as far as they and he chose.   But he grew shy, though he had favorites: I was one.   Then the captain always asked him to dinner on Monday.   Every mess in succession took up the invitation in its turn.   According to the size of the ship, you had him at your mess more or less often at dinner.   His breakfast he ate in his own stateroom—which was where a sentinel or somebody on the watch could see the door.   And whatever else he ate or drank, he ate or drank alone.   Sometimes, when the marines or sailors had any special jollification, they were permitted to invite "Plain-Buttons," as they called him. Then Nolan was sent with some officer, and the men were forbidden to speak of home while he was there.   I believe the theory was that the sight of his punishment did them good.   They called him "Plain-Buttons" because, while he always chose to wear a regulation army uniform, he was not permitted to wear the army button, for the reason that it bore either the initials or the insignia of the country he had disowned.

I remember, soon after I joined the navy, I was on shore with some of the older officers from our ship and from the "Brandywine," which we had met at Alexandria. We had leave to make a party and go up to Cairo and the Pyramids. As we jogged along (you went on donkeys then), some of the gentlemen (we boys called them "Dons," but the phrase was long since changed) fell to talking about Nolan, and some one told the system which was adopted from the first about his books and other reading. As he was almost never permitted to go on shore, even though the vessel lay in port for months, his time at the best hung heavy; and everybody was permitted to lend him books if they were not published in America and made no allusion to it. These were common enough in the old days, when people in the other hemisphere talked of the United States as little as we do of Paraguay. He had almost all the foreign papers that came into the ship, sooner or later; only somebody must go over them first, and cut out any advertisement or stray paragraph that alluded to America. This was a little cruel sometimes, when the back of what was cut out might be as innocent as Hesiod. Right in the midst of one of Napoleon's battles, or one of Canning's speeches, poor Nolan would find a great hole, because on the back of the page of that paper there had been an advertisement of a packet for New York, or a scrap from the President's message. I say this was the first time I ever heard of this plan, which afterward I had enough and more than enough to do with.   I remember it, because poor Phillips, who was of the party, as soon as the allusion to reading was made, told a story of something which happened at the Cape of Good Hope on Nolan's first voyage; and it is the only thing I ever knew of that voyage.   They had touched at the Cape, and had done the civil thing with the English Admiral and the fleet, and then, leaving for a long cruise up the Indian Ocean, Phillips had borrowed a lot of English books from an officer, which, in those days, as indeed in these, was quite a windfall. Among them, as the Devil would order, was the "Lay of the Last Minstrel," which they had all of them heard of, but which most of them had never seen.   I think it could not have been published long.   Well, nobody thought there could be any risk of anything national in that, though Phillips swore old Shaw had cut out the "Tempest" from Shakespeare before he let Nolan have it, because he said "the Bermudas ought to be ours, and, by Jove, should be one day."   So Nolan was permitted to join the circle one afternoon when a lot of them sat on deck smoking and reading aloud.   People do not do such things so often now, but when I was young we got rid of a great deal of time so.   Well, so it happened that in his turn Nolan took the book and read to the others, and he read very well, as I know.   Nobody in the circle knew a line of the poem, only it was all magic and Border chivalry, and was a thousand years ago.   Poor Nolan read steadily through the fifth canto, stopped a minute and drank something, and then began, without a thought of what was coming.

> "Breathes there the man, with soul so dead,
> Who never to himself hath said"—

It seems impossible to us that anybody ever heard this for the first time; but all these fellows did then, and poor Nolan himself went on, still unconsciously or mechanically:

> "This is my own, my native land!"

Then they all saw something was to pay; but he expected to get through, I suppose, turned a little pale, but plunged on:

> "Whose heart hath ne'er within him burned,
> As home his footsteps he hath turned
>   From wandering on a foreign strand?—
> If such there breathe, go, mark him well"—

By this time the men were all beside themselves, wishing there was any way to make him turn over two pages. But he had not quite presence of mind for that; he gagged a little, colored crimson, and staggered on:

> "For him no minstrel raptures swell;
> High though his titles, proud his name,
> Boundless his wealth as wish can claim,
> Despite these titles, power, and pelf,
> The wretch, concentred all in self"—

and here the poor fellow choked, could not go on, but started up, swung the book into the sea, vanished into his stateroom, "And, by Jove," said Phillips, "we did not see him for two months again. And I had

to make up some beggarly story to that English
surgeon why I did not return his Walter Scott to
him."

The story shows about the time when Nolan's brag-
gadocio must have broken down. At first, they said,
he took a very high tone, considered his imprisonment
a mere farce, affected to enjoy the voyage, and all that;
but Phillips said that after he came out of his stateroom he never was the same man again. He never
read aloud again, unless it was the Bible or Shakespeare, or something else he was sure of. But it was
not that merely. He never entered in with the other
young men exactly as a companion again. He was
always shy afterward, when I knew him, very seldom
spoke, unless he was spoken to, except to a very few
friends. He lighted up occasionally—I remember late
in his life hearing him fairly eloquent on something
which had been suggested to him by one of Fléchier's
sermons—but generally he had the nervous, tired look
of a heart-wounded man.

When Captain Shaw was coming home—if, as I
say, it was Shaw—rather to the surprise of everybody
they made one of the Windward Islands, and lay off
and on for nearly a week. The boys said the officers
were sick of salt junk, and meant to have turtle soup before they came home. But after several days the "Warren" came to the same rendezvous; they exchanged
signals, she sent to Phillips and these homeward-bound
men letters and papers, and told them she was outward-
bound, perhaps to the Mediterranean, and took poor
Nolan and his traps on the boat back to try his second

cruise.   He looked very blank when he was told to
get ready to join her.   He had known enough of the
signs of the sky to know that till that moment he was
going "home."   But this was a distinct evidence of
something he had not thought of, perhaps—that there
was no going home for him, even to a prison.   And
this was the first of some twenty such transfers, which
brought him sooner or later into half our best vessels,
but which kept him all his life at least some hundred
miles from the country he had hoped he might never
hear of again.

It may have been on that second cruise—it was once
when he was up the Mediterranean—that Mrs. Graff,
the celebrated Southern beauty of those days, danced
with him.   They had been lying a long time in the
Bay of Naples, and the officers were very intimate in
the English fleet, and there had been great festivities,
and our men thought they must give a great ball on
board the ship.   How they ever did it on board the
"Warren" I am sure I do not know.   Perhaps it was
not the "Warren," or perhaps ladies did not take up so
much room as they do now.   They wanted to use Nolan's stateroom for something, and they hated to do it
without asking him to the ball; so the captain said they
might ask him if they would be responsible that he did
not talk with the wrong people, "who would give him
intelligence."   So the dance went on, the finest party
that had ever been known, I dare say; for I never
heard of a man-of-war ball that was not.   For ladies
they had the family of the American consul, one or
two travelers who had adventured so far, and a nice

bevy of English girls and matrons, perhaps Lady Hamilton herself.

Well, different officers relieved each other in standing and talking with Nolan in a friendly way, so as to be sure that nobody else spoke to him. The dancing went on with spirit, and after a while even the fellows who took this honorary guard of Nolan ceased to fear any *contretemps*. Only when some English lady—Lady Hamilton, as I said, perhaps—called for a set of "American dances," an odd thing happened. Everybody then danced contra-dances. The black band, nothing loath, conferred as to what "American dances" were and started off with "Virginia Reel," which they followed with "Money-Musk," which, in its turn in those days, should have been followed by "The Old Thirteen." But just as Dick, the leader, tapped for his fiddles to begin, and bent forward, about to say, in true negro state, " 'The Old Thirteen,' gentlemen and ladies !" as he had said " 'Virginny Reel,' if you please !" and " 'Money-Musk,' if you please !" the captain's boy tapped him on the shoulder, whispered to him, and he did not announce the name of the dance. He merely bowed, began on the air, and they all fell to—the officers teaching the English girls the figure, but not telling them why it had no name.

But that is not the story I started to tell. As the dancing went on, Nolan and our fellows all got at ease, as I said—so much so, that it seemed quite natural for him to bow to that splendid Mrs. Graff, and say :

"I hope you have not forgotten me, Miss Rutledge. Shall I have the honor of dancing?"

He did it so quickly that Fellows, who was with him, could not hinder him. She laughed and said: "I am not Miss Rutledge any longer, Mr. Nolan, but I will dance all the same," just nodded to Fellows, as if to say he must leave Mr. Nolan to her, and led him off to the place where the dance was forming.

Nolan thought he had got his chance. He had known her at Philadelphia, and at other places had met her, and this was a godsend. You could not talk in contra-dances, as you do in cotillons, or even in the pauses of waltzing, but there were chances for tongues and sounds, as well as for eyes and blushes. He began with her travels, and Europe, and Vesuvius, and the French, and then, when they had worked down, and had that long talking time at the bottom of the set, he said boldly, a little pale, she said, as she told me the story years after:

"And what do you hear from home, Mrs. Graff?"

And that splendid creature looked through him. Jove! how she must have looked through him!

"Home!! Mr. Nolan!!! I thought you were the man who never wanted to hear of home again!" And she walked directly up the deck to her husband, and left poor Nolan alone, as he always was. He did not dance again. I can not give any history of him in order; nobody can now, and, indeed, I am not trying to.

These are the traditions, which I sort out, as I believe them, from the myths which have been told about this

man for forty years.   The lies that have been told
about him are legion.   The fellows used to say he
was the "Iron Mask," and poor George Pons went to
his grave in the belief that this was the author of
"Junius," who was being punished for his celebrated
libel on Thomas Jefferson.   Pons was not very strong
in the historical line.

A happier story than either of these I have told is
of the war.   That came along soon after.   I have heard
this affair told in three or four ways, and, indeed, it
may have happened more than once.   But which ship
it was on I can not tell.   However, in one, at least, of
the great frigate duels with the English, in which the
navy was really baptized, it happened that a round
shot from the enemy entered one of our ports square,
and took right down the officer of the gun himself, and
almost every man of the gun's crew.   Now you may
say what you choose about courage, but that is not a
nice thing to see.   But, as the men who were not
killed picked themselves up, and as they and the surgeon's people were carrying off the bodies, there appeared Nolan, in his shirt-sleeves, with the rammer in
his hand, and, just as if he had been the officer, told
them off with authority—who should go to the cock-
pit with the wounded men, who should stay with him—
perfectly cheery, and with that way which makes men
feel sure all is right and is going to be right.   And he
finished loading the gun with his own hands, aimed it,
and bade the men fire.   And there he stayed, captain of
that gun, keeping those fellows in spirits, till the enemy
struck, sitting on the carriage while the gun was cool-

ing, though he was exposed all the time, showing them easier ways to handle heavy shot, making the raw hands laugh at their own blunders, and when the gun cooled again, getting it loaded and fired twice as often as any other gun on the ship. The captain walked forward by way of encouraging the men, and Nolan touched his hat and said:

"I am showing them how we do this in the artillery, sir."

And this is the part of the story where all the legends agree. The commodore said:

"I see you do, and I thank you, sir; and I shall never forget this day, sir, and you never shall, sir."

And after the whole thing was over, and he had the Englishman's sword, in the midst of the state and ceremony of the quarterdeck, he said:

"Where is Mr. Nolan? Ask Mr. Nolan to come here."

And when Nolan came, he said:

"Mr. Nolan, we are all very grateful to you to-day; you are one of us to-day; you will be named in the despatches."

And then the old man took off his own sword of ceremony, and gave it to Nolan, and made him put it on. The man told me this who saw it. Nolan cried like a baby, and well he might. He had not worn a sword since that infernal day at Fort Adams. But always afterward, on occasions of ceremony, he wore that quaint old French sword of the commodore's.

The captain did mention him in the despatches. It was always said he asked that he might be pardoned.

He wrote a special letter to the Secretary of War. But nothing ever came of it. As I said, that was about the time when they began to ignore the whole transaction at Washington, and when Nolan's imprisonment began to carry itself on because there was nobody to stop it without any new orders from home.

I have heard it said that he was with Porter when he took possession of the Nukahiva Islands. Not this Porter, you know, but old Porter, his father, Essex Porter—that is, the old Essex Porter, not this Essex. As an artillery officer, who had seen service in the West, Nolan knew more about fortifications, embrasures, ravelins, stockades, and all that, than any of them did; and he worked with a right good will in fixing that battery all right. I have always thought it was a pity Porter did not leave him in command there with Gamble. That would have settled all the question about his punishment. We should have kept the islands, and at this moment we should have one station in the Pacific Ocean. Our French friends, too, when they wanted this little watering-place, would have found it was preoccupied. But Madison and the Virginians, of course, flung all that away.

All that was near fifty years ago. If Nolan was thirty then, he must have been near eighty when he died. He looked sixty when he was forty. But he never seemed to me to change a hair afterward. As I imagine his life, from what I have seen and heard of it, he must have been in every sea, and yet almost never on land. He must have known, in a formal way, more officers in our service than any man living knows. He told me once, with a grave smile, that no man in the world lived so methodical a life as he. "You know the boys say I am the Iron Mask, and you know how busy he was." He said it did not do for any one to try to read all the time, more than to do anything else all the time, but that he read just five hours a day. "Then," he said, "I keep up my note-books, writing in them at such and such hours from what I have been reading, and I include in these my scrap-books." These were very curious indeed. He had six or eight, of different subjects. There was one of History, one of Natural Science, one which he called "Odds and Ends." But they were not merely books of extracts from newspapers. They had bits of plants and ribbons, shells tied on, and carved scraps of bone and wood, which he had taught the men to cut for him, and they were beautifully illustrated. He drew admirably. He had some of the funniest draw-ings there, and some of the most pathetic that I have ever seen in my life. I wonder who will have Nolan's scrap-books.

Well, he said his reading and his notes were his profession, and that they took five hours and two hours respectively of each day. "Then," said he, "every man should have a diversion as well as a pro-fession. My Natural History is my diversion." That took two hours a day more. The men used to bring him birds and fish, but on a long cruise he had to satisfy himself with centipedes and cockroaches and such small game. He was the only naturalist I ever met who knew anything about the habits of the housefly and the mosquito. All those people can tell you whether they are *Lepidoptera* or *Steptopotera;* but as for telling you how you can get rid of them, or how they get away from you when you strike at them —why, Linnæus knew as little of that as John Foy, the idiot, did.

These nine hours made Nolan's regular daily "occupation." The rest of the time he talked or walked. Till he grew very old, he went aloft a great deal. He always kept up his exercise, and I never heard that he was ill. If any other man was ill, he was the kindest nurse in the world; and he knew more than half the surgeons do. Then, if anybody was sick or died, or if the captain wanted him to, on any other occasion, he was always ready to read prayers. I have said that he read beautifully.

My own acquaintance with Philip Nolan began six or eight years after the English war, on my first voyage after I was appointed a midshipman. It was in the first days after our Slave-Trade treaty, while the Reigning House, which was still the House of Virginia, had still a sort of sentimentalism about the suppression of the horrors of the Middle Passage, and something was sometimes done that way. We were in the South Atlantic on that business. From the time I joined, I believe I thought Nolan was a sort of lay chaplain—a chaplain with a blue coat. I never asked about him. Everything in the ship was strange to me. I knew it was green to ask questions, and I suppose I thought there was a "Plain-Buttons" on every ship. We had him to dine in our mess once a week, and the caution was given that on that day nothing was to be said about home. But if they had told us not to say anything about the planet Mars or the Book of Deuteronomy, I should not have asked why; there were a great many things which seemed to me to have as little reason.

I first came to understand anything about "the man without a country" one day when we overhauled a dirty little schooner which had slaves on board An officer was sent to take charge of her, and, after a few minutes, he sent back his boat to ask that some one might be sent him who could speak Portuguese. We were all looking over the rail when the message came, and we all wished we could interpret, when the captain asked who spoke Portuguese. But none of the officers did, and just as the captain was sending forward to ask if any of the people could, Nolan stepped out and said he should be glad to interpret, if the captain wished, as he understood the language. The captain thanked him, fitted out another boat with him, and in this boat it was my luck to go. When we got there it was such a scene as you seldom see, and never want to. Nastiness beyond account, and chaos run loose in the midst of the nastiness. There were not a great many of the negroes; but by way of making what there were understand that they were free, Vaughan had had their handcuffs and ankle-cuffs knocked off, and, for convenience' sake, was putting them upon the rascals of the schooner's crew. The negroes were, most of them, out of the hold, and swarming all round the dirty deck, with a central

throng surrounding Vaughan and addressing him in
every dialect and *patois* of a dialect, from the Zulu
click up to the Parisian of Beledeljereed.

As we came on deck, Vaughan looked down from a
hogshead, on which he had mounted in desperation,
and said:

"For God's love, is there anybody who can make
these wretches understand something? The men gave
them rum, and that did not quiet them. I knocked
that big fellow down twice, and that did not soothe
him. And then I talked Choctaw to all of them together, and I'll be hanged if they understood that as
well as they understood the English."

Nolan said he could speak Portuguese, and one or
two fine-looking Kroomen were dragged out, who, as
it had been found already, had worked for the Portuguese on the coast at Fernando Po.

"Tell them they are free," said Vaughan. "And
tell them that these rascals are to be hanged as soon
as we can get rope enough."

Nolan "put that into Spanish"—that is, he explained it in such Portuguese as the Kroomen could
understand, and they in turn to such of the negroes
as could understand them. Then there was such a
yell of delight, clinching of fists, leaping and dancing, kissing of Nolan's feet, and a general rush
made to the hogshead by way of spontaneous
worship of Vaughan, as the *deus ex machina* of the
occasion.

"Tell them," said Vaughan, well pleased, "that I
will take them all to Cape Palmas."

This did not answer so well. Cape Palmas was practically as far from the homes of most of them as New Orleans or Rio Janeiro was—that is, they would be eternally separated from home there. And their interpreters, as we could understand, instantly said, *"Ah, non Palmas,"* and began to propose infinite other expedients in most voluble language. Vaughan was rather disappointed at this result of his liberality, and asked Nolan eagerly what they said. The drops stood on poor Nolan's white forehead, as he hushed the men down, and said:

"He says, 'Not Palmas.' He says, 'Take us home, take us to our own country, take us to our own house, take us to our own pickaninnies and our own women.' He says he has an old father and mother who will die if they do not see him. And this one says he left his people all sick, and paddled down to Fernando to beg the white doctor to come and help them, and that these devils caught him in the bay just in sight of home, and that he has never seen anybody from home since then. And this one says," choked out Nolan, "that he has not heard a word from his home in six months, while he has been locked up in that infernal barracoon."

Vaughan always said he grew gray himself while Nolan struggled through this interpretation. I, who did not understand anything of the passion involved in it, saw that the very elements were melting with fervent heat, and that something was to pay some-where. Even the negroes themselves stopped howl-ing, as they saw Nolan's agony and Vaughan's al-

most equal agony of sympathy. As quick as he could
get words, he said:

"Tell them yes, yes, yes; tell them they shall go to
the Mountains of the Moon if they will. If I sail the
schooner through the Great White Desert, they shall
go home!"

And after some fashion Nolan said so. And then
they all fell to kissing him again, and wanted to rub
his nose with theirs.

But he could not stand it long, and, getting
Vaughan to say he might go back, he beckoned me
down into our boat. As we lay back in the stern-
sheets and the men gave way, he said to me: "Young-
ster, let that show you what it is to be without a family, without a home, and without a country. And if
you are ever tempted to say a word or to do a thing
that shall put a bar between you and your family, your
home, and your country, pray God in His mercy to
take you that instant home to His own heaven. Stick
by your family, boy; forget you have a self, while you
do everything for them. Think of your home, boy;
write and send and talk about it. Let it be nearer
and nearer to your thought the further you have to
travel from it; and rush back to it when you are free,
as that poor black slave is doing now. And for your
country, boy," and the words rattled in his throat,
"and for that flag," and he pointed to the ship, "never
dream a dream but of serving her as she bids you,
though the service carry you through a thousand
hells. No matter what happens to you, no matter who
flatters you or who abuses you, never look at another

flag, never let a night pass but you pray God to bless that flag. Remember, boy, that behind all these men you have to do with, behind officers, and government, and people even, there is the Country Herself, your Country, and that you belong to Her as you belong to your own mother. Stand by Her, boy, as you would stand by your mother, if those devils there had got hold of her to-day!"

I was frightened to death by his calm, hard passion, but I blundered out that I would, by all that was holy, and that I had never thought of doing anything else. He hardly seemed to hear me, but he did, almost in a whisper, say: "Oh, if anybody had said so to me when I was of your age!"

I think it was this half-confidence of his, which I never abused, for I never told this story till now, which afterward made us great friends. He was very kind to me. Often he sat up, or even got up, at night, to walk the deck with me, when it was my watch. He explained to me a great deal of my mathematics, and I owe to him my taste for mathematics. He lent me books, and helped me about my reading. He never alluded so directly to his story again, but from one and another officer I have learned, in thirty years, what I am telling. When we parted from him in St. Thomas harbor at the end of our cruise I was more sorry than I can tell. I was very glad to meet him again in 1830; and later in life, when I thought I had some influence in Washington, I moved heaven and earth to have him discharged. But it was like getting a ghost out of prison. They pretended there was no

such man, and never was such a man. They will say
so at the Department now! Perhaps they do not
know. It will not be the first thing in the service of
which the Department appears to know nothing!

There is a story that Nolan met Burr once on one
of our vessels, when a party of Americans came on
board in the Mediterranean. But this I believe to be
a lie; or, rather, it is a myth, *ben trovato,* involving a
tremendous blowing-up with which he sunk Burr,
asking him how he liked to be "without a country."
But it is clear from Burr's life that nothing of the
sort could have happened, and I mention this only as
an illustration of the stories which get a-going where
there is the least mystery at bottom.

So poor Philip Nolan had his wish fulfilled. I
know but one fate more dreadful: it is the fate reserved for those men who shall have one day to exile
themselves from their country because they have attempted her ruin, and shall have at the same time to
see the prosperity and honor to which she rises when
she has rid herself of them and their iniquities. The
wish of poor Nolan, as we all learned to call him,
not because his punishment was too great, but because his repentance was so clear, was precisely the
wish of every Bragg and Beauregard who broke a
soldier's oath two years ago, and of every Maury and
Barron who broke a sailor's. I do not know how
often they have repented. I do know that they
have done all that in them lay that they might have
no country, that all the honors, associations, memories, and hopes which belong to "country" might be

broken up into little shreds and distributed to the winds. I know, too, that their punishment, as they vegetate through what is left of life to them in wretched Boulognes and Leicester Squares, where they are destined to upbraid each other till they die, will have all the agony of Nolan's, with the added pang that every one who sees them will see them to despise and to execrate them. They will have their wish, like him.

For him, poor fellow, he repented of his folly, and then, like a man, submitted to the fate he had asked for. He never intentionally added to the difficulty or delicacy of the charge of those who had him in hold. Accidents would happen, but they never happened from his fault. Lieutenant Truxton told me that, when Texas was annexed, there was a careful discussion among the officers, whether they should get hold of Nolan's handsome set of maps and cut Texas out of it—from the map of the world and the map of Mexico. The United States had been cut out when the atlas was bought for him. But it was voted, rightly enough, that to do this would be virtually to reveal to him what had happened, or, as Harry Cole said, to make him think old Burr had succeeded. So it was from no fault of Nolan's that a great botch happened at my own table, when, for a short time, I was in command of the "George Washington" corvette, on the South American station. We were lying in the La Plata, and some of the officers, who had been on shore and had just joined again, were entertaining us with accounts of their misadventures in riding the half-wild horses of Buenos Ayres. Nolan was at table, and was in an unusually bright and talkative mood. Some story of a tumble reminded him of an adventure of his own when he was catching wild horses in Texas with his adventurous cousin, at a time when he must have been quite a boy. He told the story with a good deal of spirit—so much so that the silence which often follows a good story hung over the table for an instant, to be broken by Nolan himself. For he asked perfectly unconsciously:

"Pray, what has become of Texas? After the Mexicans got their independence, I thought that province of Texas would come forward very fast. It is really one of the finest regions on earth; it is the Italy of this continent. But I have not seen or heard a word of Texas for near twenty years."

There were two Texan officers at the table. The reason he had never heard of Texas was that Texas and her affairs had been painfully cut out of his newspapers since Austin began his settlements, so that, while he read of Honduras and Tamaulipas, and, till quite lately, of California, this virgin province, in which his brother had traveled so far, and, I believe, had died, had ceased to be to him. Waters and Williams, the two Texas men, looked grimly at each other and tried not to laugh. Edward Morris had his attention attracted by the third link in the chain of the captain's chandelier. Watrous was seized with a convulsion of sneezing. Nolan himself saw that something was to pay, he did not know what. And I, as master of the feast, had to say:

"Texas is out of the map, Mr. Nolan. Have you seen Captain Back's curious account of Sir Thomas Roe's Welcome?"

After that cruise I never saw Nolan again. I wrote to him at least twice a year, for in that voyage we became even confidentially intimate; but he never wrote to me. The other men tell me that in those fifteen years he *aged* very fast, as well he might, indeed, but that he was still the same gentle, uncomplaining, silent sufferer that he ever was, bearing as best he could his self-appointed punishment—rather less social, perhaps, with new men whom he did not know, but more anxious, apparently, than ever to serve and befriend and teach the boys, some of whom fairly seemed to worship him. And now it seems the dear old fellow is dead. He has found a home at last, and a country.

Since writing this, and while considering whether or no I would print it, as a warning to the young Nolans and Vallandighams and Tatnalls of to-day, I have received from Danforth, who is on board the "Levant," a letter which gives an account of Nolan's last hours. It removes all my doubts about telling this story.

To understand the first words of the letter, the nonprofessional reader should remember that after 1817 the position of every officer who had Nolan in charge was one of the greatest delicacy. The government had failed to renew the order of 1807 regarding him. What was a man to do? Should he let him go? What, then, if he were called to account by the Department for violating the order of 1807? Should he keep him? What, then, if Nolan should be liberated some day, and should bring an action for false imprisonment or kidnapping against every man who had had him in charge? I urged and pressed this upon Southard, and I have reason to think that other officers did the same thing. But the Secretary always said, as they so often do at Washington, that there were no special orders to give, and that we must act on our own judgment. That means, "If you succeed, you will be sustained; if you fail, you will be disavowed." Well, as Danforth says, all that is over now, though I do not know but I expose myself to a criminal prosecution on the evidence of the very revelation I am making.

Here is the letter:

"LEVANT, 2° 2′ S. @ 131° W.

"*Dear Fred*—I try to find heart and life to tell you that it is all over with dear old Nolan. I have been with him on this voyage more than I ever was, and I can understand wholly now the way in which you used to speak of the dear old fellow. I could see that he was not strong, but I had no idea the end was so near. The doctor has been watching him very carefully, and yesterday morning came to me and told me that Nolan was not so well, and had not left his stateroom—a thing I never remember before. He had let the doctor come and see him as he lay there—the first time the doctor had been in the stateroom—and he said he should like to see me. Oh, dear! do you remember the mysteries we boys used to invent about his room in the old 'Intrepid' days? Well, I went in, and there, to be sure, the poor fellow lay in his berth, smiling pleasantly as he gave me his hand, but looking very frail. I could not help a glance round, which showed me what a little shrine he had made of the box he was lying in. The Stars and Stripes were triced up above and around a picture of Washington, and he had painted a majestic eagle, with lightnings blazing from his beak and his foot just clasping the whole globe, which his wings overshadowed. The dear old boy saw my glance, and said, with a sad smile, 'Here, you see, I have a country!' And then he pointed to the foot of his bed, where I had not seen before a great map of the United States, as he had drawn it from memory, and which he had there to look upon as he lay. Quaint, queer old names were on it, in large letters: 'Indiana Territory,' 'Mississippi Territory,' and 'Louisiana Territory,' as I suppose our fathers learned such things. But the old fellow had patched in Texas, too; he had carried his western boundary all the way to the Pacific, but on that shore he had defined nothing.

" 'Oh, Danforth,' he said, 'I know I am dying. I can not get home. Surely you will tell me something now? Stop! Stop! Do not speak till I say what I am sure you know, that there is not in this ship, that there is not in America—God bless her!— a more loyal man than I. There can not be a man who loves the old flag as I do, or prays for it as I do, or hopes for it as I do. There are thirty-four stars in it now, Danforth. I thank God for that, though I do not know what their names are. There has never been one taken away; I thank God for that. I know by that that there has never been any successful Burr. Oh, Danforth, Danforth,' he sighed out, 'how like a wretched night's dream a boy's idea of personal fame or of separate sovereignty seems, when one looks back on it after such a life as mine! But tell me—tell me something—tell me everything, Danforth, before I die!'

"Ingham, I swear to you that I felt like a monster that I had not told him everything before. Danger or no danger, delicacy or no delicacy, who was I, that I should have been acting the tyrant all this time over this dear, sainted old man, who had years ago expiated, in his whole manhood's life, the madness of a boy's treason? 'Mr. Nolan,' said I, 'I will tell you everything you ask about. Only, where shall I begin?'

"Oh, the blessed smile that crept over his white face! And he pressed my hand and said, 'God bless you! Tell me their names,' he said, and he pointed to the stars on the flag. 'The last I know is Ohio. My father lived in Kentucky. But I have guessed Michigan and Indiana and Mississippi—that was where Fort Adams is. They make twenty. But where are your other fourteen? You have not cut up any of the old ones, I hope?'

"Well, that was not a bad text, and I told him the names in as good order as I could, and he bade me take down his beautiful map and draw them in as I best could with my pencil. He was wild with delight about Texas—told me how his cousin died there; he had marked a gold cross near where he supposed his grave was; and he had guessed at Texas. Then he was delighted as he saw California and Oregon. That, he said, he had suspected partly, because he had never been permitted to land on that shore, though the ships were there so much. 'And the men,' said he, laughing, 'brought off a good deal besides furs.' Then he went back—heavens, how far!—to ask about the 'Chesapeake,' and what was done to Barron for surrendering her to the 'Leopard,' and whether Burr ever tried again—and he ground his teeth with the only passion he showed. But in a moment that was over, and he said, 'God forgive me, for I am sure I forgive him.' Then he asked about the old war—told me the true story of his serving the gun the day we took the 'Java' —asked about dear old David Porter, as he called him. Then he settled down more quietly, and very happily, to hear me tell in an hour the history of fifty years.

"How I wished it had been somebody who knew something! But I did as well as I could. I told him of the English war. I told him about Fulton and the steamboat beginning. I told him about old Scott, and Jackson—told him all I could think of about the Mississippi, and New Orleans, and Texas, and his own old Kentucky. And what do you think he asked? 'Who was in command of the Legion of the West!' I told him it was a very gallant officer named Grant, and that, by our last news, he was about to establish his headquarters at Vicksburg. Then, 'Where was Vicksburg?' I worked that out on the map; it was about a hundred miles, more or less, above his old Fort Adams, and I thought Fort Adams must be a ruin now. 'It must be at old Vick's plantation, at Walnut Hills,' said he; 'well, that is a change!'

"I tell you, Ingham, it was a hard thing to condense the history of half a century into that talk with a sick man. And I do not now know what I told him—of emigration, and the means of it—of steamboats, and railroads, and telegraphs—of inventions, and books, and literature—of the colleges, and West Point, and the Naval School—but with the queerest interruptions that ever you heard. You see, it was Robinson Crusoe asking all the accumulated questions of fifty-six years!

"I remember he asked, all of a sudden, who was President now. And when I told him, he asked if Old Abe was General Benjamin Lincoln's son. He said he met old General Lincoln, when he was quite a boy himself, at some Indian treaty. I said no, that Old Abe was a Kentuckian like himself, but I could not tell him of what family; he had worked up from the ranks. 'Good for him!' cried Nolan; 'I am glad of that. As I have brooded and wondered, I have thought our danger was in keeping up those regular successions in the first families.' Then

I got talking about my visit to Washington. I told him of meeting the Oregon Congressman, Harding; I told him about the Smithsonian, and the exploring Expedition; I told him about the Capitol, and the statues for the pediment, and Crawford's Liberty, and Greenough's Washington. Ingham, I told him everything I could think of that would show the grandeur of his country and its prosperity ; but I could not make up my mouth to tell him a word about this infernal rebellion.

"And he drank it in and enjoyed it as I can not tell you. He grew more and more silent, yet I never thought he was tired or faint. I gave him a glass of water, but he just wet his lips, and told me not to go away. Then he asked me to bring the Presbyterian 'Book of Public Prayer,' which lay there, and said, with a smile, that it would open at the right place—and so it did. There was his double red mark down the page. And I knelt down and read, and he repeated with me, 'For ourselves and our country, oh, gracious God, we thank Thee that, notwithstanding our manifold transgressions of Thy holy laws, Thou hast continued to us Thy marvelous kindness'—and so to the end of that thanksgiving. Then he turned to the end of the same book, and I read the words more familiar to me: 'Most heartily we beseech Thee with Thy favor to behold and bless Thy servant, the President of the United States, and all others in authority'—and the rest of the Episcopal collect. 'Danforth,' said he, 'I have repeated those prayers night and morning, it is now fifty-five years.' And then he said he would go to sleep.

"He bent me down over him and kissed me, and he said, 'Look in my Bible, Danforth, when I am gone.' And I went away.

"But I had no thought it was the end. I thought he was tired and would sleep. I knew he was happy, and I wanted him to be alone.

"But in an hour, when the doctor went in gently, he found Nolan had breathed his life away with a smile. He had something pressed close to his lips. It was his father's badge of the Order of the Cincinnati.

"We looked in his Bible, and there was a slip of paper at the place where he had marked the text:

" 'They desire a country, even a heavenly: wherefore God is not ashamed to be called their God: for He hath prepared for them a city.'

"On this slip of paper he had written:

" 'Bury me in the sea; it has been my home, and I love it. But

will not some one set up a stone for my memory at Fort Adams
or at Orleans, that my disgrace may not be more than I ought
to bear? Say on it:

"'In Memory of

"'PHILIP NOLAN,

"'Lieutenant in the Army of the United States.

"'He loved his country as no other man has
loved her; but no man deserved
less at her hands.'"

A BRACE OF BOYS

BY FITZ HUGH LUDLOW

Fitz Hugh Ludlow (born in 1837, in Pough-keepsie, N. Y., died in 1870), fortunately for American literature, entered into authorship at an early age, publishing when twenty-one "The Hasheesh-Eater," which achieved instant popularity. The book was signifi-cant of the author's end: thirteen years later he died a victim of the opium habit. Mr. Ludlow published a number of stories, chiefly in "Harper's Monthly," all of which show him to have been a man of keen sense of humor, refined feeling, remarkable insight into character, and deeply religious nature. "A Brace of Boys," while it deals largely with juvenile character, is a story for adults. It is a love romance of the delightful order to which John Habberton's "Helen's Babies" belongs—where the guileless "enfant ter-rible" performs the office of designing Cupid.

A BRACE OF BOYS

BY FITZ HUGH LUDLOW

I AM a bachelor uncle. That, as a mere fact, might happen to anybody; but I am a bachelor uncle by internal fitness. I am one essentially, just as I am an individual of the Caucasian division of the human race; and if, through untoward circumstances—which Heaven forbid—I should lose my present position, I shouldn't be surprised if you saw me out in the "Herald" under "Situations Wanted—Males." Thanks to a marrying tendency in the rest of my family, I have now little need to advertise, all the business being thrown into my way which a single member of my profession can attend to.

I suppose you won't agree with me; but, do you know, sometimes I think it's better than having children of one's own? People tell me that I'd feel very differently if I did have any. Perhaps so, but then, too, I might be unwise with them; I might bother them into mischief by trying to keep them out. I might be avaricious of them—might be tempted to lock them up in my own stingy old nursery-chest instead of paying them out to meet the bills of humanity and keep the Lord's business moving. I might forget, when I had spent my life in fining their gold and polishing their graven-work, that they were still vessels for the Master's use—I only the Butler—the sweetness and the spirit with which they brimmed all belonging to His lips who tasted bitterness for me. Then, if seeking to drain another's wine, I raised the chalice to my lips and found it gall, or felt it steal into my old veins to poison the heart and paralyze the hand which had kept it from the Master, what further good would there be for me in the world? Who doesn't know, in some friend's house, a closet containing that worst of skeletons—the skeleton which, in becoming naked, grim and ghastly, tears its way through our own flesh and blood?

To be an uncle is a different kind of thing. There you have nothing of the excitement of responsibility to shake your judgment. That's what makes us bachelor uncles so much better judges of what's good for children and their fathers and mothers. We know that nobody will blame us if our nephews unjoint their knuckles or cut their fingers off; so we give them five-bladed knives and boxing gloves. This involves getting thanked at the time, which is pleasant; and if no catastrophe occurs, when they have grown stout and ingenious, with what calm satisfaction we hear people say, "See what a pretty windmill the child's whittled out with Uncle Ned's birthday present!" or, "That boy's grown an inch round the chest since you set him sparring!" Uncles never get stale. They don't come every day like parents and plain pudding; they're a sort of holiday relative with a plummy, Christmas flavor about them. Everybody hasn't got them; they are not so rare as the meteoric showers, but as occasional as a particularly fine day, and whenever they come to a house they're in the nature of a pleasant surprise.

I meander, like a desultory, placid river of an old bachelor as I am, through the flowery mead of several nurseries. I am detained by all the little roots that run down into me to drink happiness, but I linger longest among the children of my sister Lu.

Lu married Mr. Lovegrove. He is a merchant, retired, with a fortune amassed by the old-fashioned slow process of trade, and regards the mercantile life of the present day only as so much greed and gambling Christianly baptized. For the ten years elapsing since he sold out of Lovegrove, Cashdown, & Co., he has devoted himself to his family and a revival of letters, taking up again the Latin and Greek which he had not looked at since his college days, until he dismissed teas and silks to adorn a suburban villa with a spectacle of a prime Christian parent and Pagan scholar. Lu is my favorite sister; Lovegrove an unusually good article of brother-in-law; and I can not say that any of my nieces and nephews interest me more than their two children, Daniel and Billy, who are more unlike than words can paint them. They are far apart in point of years; Daniel is twenty-two, Billy eleven. I was reminded of this fact the other day by Billy, as he stood between my legs, scowling at his book of sums.

" 'A boy has 85 turnips and gives his sister 30'— pretty present for a girl, isn't it?" said Billy with an air of supreme contempt. "Could *you* stand such stuff —say?"

I put on my instructive face and answered: "Well, my dear Billy, you know that arithmetic is necessary to you if you mean to be an industrious man and succeed in business. Suppose your parents were to lose all their property, what would become of them without a little son who could make money and keep accounts?"

"Oh!" said Billy with surprise. "Hasn't father got enough stamps to see him through?"

"He has now, I hope; but people don't always keep them. Suppose they should go by some accident when your father was too old to make any more stamps for himself?"

"You haven't thought of brother Daniel——"

True; for nobody ever had, in connection with the active employments of life.

"No, Billy," I replied; "I forgot him; but then, you know, Daniel is more of a student than a business man, and——"

"Oh, Uncle Teddy! you don't think I meant he'd support them? I meant I'd have to take care of father and mother and of all when they'd all got to be old people together. Just think! I'm eleven and he's twenty-two; so he is just twice as old as I am. How old are you?"

"Forty, Billy, last August."

"Well, you aren't so awful old, and when I get to be as old as you Daniel will be eighty. Seth Kendall's grandfather isn't more than that, and he has to be fed with a spoon, and a nurse puts him to bed and wheels him around in a chair like a baby. That takes the stamps, *I* bet! Well, I'll tell you how I'll keep my accounts; I'll have a stick like Robinson Crusoe, and every time I make a toadskin I'll gouge a piece out of one side of the stick, and every time I spend one I'll gouge a piece out of the other."

"Spend a what!" said the gentle and astonished voice of my sister Lu, who, unperceived, had slipped into the room.

"A toadskin, ma," replied Billy, shutting up Colburn with a farewell glance of contempt.

"Dear! dear! where does the boy learn such horrid words?"

"Why, ma! don't you know what a toadskin is? Here's one," said Billy, drawing a dingy five-cent stamp from his pocket. And don't I wish I had lots of 'em!"

"Oh!" sighed his mother, "to think I should have a child so addicted to slang! How I wish he were like Daniel!"

"Well, mother," replied Billy, "if you wanted two boys just alike you'd oughter had twins. There ain't any use of my trying to be like Daniel now when he's got eleven years the start. Whoop! There's a dog-fight! Hear 'em! It's Joe Casey's dog—I know his bark!"

With these words my nephew snatched his Glengarry bonnet from the table and bolted downstairs to see the fun.

"What will become of him?" said Lu hopelessly; "he has no taste for anything but rough play; and then such language as he uses! Why *isn't* he like Daniel?"

"I suppose because his Maker never repeats himself. Even twins often possess strongly marked individualities. Don't you think it would be a good plan to learn Billy better before you try to teach him? If you do you'll make something as good of him as Daniel; though it will be rather different from that model."

"Remember, Ned, that you never did like Daniel as well as you do Billy. But we all know the proverb about old maids' daughters and old bachelors' sons. I wish you had Billy for a month—then you'd see."

"I'm not sure that I'd do any better than you. I might err as much in other directions. But I'd try to start right by acknowledging that he was a new problem, not to be worked without finding the value of 'x' in his particular instance. The formula which solves one boy will no more solve the next one than the rule of three will solve a question in calculus—or, to rise into your sphere, than the receipt for one-two-three-four cake will conduct you to a successful issue through plum pudding—"

I excel in metaphysical discussions, and was about giving further elaboration of my favorite idea when the door burst open. Master Billy came tumbling in with a torn jacket, a bloody nose, the trace of a few tears in his eyes, and the mangiest of cur dogs in his hands.

"Oh my! my!! my!!!" exclaimed his mother.

"Don't you get scared, ma!" cried Billy, smiling a stern smile of triumph; I smashed the nose off him! He won't sass me again for nothing *this* while! Uncle Teddy, d'ye know it wasn't a dog-fight after all? There was that nasty good-for-nothing Joe Casey 'n' Patsy Grogan and a lot of bad boys from Mackerelville; and they'd caught this poor little ki-oodle and tied a tin pot to his tail and were trying to set Joe's dog on him, though he's ten times littler—"

"You naughty, naughty boy! How did you suppose your mother'd feel to see you playing with those ragamuffins?"

"Yes, I *played* 'em! I polished 'em—that's the play I did! Says I, 'Put down that poor little pup! Ain't you ashamed of yourself, Patsy Grogan?' 'I guess you don't know who I am,' says he. That's the way they always say, Uncle Teddy, to make a fellow think they're some awful great fighters. So says I again, 'Well, you put down that dog or I'll show you who *I* am'; and when he held on, I let him have it. Then he dropped the pup, and as I stooped to pick it up he gave me one on the bugle."

"*Bugle!* Oh! oh! oh!"

"The rest pitched in to help him; but I grabbed the pup, and while I was trying to give as good as I got— only a fellow can't do it well with only one hand, Uncle Teddy—up came a policeman and the whole crowd ran away. So I got the dog safe, and here he is!"

With that Billy set down his "ki-oodle," bade farewell to every fear, and wiped his bleeding nose. The unhappy beast slunk back between the legs of his preserver and followed him out of the room, as Lu, with an expression of maternal despair, bore him away for the correction of his dilapidated raiment and depraved associations. I felt such sincere pride in this young Mazzini of the dog-nation that I was vexed at Lu for bestowing on him reproof instead of congratulation; but she was not the only conservative who fails to see a good cause and a heroic heart under a bloody nose and torn jacket. I resolved that if Billy was punished, he should have his recompense before long in an extra holiday at Barnum's or the Hippotheatron.

You already have some idea of my other nephew if you have noticed that none of us, not even that habitual disrespecter of dignities, Billy, ever called him Dan. It would have seemed as incongruous as to call Billy William. He was one of those youths who never give their parents a moment's uneasiness; who never have to have their wills broken, and never forget to put on their rubbers or take an umbrella. In boyhood he was intended for a missionary. Had it been possible for him to go to Greenland's icy mountains without catching cold, or to India's coral strand without getting bilious, his parents would have carried out their pleasing dream of contributing him to the world's evangelization. Lu and Mr. Lovegrove had no doubt that he would have been greatly blessed if he could have stood it. They brought him up in the most careful manner, and I can not recollect the time when he was not president, secretary, or something in some society of small yet good children. He was not only an exemplar to whom all Lu's friends pointed their own nursery as the little boy who could

say most hymns and sit stillest in church, but he was
a reproof even unto his elders. One Sunday afternoon, in the Connecticut village where my brother-in-
law used to spend his summers, when half of the con-
gregation was slumbering under the combined effect
of the heat, a lunch of cheese and apples, and the sermon, my nephew, then aged five, sat bolt upright in
the pew, winkless as a deacon hearing a new candi-
date suspected of shakiness on a "a card'nal p'int,"
and mortified almost to death poor old Mrs. Pringle,
who, compassionating his years, had handed him a
sprig of her "meetin'-seed" over the back of the seat,
by saying, in a loud and stern voice: "I don't eat
things in church."

I should have spanked the boy when I got home, but
Lu, with tears in her eyes, quoted something about the
mouths of babes and sucklings.

Both she and his father always encouraged old
manners in him. I think they took such pride in rais-
ing a peculiarly pale boy as a gardener does in getting a nice blanch on his celery, and, so long as he
was not absolutely sick, the graver he was, the better.
He was a sensitive plant, a violet by a mossy stone,
and all that sort of thing. But when in his tenth
year he had the measles, and was narrowly carried
through, Lu got a scare about him. During his con-
valescence, reading aloud a life of Henry Martyn to
amuse him, she found in it a picture of that young
apostle preaching to a crowd of Hindus without
any boots on. An American mother's association of
such behavior with croup and ipecac was too strong

to be counteracted by known climatic facts; and from that hour, as she never had before, Lu realized that being a missionary might involve going to carry the gospel to the heathen in your stocking-feet.

When they had decided that such a life would not do for him, his training had almost entirely unfitted him for any other active calling. The strict propriety with which he had been brought up had resulted in weak lungs, poor digestion, sluggish circulation, and torpid liver. Moreover, he was troubled with the painfulest bashfulness which ever made a mother think her child too ethereal, or a dispassionate outsider regard him as too flimsy, for this world. These were weights enough to carry, even if he had not labored under that heaviest of all, a well-stored mind.

No misnomer that last to any one who has ever frequented the Atlantic Docks, or seen storage in any large port of entry. How does a storehouse look? It's a vast, dark, cold chamber—dust an inch deep on the floor, cobwebs festooning the girders—and piled from floor to ceiling on the principle of getting the largest bulk into the least room, with barrels, boxes, bales, baskets, chests, crates, and carboys—merchandise of all description, from the rough, raw material to the most exquisite *choses de luxe*. The inmost layers are inextricable without pulling down the outer ones. If you want a particular case of broadcloth you must clear yourself an alleyway through a hundred tierces of hams, and last week's entry of clayed sugars is inaccessible without tumbling on your head a mountain of Yankee notions.

In my nephew's unfortunate youth such storage as
this had minds. As long as the crown of his brain's
arch was not crushed in by some intellectual Fur-
man Street disaster, those stevedores of learning, the
schoolmasters, kept on unloading the Rome and Athens
lighters into a boy's crowded skull, and breaking out
of the hold of that colossal old junk, The Pure Mathematics, all the formulas which could be crowded into
the interstices between his Latin and Greek.

At the time I introduce Billy, both Lu and her
husband were much changed. They had gained a
great deal in width of view and liberality of judgment. They read Dickens and Thackeray with avid-
ity; went now and then to the opera; proposed to let
Billy take a quarter at Dodworth's; had statues in
their parlor without any thought of shame at their
lack of petticoats, and did multitudes of things which,
in their early married life, they would have considered shocking. Part of this change was due to the
great increase of travel, the wonderful progress in
art and refinement which has enlarged this generation's thought and corrected its ignorant opinions; infusing cosmopolitanism into our manners by a revolution so gradual that its subjects were a new people
before their combativeness became alarmed, yet so
rapid that a man of thirty can scarcely believe his
birthday, and questions whether he has not added
his life up wrong by a century or so when he compares
his own boyhood with that of the present day. But a
good deal of the transformation resulted from the
means of gratifying elegant tastes, the comfort, lux-

ury, and culture which came with Lovegrove's retirement on a fortune. They had mellowed on the
sunny shelves of prosperity, like every good thing
which has an astringent skin when it is green. They
would greatly have liked to see Daniel shine in society. Of his erudition they were proud, even to
worship. The young man never had any business,
and his father never seemed to think of giving him
any; knowing, as Billy would say, that he had stamps
enough to "see him through." If Daniel liked, his
father would have endowed a professorship in some
college and have given him the chair; but that would
have taken him away from his own room and the
family physician.

Daniel knew how much his parents wished him to
make a figure in the world, and only blamed himself
for his failure, magnanimously forgetting that they
had crushed out the faculties which enable a man to
mint the small change of everyday society in the exclusive cultivation of such as fit him for smelting its
ponderous ingots. With that merciful blindness which
alone prevents all our lives from becoming a horror of
nerveless reproach, his parents were equally unaware
of their share in the harm done him, when they
ascribed to his delicate organization the fact that, at
an age when love runs riot in all healthy blood, he
could not see a balmoral without his cheeks rivaling
the most vivid stripe in it. They flattered themselves
that he would outgrow his bashfulness, but Daniel
had no such hope, and frequently confided in me that
he thought he should never marry at all.

About two hours after Billy's disappearance under
his mother's convoy, the defender of the oppressed
returned to my room bearing the dog under his arm.
His cheeks shone with washing like a pair of waxy
Spitzenbergs, and other indignities had been offered
him to the extent of the brush and comb. He also
had a whole jacket on.

"Well, Billy," said I, "what are you going to do
with your dog?"

"I don't know what I'm going to do. I've a great
mind to be a bad, disobedient boy with him, and *not*
have my days long in the land which the Lord my
God giveth me."

"O Billy!"

"I can't help it. They won't be long if I don't mind
ma, she says; and she wants me to be mean, and put
Crab out in the street to have Patsy catch him and tie
coffee-pots to his tail. I—I—I—"

Here my small nephew dug his fist into his eye and
looked down.

I told Billy to stop where he was, and went to in-
tercede with Lu. She was persuaded to entertain the
angels of magnanimity and heroism in the disguise of
a young fighting character, and to accept my surety
for the behavior of his dog. Billy and I also obtained
permission to go out together and be gone the entire
afternoon. We put Crab on a comfortable. bed of
rags in an old shoe box, and then strolled, hand-in-
hand, across that most delightful of New York breath-
ing-places, Stuyvesant Square.

"Uncle Teddy!" exclaimed Billy with ardor; "I

wish I could do something to show you how much I
think of you for being so good to me. I don't know
how. Would it make you happy if I was to learn a
hymn for you—a smashing big hymn—six verses,
long metre, and no grumbling?"

"No, Billy; you make me happy enough just by
being a good boy."

"Oh, Uncle Teddy!" replied Billy decidedly, "I'm
afraid I can't do it. I've tried so often and I always
make such an awful mess of it."

"Perhaps you get discouraged too easily—"

"Well, if a savings-bank won't do it, there ain't any
chance for a boy. I got father to get me a savings-
bank once and began being good just as hard as ever
I could for three cents a day. Every night I got 'em,
I put 'em in reg'lar, and sometimes I'd keep being
good three whole days running. That made a sight
of money, I tell you. Then I'd do something, ma said,
to kick my pail of milk over, and those nights I didn't
get anything. I used to put in most of my marble
and candy money, too."

"What were you going to do with it?"

"It was for an Objeck, Uncle Teddy. That's a
kind of Indian, you know, that eats people and wants
the gospel. That's what pa says, anyway; I didn't
ever see one."

"Well, didn't that make you happy—to help the
poor little heathen children?"

"Oh, does it, Uncle Teddy? They never got a cent
of it. One time I was good so long I got scared. I
was afraid I'd never want to fly my kite on a roof

again or go anywhere where I oughtn't, or have any fun. I couldn't see any use of going and saving my money to send out to the Objecks if it was going to make good boys of 'em. It was awful hard for me to have to be a good boy, and it must be worse for them 'cause they ain't used to it. So when there wasn't anybody upstairs I went and shook a lot of pennies out of my chimney and bought ever so much taffy and marbles and popcorn. Was that awful mean, Uncle Teddy?"

The question involved such complications that I hesitated. Before I could decide what to answer Billy continued:

"Ma said it was robbing the heathen, and didn't I get it? I thought if it was robbing I'd have a cop after me."

"What's a 'cop'?"

"That's what the boys call a policeman, Uncle Teddy; and then I should be taken away and put in an awful black place underground, like Johnny Wilson when he broke Mrs. Perkins's window. I was scared, I tell you. But I didn't get anything worse than a whipping, and having my savings bank taken away from me with all that was left in it. I haven't tried to be good since, much."

We now got into a Broadway stage going down, and being unable, on account of the noise, to converse further upon those spiritual conflicts of Billy's which so much interested me, we amused ourselves with looking out until just as we reached the Astor House, when he asked me where we were going.

"Where do you guess?" said I.

He cast a glance through the front window and his face became irradiated. Oh, there's nothing like the simple, cheap luxury of pleasing a child, to create sunshine enough for the chasing away of the bluest adult devils!

"We're going to Barnum's," said Billy, involuntarily clapping his hands.

So we were; and, much as stuck-up people pretend to look down at the place, I frequently am. Not only so, but I always see that class largely represented there when I do go. To be sure, they always make believe that they only come to amuse the children, or because their country cousins visit them; and never fail to refer to the vulgar set one finds there, and the fact of the animals smelling like anything but Jockey Club; yet I notice that after they've been in the hall three minutes they're as much interested as any of the people they come to poh-poh, and only put on the high-bred air when they fancy some of their own class are looking at them. I boldly acknowledge that I go because I like it. I am especially happy, to be sure, if I have a child along to go into ecstasies and give me a chance, *by* asking questions, for the exhibition of that fund of information which is said to be one of my chief charms in the social circle, and on several occasions has led that portion of the public immediately about the Happy Family into the erroneous impression that I was Mr. Barnum explaining his five hundred thousand curiosities.

On the present occasion we found several visitors of

the better class in the room devoted to the Aquarium.
Among these was a young lady, apparently about nineteen, in a tight-fitting basque of black velvet, which
showed her elegant figure to fine advantage, a skirt
of garnet silk, looped up over a pretty Balmoral, and
the daintiest imaginable pair of kid walking-boots.
Her height was a trifle over the medium, her eyes,
a soft expressive brown, shaded by masses of hair
which exactly matched their color, and, at that rat-
and-miceless day, fell in such graceful abandon as to
show at once that nature was the only maid who
crimped their waves into them. Her complexion was
rosy with health and sympathetic enjoyment; her
mouth was faultless, her nose sensitive, her manners
full of refinement, and her voice musical as a wood-
robin's, when she spoke to the little boy of six at her
side, to whom she was revealing the palace of the great
show-king. Billy and I were flattening our noses
against the abode of the balloon-fish and determining
whether he looked most like a horse-chestnut burr or
a ripe cucumber, when his eyes and my own simul-
taneously fell on the child and lady. In a moment, to
Billy the balloon-fish was as though he had not been.

"That's a pretty little boy!" said I. And then I
asked Billy one of those senseless routine questions
which must make children look at us, regarding the
scope of our intellects very much as we look at Bush-
men.

"How would you like to play with him?"

"Him!" replied Billy scornfully, "that's his first
pair of boots; see him pull up his little breeches to

show the red tops to them! But, crackey! isn't *she* a
smasher!"

After that we visited the wax figures and the
sleepy snakes, the learned seal, and the glass-blowers.
Whenever we passed from one room into another,
Billy could be caught looking anxiously to see if the
pretty girl and child were coming, too.

Time fails me to describe how Billy was lost in
astonishment at the Lightning Calculator—wanted me
to beg the secret of that prodigy for him to do his
sums by—finally thought he had discovered it, and
resolved to keep his arm whirling all the time he
studied his arithmetic lesson the next morning.
Equally inadequate is it to relate in full how he became so confused among the waxworks that he
pinched the solemnest showman's legs to see if he was
real, and perplexed the beautiful Circassian to the
verge of idiocy by telling her he had read all about
the way they sold girls like her in his geography.

We had reached the stairs to that subterranean
chamber in which the Behemoth of Holy Writ was
wallowing about without a thought of the dignity
which one expects from a canonical character. Billy
had always languished upon his memories of this di-
verting beast, and I stood ready to see him plunge
headlong the moment that he read the signboard at
the head of the stairs. When he paused and hesitated there, not seeming at all anxious to go down till
he saw the pretty girl and the child following after—
a sudden intuition flashed across me. Could it be
possible that Billy was caught in that vortex which

whirled me down at ten years—a little boy's first love?

We were lingering about the elliptical basin, and catching occasional glimpses between bubbles of a vivified hair trunk of monstrous compass, whose knobby lid opened at one end and showed a red morocco lining, when the pretty girl, in leaning over to point out the rising monster, dropped into the water one of her little gloves, and the swash made by the hippopotamus drifted it close under Billy's hand. Either in play, or as a mere coincidence, the animal followed it. The other children about the tank screamed and started back as he bumped his nose against the side; but Billy manfully bent down and grabbed the glove, not an inch from one of his big tusks, then marched around the tank and presented it to the lady with a chivalry of manner in one of his years quite surprising.

"That's a real nice boy—you said so, didn't you, Lottie? And I wish he'd come and play with me," said the little fellow by the young lady's side, as Billy turned away, gracefully thanked, to come back to me with his cheeks roseate with blushes.

As he heard this, Billy sidled along the edge of the tank for a moment, then faced about and said:

"P'rhaps I will some day—where do you live?"

"I live on East Seventeenth Street with papa—and Lottie stays there too now—she's my cousin: where d'you live?"

"Oh, I live close by—right on that big green square where I guess the nurse takes you once in a while," said Billy patronizingly. Then, looking up pluckily at the young lady, he added, "I never saw you out there."

"No, Jimmy's papa has only been in his new house a little while, and I've just come to visit him."

"Say, will you come and play with me some time?" chimed in the inextinguishable Jimmy. I've got a cooking stove—for real fire—and blocks and a ball with a string."

Billy, who belonged to a club for the practice of the great American game, and was what A. Ward would call the most superior battest among the I. G. B. B. C., or "Infant Giants," smiled from that altitude upon Jimmy, but promised to go and play with him the next Saturday afternoon.

Late that evening, after we had got home and dined, as I sat in my room over Pickwick, with a sedative cigar, a gentle knock at the door told of Daniel. I called "Come in!" and, entering with a slow dejected air, he sat down by my fire. For ten minutes he remained silent, though occasionally looking up as if about to speak, then dropping his head again to ponder on the coals. Finally I laid down Dickens, and spoke myself.

"You don't seem well to-night, Daniel?"

"I don't feel very well, uncle."

"What's the matter, my boy?"

"Oh—ah—I don't know. That is, I wish I knew how to tell you."

I studied him for a few moments with kindly curiosity, then answered: "Perhaps I can save you the trouble by cross-examining it out of you. Let's try

the method of elimination. I know that you are not
harassed by any economical considerations, for you've
all the money you want; and I know that ambition
doesn't trouble you, for your tastes are scholarly.
This narrows down the investigation of your symptoms—listlessness, general dejection, and all—to three
causes: Dyspepsia, religious conflicts, love. Now is
your digestion awry?"

"No, sir, good as usual. I'm not melancholy on
religion and—"

"You don't tell me you're in love?"

"Well — yes — I suppose that's about it, Uncle
Teddy."

I took a long breath to recover from my astonishment at this unimaginable revelation, then said:

"Is your feeling returned?"

"I really don't know, uncle. I don't believe it
is. I don't see how it can be. I never did anything
to make her love me. What is there in me to love!
I've borne enough for her—that is, nothing that could
do her any good—though I've endured on her account,
I may say, anguish. So, look at it any way you please,
I neither am, do, nor suffer anything that can get a
woman's love."

"Oh, you man of learning! Even in love you tote
your grammar along with you, and arrange a divine
passion under the active, passive, and neuter!"

Daniel smiled faintly.

"You've no idea, Uncle Teddy, that you are twitting
on facts; but you hit the truth there; indeed you do.
If she were a Greek or Latin woman I could talk

Anacreon or Horace to her. If women only understood the philosophy of the flowers as well as they do
the poetry—"

"Thank God they don't, Daniel!" sighed out I de-
voutly.

"Never mind—in that case I could entrance her for
hours, talking about the grounds of difference between
Linnæus and Jussieu. Women like the star business,
they say—and I could tell her where all the constella-
tions are; but sure as I tried to get off any sentiment
about them, I'd break down and make myself ridicu-
lous. But what earthly chance would the greatest
philosopher that ever lived have with the woman he
loved, if he depended for her favor on his ability to
analyze her bouquet or tell her when she might look
out for the next occultation of Orion? I can't talk
bread and butter. I can't do anything that makes a
man even tolerable to a woman!"

"I hope you don't mean that nothing but bread and
butter talk is tolerable to a woman!"

"No; but it's necessary to some extent—at any rate
the ability is—in order to succeed in society; and it is
in society men first meet and strike women. And
Uncle Teddy! I'm such a fish out of water in society!
—such a dreadful floundering fish! When I see her
dancing gracefully as a swan swims, and feel that fellows, like little Jack Mankyn, 'who don't know twelve
times,' can dance to her perfect admiration; when I
see that she likes ease of manners—and all sorts of
men without an idea in their heads have that—while
I turn all colors when I speak to her, and am clumsy,

and abrupt, and abstracted, and bad at repartee—Uncle Teddy! sometimes (though it seems so ungrateful to father and mother, who have spent such pains for me)—sometimes, do you know, it seems to me as if I'd exchange all I've ever learned for the power to make a good appearance before her!"

"Daniel, my boy, it's too much a matter of reflection with you! A woman is not to be taken by laying plans. If you love the lady (whose name I don't ask you because I know you'll tell me as soon as you think best), you must seek her companionship until you're well enough acquainted with her to have her regard you as something different from the men whom she meets merely in society, and judge your qualities by another standard than that she applies to them. If she's a sensible girl (and God forbid you should marry her otherwise!) she knows that people can't always be dancing, or holding fans, or running after orange ice. If she's a girl capable of appreciating your best points (and woe to you if you marry a girl who can't!), she'll find them out upon closer intimacy, and once found they'll a hundred times outweigh all brilliant advantages kept in the showcase of fellows who have nothing on the shelves. When this comes about, you will pop the question unconsciously, and, to adopt Milton, she will drop into your lap, 'gathered—not harshly plucked.' "

"I know that's sensible, Uncle Teddy, and I'll try. Let me tell you the sacredest of secrets—regularly every day of my life I send her a little poem fastened round the prettiest bouquet I can get at Hanfts'."

"Does she know who sends them?"

"She can't have any idea. The German boy that takes them knows not a word of English except her name and address. You'll forgive me, Uncle, for not mentioning her name yet? You see she may despise or hate me some day when she knows who it is that has paid her these attentions; and then I'd like to be able to feel that at least I've never hurt her by any absurd connection with myself."

"Forgive you? Nonsense! The feeling does your heart infinite credit, though a little counsel with your head would show you that your only absurdity is self-depreciation."

Daniel bade me good-night. As I put out my cigar and went to bed, my mind reverted to the dauntless little Hotspur who had spent the afternoon with me, and reversed his mother's wish, thinking: "Oh, if Daniel were more like Billy!"

It was always Billy's habit to come and sit with me while I smoked my after-breakfast cigar, but the next morning did not see him enter my room till St. George's hands pointed to a quarter of nine.

"Well, Billy Boy Blue, come blow your horn; what haystack have you been under till this time of day? We shan't have a minute to look over our spelling together, and I know a boy who is going in for promotion next week. Have you had your breakfast and taken care of Crab?"

"Yes, sir, but I didn't feel like getting up this morning."

"Are you sick?"

"No-o-o—it isn't that; but you'll laugh at me if I tell you."

"Indeed, I won't, Billy!"

"Well"—his voice dropped to a whisper and he stole close to my side—"I had such a nice dream about *her* just the last thing before the bell rang; and when I woke up I felt so queer—so kinder good and kinder bad—and I wanted to see her so much, that if I hadn't been a big boy, I believe I should have blubbered. I tried ever so much to go to sleep and see her again; but the more I tried the more I couldn't. After all, I had to get up without it, though I didn't want any breakfast, and only ate two buckwheat cakes, when I always eat six, you know, Uncle Teddy. Can you keep a secret?"

"Yes, dear, so you couldn't get it out of me if you were to shake me upside down like a savings-bank."

"Oh, ain't you mean! That was when I was small I did that. I'll tell you the secret, though—that girl and I are going to get married. I mean to ask her the first chance I get. Oh, isn't she a smasher!"

"My dear Billy, shan't you wait a little while to see if you always like her as well as you do now? Then, too, you'll be older."

"I'm old enough, Uncle Teddy, and I love her dearly. I am as old as the Kings of France used to be when they got married—I read it in Abbott's history. But there's the clock striking nine! I must run or I shall get a tardy mark and perhaps she'll want to see my certificate some time."

So saying, he kissed me on the cheek and set off for

school as fast as his legs could carry him. Oh, Love, omnivorous Love, that sparest neither the dotard leaning on his staff nor the boy with pantaloons buttoning on his jacket—omnipotent Love, that, after parents and teachers have failed, in one instant can make Billy try to become a good boy!

With both of my nephews hopelessly enamored and myself the confidant of both, I had my hands full. Daniel was generally dejected and distrustful; Billy buoyant and jolly. Daniel found it impossible to overcome his bashfulness, was spontaneous only in sonnets, brilliant only in bouquets. Billy was always coming to me with pleasant news, told in his slangy New York boy vernacular. One day he would exclaim: "Oh, I'm getting on prime! I got such a smile off her this morning as I went by the window!" Another day he wanted counsel how to get a valentine to her—because it was too big to shove in a lamppost and she might catch him if he left it on the steps, rang the bell, and ran away. Daniel wrote his own valentine, but, despite its originality, that document gave him no such comfort as Billy got from twenty-five cents' worth of embossed paper, pink cupids, and doggerel.

Finally Billy announced to me that he had been to play with Jimmy and got introduced to his girl.

Shortly after this Lu gave what they call "a little company"—not a party, but a reunion of forty or fifty people with whom the family were well acquainted, several of them living in our immediate neighborhood. There was a goodly proportion of young folk and there was to be dancing; but the music

was limited to a single piano played by the German
exile usual on such occasions, and the refreshments did
not rise to the splendor of a costly supper. This kind
of compromise with fashionable gayety was wisely
deemed by Lu the best method of introducing Daniel
to the *beau monde*—a push given the timid eaglet by
the maternal bird, with a soft tree-top between him
and the vast expanse of society. How simple was the
entertainment may be inferred from the fact that Lu
felt somewhat discomposed when she got a note from
one of her guests asking leave to bring along her
niece who was making her a few weeks' visit. As a
matter of course, however, she returned answer to
bring the young lady and welcome.

Daniel's dressing-room having been given up to the
gentlemen, I invited him to make his toilet in mine,
and indeed, wanting him to create a favorable impression, became his valet *pro tem.*, tying his cravat and
teasing the divinity-student look out of his side hair.
My little dandy Billy came in for another share of
attention, and when I managed to button his jacket
for him so that it showed his shirt studs "like a
man's," Count d'Orsay could not have felt a greater
sense of his sufficiency for all the demands of the gay
world.

When we reached the parlor we found Pa and
Ma Lovegrove already receiving. About a score of
guests had arrived. Most of them were old married
couples which, after paying their devoirs, fell in two
like unriveted scissors, the gentlemen finding a new
pivot in pa and the ladies in ma, where they mildly

opened and shut upon such questions as severally
concerned them, such as "The way gold closed" and
"How the children were."

Besides the old married people there were several
old young men, of distinctly hopeless and unmarried
aspect, who, having nothing in common with the other
class, nor sufficient energy of character to band themselves for mutual protection, hovered dejectedly about
the arch pillars or appeared to be considering whether
on the whole it would not be feasible and best to sit
down on the centre-table. These subsisted upon such
crumbs of comfort as Lu could get an occasional
chance to throw them by rapid sorties of conversation
—became galvanically active the moment they were
punched up and fell flat the moment the punching was
remitted. I did all I could for them, but, having
Daniel in tow, dared not sail too near the edge of the
Doldrums, lest he should drop into sympathetic stag-
nation and be taken preternaturally bashful with his
sails all aback, just as I wanted to carry him gallantly
into action with some clipper-built cruiser of a nice
young lady. Finally, Lu bethought herself of that
last plank of drowning conversationalists, the photo-
graph album. All the dejected young men made for
it at once, some reaching it just as they were about to
sink for the last time, but all getting a grip on it
somehow and staying there, in company with other
people's babies whom they didn't know, and celebri-
ties whom they knew to death, until, one by one, they
either stranded upon a motherly dowager by the Fire-
Place Shoals, or were rescued from the Sofa Reef by

some gallant wrecker of a strong-minded young lady,
with a view of taking salvage out of them in the
German.

Besides these, were already arrived a dozen nice
little boys and girls who had been invited to make it
pleasant for Billy. I had to remind him of the fact
that they were his guests, for, in comparison with the
queen of his affections, they were in danger of being
despised by him as small fry.

The younger ladies and gentlemen—those who had
fascinations to disport or were in the habit of dis-
porting what they considered such—were probably
still at home consulting the looking-glass until that
oracle should announce the auspicious moment for
their setting forth.

Daniel was in conversation with a perfect godsend
of a girl who understood Latin and had taken up
Greek.

Billy was taking a moment's vacation from his
boys and girls, busy with "Old Maid" in the extension room, and whispering, with his hand in mine,
"Oh, don't I wish *she* were here!" when a fresh in-
voice of ladies, just unpacked from the dressing-room,
in all the airy elegance of evening costume, floated
through the door. I heard Lu say:

"Ah, Mrs. Rumbullion! happy to see your niece,
too. How do you do, Miss Pilgrim?"

At this last word Billy jumped as if he had been
shot, and the bevy of ladies opening about Sister Lu
disclosed the charming face and figure of the pretty
girl we had met at Barnum's.

Billy's countenance rapidly changed from astonishment to joy.

"Isn't that splendid, Uncle Teddy? Just as I was wishing it! It's just like the fairy books!" and, rushing up to the party of new-comers, "My dear Lottie!" cried he, "if I had only known you were coming I'd have come after you!"

As he caught her by the hand, I was pleased to see her soft eyes brighten with gratification at his enthusiasm, but my sister Lu looked on, naturally with astonishment in every feature.

"Why Billy!" said she, "you ought not to call a strange young lady '*Lottie.*' Miss Pilgrim, you must excuse my wild boy—"

"And you must excuse my mother, Lottie," said Billy, affectionately patting Miss Pilgrim's rose kid, "for calling you a strange young lady. You are not strange at all—you're just as nice a girl as there is."

"There are no excuses necessary," said Miss Pilgrim, with a bewitching little laugh. "Billy and I know each other intimately well, Mrs. Lovegrove, and I confess that when I heard the lady Aunt had been invited to visit was his mother, I felt all the more willing to infringe on etiquette this evening, by coming where I had no previous introduction."

"Don't you care!" said Billy encouragingly, "I'll introduce you to every one of our family; I know 'em if you don't."

At this moment I came up as Billy's reinforcement, and, fearing lest, in his enthusiasm, he might forget the canon of society which introduced a gentleman to a lady, not a lady to him, I ventured to suggest it delicately by saying, "Billy, will you grant me the favor of a presentation to Miss Pilgrim?"

"In a minute, Uncle Teddy," answered Billy, considerably lowering his voice. "The older people first"; and after this reproof I was left to wait in the cold until he had gone through the ceremony of introducing to the young lady his father and his mother.

Billy, who had now assumed entire guardianship of Miss Pilgrim, with an air of great dignity intrusted her to my care, and left us promenading while he went in search of Daniel. I, myself, looked in vain for that youth, whom I had not seen since the entrance of the last comers. Miss Pilgrim and I found a congenial common ground in Billy, whom she spoke of as one of the most delightfully original boys she had ever met; in fact, altogether the most fascinating young gentleman she had seen in New York society. You may be sure it wasn't Billy's left ear which burned when I made my responses.

In five minutes he reappeared to announce, in a tone of disappointment, that he could find Daniel nowhere. He could see a light through his keyhole, but the door was locked and he could get no admittance. Just then Lu came up to present a certain—no, an uncertain—young man of the fleet stranded on parlor furniture earlier in the evening. To Lu's great astonishment, Miss Pilgrim asked Billy's permission to leave him. It was granted with all the courtesy of a *preux chevalier,* on the condition, readily assented to, that she should dance one Lancers with him during the evening.

"Dear me!" exclaimed Lu, after Billy had gone back like a superior being, to assist at the childish amusement of his contemporaries, "would anybody ever suppose that was our Billy?"

"I should, my dear sister," said I, with proud satisfaction; "but you remember I always was just to Billy."

Left free, I went myself to hunt up Daniel. I found his door locked and a light showing through the keyhole, as Billy had said. I made no attempt to enter by knocking; but, going to my room and opening the window next his, I leaned out as far as I could, shoved up his sash with my cane and pushed aside his curtain. Such an unusual method of communication could not fail to bring him to the window with a rush. When he saw me, he trembled like a guilty thing, his countenance fell, and, no longer able to feign absence, he unlocked his door and let me enter by the normal mode.

"Why, Daniel Lovegrove, my nephew, what does this mean; are you sick?"

"Uncle Edward, I am not sick, and this means that I am a fool. Even a little boy like Billy puts me to shame. I feel humbled to the very dust. I wish I'd been a missionary and got massacred by savages. Oh, that I'd been permitted to wear damp stockings in childhood, or that my mother hadn't carried me through the measles! If it weren't wrong to take my life into my own hands, I'd open that window and

—and—sit in a draught this very evening! Oh, yes!
I'm just that bitter! Oh! Oh! Oh!"

And Daniel paced the floor with strides of frenzy.

"Well, my dear fellow, let's look at the matter
calmly for a minute. What brought on this sudden
attack? You seemed doing well enough the first ten
minutes after we came down. I was only out of your
sight long enough to speak to the Rumbullion party
who had just come in, and when I turned you were
gone. Now you are in this fearful condition. What
is there in the Rumbullions to start you off on such
a bender of bashfulness as this which I here
behold?"

"Rumbullions indeed!" said Daniel. A hundred
Rumbullions could not make me feel as I do; but *she*
can shake me into a whirlwind with her little finger,
and *she* came with the Rumbullions!"

"What! D'you—Miss Pilgrim?"

"Miss Pilgrim!"

I labored with Daniel for ten minutes, using every
encouragement and argument I could think of, and
finally threatened him that I would bring up the whole
Rumbullion party, Miss Pilgrim included, telling
them that he invited them to look at his conchological
cabinet, unless he instantly shook the ice out of his
manner and accompanied me downstairs. This dreadful menace had the desired effect. He knew that I
would not scruple to fulfil it; and at the same time
that it made him surrender it also provoked him with
me to a degree which gave his eyes and cheeks as fine
a glow as I could have wished for the purpose of a

favorable impression. The stimulus of wrath was good for him, and there was little tremor in his knees when he descended the stairs. Well-a-day—so Daniel and Billy were rivals!

The latter gentleman met us at the foot of the staircase.

"Oh, there you are, Daniel!" said he, cheerily. "I was just going to look for you and Uncle Teddy. We wanted you for the dances. We have had the Lancers twice and three round dances; and I danced the second Lancers with Lottie. Now we're going to play some games to amuse the children, you know," he added loftily with the adult gesture of pointing his thumb over his shoulder at the extension room. "Lottie's going to play, too, so will you and Daniel, won't you, uncle? Oh, here comes Lottie now! This is my brother, Miss Pilgrim; let me introduce him to you. I'm sure you'll like him. There's nothing he don't know."

Miss Pilgrim had just come to the newel post of the staircase, and when she looked into Daniel's face blushed like the red, red rose, losing her self-possession perceptibly more than Daniel.

The courage of weak warriors and timid gallants mounts as the opposite party's falls, and Daniel made out to say, in a firm tone, that it was long since he had enjoyed the pleasure of meeting Miss Pilgrim.

"Not since Mrs. Cramcroud's last sociable, I think," replied Miss Pilgrim, her cheeks and eyes still playing the telltale.

"Oho! so you don't want any introduction," exclaimed Master Billy. I didn't know you knew each other, Lottie."

"I have met Mr. Lovegrove in society. Shall we go and join in the plays?"

"To be sure we shall!" cried Billy. "You needn't mind; all the grown people are going to."

On entering the parlor we found it as he had said. The guests being almost all well acquainted with each other, at the solicitation of jolly little Mrs. Bloomingal, Sister Lu had consented to make a pleasant Christmas kind of time of it, in which everybody was permitted to be young again and romp with the rompiest. We played Blindman's-buff till we tired of that— Daniel, to Lu's great delight, coming out splendidly as Blindman, and evincing such "cheek" in the style he hunted down and caught the ladies, as satisfied me that nothing but his sight stood in the way of his making an audacious figure in the world. Then a pretty little girl, Tilly Turtelle, who seemed quite a premature flirt, proposed "Doorkeeper"—a suggestion accepted with great *éclat* by all the children, several grown people assenting.

To Billy—quite as much on account of his shining prominence in the executive faculties of his character, as host—was committed the duty of counting out the first person to be sent into the hall. There were so many of us that "Aina-maina-mona-mike" would not go quite around; but with that promptness of expedient which belongs to genius, Billy instantly added on "Intery-mintery-cutery-corn," and the last word of the cabalistic formula fell upon me, Edward Bal-

bus. I disappeared into the entry amid peals of
happy laughter from both old and young, calling,
when the door opened again to ask me who I wanted,
for the pretty, lisping flirt who had proposed the
game. After giving me a coquettish little chirrup of
a kiss and telling me my beard scratched, she bade me,
on my return, send out to her "Mither Billy Lovegrove." I obeyed her; my youngest nephew retired
and, after a couple of seconds, during which Tilly
undoubtedly got what she proposed the game for,
Billy being a great favorite with the little girls, she
came back pouting and blushing, to announce that he
wanted Miss Pilgrim. The young lady showed no
mock modesty, but arose at once and laughingly went
out to her youthful admirer, who, as I afterward
learned, embraced her ardently and told her he loved
her better than any girl in the world. As he turned
to go back she told him that he might send to her one
of her juvenile cousins, Reginald Rumbullion. Now,
whether because on this youthful Rumbullion's account Billy had suffered the pangs of that most terrible passion, jealousy, or from his natural enjoyment
of playing practical jokes destructive of all dignity in
his elders, Billy marched into the room, and, having
shut the door behind him, paralyzed the crowded parlor by an announcement that Mr. Daniel Lovegrove
was wanted.

I was standing at his side and could feel him tremble—see him turn pale.

"Dear me!" he whispered, in a choking voice; "can
she mean me?"

"Of course she does," said I. "Who else? Do you hesitate? Surely you can't refuse such an invitation from a lady."

"No; I suppose not," said he, mechanically. And, amid much laughter from the disinterested, while the faces of Mrs. Rumbullion and his mother were spectacles of crimson astonishment, he made his exit from the room. Never in my life did I so much long for that instrument, described by Mr. Samuel Weller—a pair of patent, double-million magnifying microscopes of hextery power, to see through a deal door. Instead of this I had to learn what happened only by report.

Lottie Pilgrim was standing under the hall burners with her elbow on the newel-post, more vividly charming than he had ever seen her before, at Mrs. Cramcroud's sociable or elsewhere. When startled by the apparition of Mr. Daniel Lovegrove instead of little Rumbullion whom she was expecting—she had no time to exclaim or hide her mounting color, none at all to explain to her own mind the mistake that had occurred, before his arm was clasped around her waist and his lips so closely pressed to hers that, through her soft, thick hair she could feel the throbbing of his temples. As for Daniel, he seemed in a walking dream, from which he waked to see Miss Pilgrim looking into his eyes with utter, though not incensed stupefaction—to stammer, "Forgive me! do forgive me! I thought you were in earnest."

"So I was," she said tremulously, as soon as she could catch her voice, "in sending for my cousin Reginald."

"Oh dear, what shall I do! Believe me, I was told you wanted me. Let me go and explain it to mother. She will tell the rest—I couldn't do it—I'd die of mortification. Oh, that wretched boy Billy!"

On the principle already mentioned, his agitation reassured her.

"Don't try to explain it now—it may get Billy a scolding. Are there any but intimate family friends here this evening?"

"No—I believe—no—I'm sure," replied Daniel, collecting his faculties.

"Then I don't mind what they think. Perhaps they'll suppose we've known each other long; but we'll arrange it by and by. They'll think the more of it the longer we stay out here—hear them laugh! I must run back now. I'll send you somebody."

A round of juvenile applause greeted her as she hurried into the parlor, and a number of grown people smiled quite musically. Her quick woman's wit told her how to retaliate and divide the embarrassment of the occasion. As she passed me she said in an undertone:

"Answer quick! Who is that fat lady on the sofa who laughed so loud?"

"Mrs. Cromwell Craggs," said I, quietly.

Miss Pilgrim made a satirically low courtesy and spoke in a modest but distinct voice:

"I really must be excused for asking. I'm a stranger, you know; but is there such a lady here as Mrs. Craggs—Mrs. *Cromwell* Craggs? For, if so, the present doorkeeper would like to see Mrs. Cromwell Craggs."

Then came the turn of the fat lady to be laughed at; but out she had to go and get kissed like the rest of us. Before the close of the evening Billy was made as jealous as his parents and I were surprised to see Daniel in close conversation with Miss Pilgrim among the geraniums and fuchsias of the conservatory.

"A regular flirtation," said Billy, somewhat indignantly. The conclusion which they arrived at was that after all no great harm had been done, and that the dear little fellow ought not to be peached on for his fun. If I had known at the time how easily they forgave him, I should have suspected that the offence Billy had led Daniel into committing was not unlikely to be repeated on the offender's own account; but so much as I could see showed me that the ice was broken.

Billy's jealousy did not outlast the party. He became more and more interested in "his girl," and often went in the afternoon, after getting out of school, ostensibly to play with Jimmy. Daniel's calls, according to adult etiquette, made in the evening, did not interfere with my younger nephew's, and as neither knew that the other, after his fashion, was his most uncompromising rival, my position, as the confidant of both, was one of extreme delicacy. But the matter was more speedily settled than I expected.

Billy came to me one day and told me that he intended to get married immediately; that he was going to speak to his Lottie that very afternoon. He was prepared to meet every objection. He had asked his father if he might, and his father said yes, if he had money enough to support a wife—and Billy thought he had. He'd saved up all the money his Uncle Jim and Aunt Jane had sent him for Christmas; and besides, if he were once married, his father wouldn't see him want for stamps, he knew. Then, too, he was going to leave school and be a merchant next year— and I'd help him now and then, if he got hard up, wouldn't I? If he were driven to it, he could be a good boy again, and save up the money to buy Lottie presents with, instead of giving it to nasty old "Objecks." He was so much older than when he had the savings-bank that he ought to have at least ten cents a day now for being good; didn't I think that was fair? As to his age, if Lottie loved him, he didn't care—anyway he would be lots bigger than she was before long—and he'd often heard his ma say she approved of early marriages; hers and pa's was one. So he ran off up Livingston Place, the most undaunted lover that ever put an extra shine on his proposal boots, or spent half an hour on the bow of his popping necktie.

Shortly after, Daniel went into the street. Not meaning to call upon his *inamorata,* but drawn by the irresistible fascination of passing her house, he strolled in the direction that Billy had gone. As he came to the Rumbullions', something suddenly bade him enter—a whim he called it, but not his own—one of the whims of destiny which are always gratified.

"Yes, sir," said the servant, "Miss Pilgrim is in, I will call her."

His step was always light. . He passed noiselessly
into the front parlor and sat down among the heavy
brocatelle curtains which shadowed the recess of one
of the windows. He supposed Miss Pilgrim to be upstairs, and while his heart fluttered, expecting her foot-
fall at the particular door, he heard an earnest boyish
voice in the inside room. Looking from his concealment he beheld Miss Pilgrim on a sofa in the pier and
sitting by her side, with her hand clasped in his, his
brother Billy. Before he could avoid it, he became
aware that Billy was unconsciously but eagerly fore-
stalling him.

"Now, Lottie, my dear Lottie! I wish you would!
I'll do everything I can to make you happy. If you'll
only marry me, I'll be good all the time! Come now!
Say yes! Father's got a really nice place over the
stable—they only use it for a tool room now; we could
clear it out and have it scrubbed and go to housekeep-
ing right away. Ma'd let us have all her old set of
china. I've got a silver mug Uncle Teddy gave me
and a napkin ring and four spoons. As soon as I
make my money I'll buy you a nice carriage and
horses, any color you want 'em. Oh, my darling,
darling Lottie, I do love you so much and we could
have such a splendid time! Do say yes, Lottie—
please, *do* please!"

Miss Pilgrim looked at the earnest little suitor with
a face in which tender interest and compassion quite
overrode any sense of the whimsicality of the situation which might lurk there. Daniel's astonishment
at the sight was so great that he realized the entire

state of the case before he could recover himself sufficiently to rise and go into the back room.

Billy jumped up and looked defiantly at the intruder. Miss Pilgrim blushed violently, but turned away her head to avoid the exhibition of a still more convulsing emotion than embarrassment.

"I must beg your pardon, Miss Pilgrim—and yours, too, Billy," began Daniel in a hesitating way, hardly knowing how to treat the posture in which he found things, "but—you see—the fact is the servant said she'd go to announce me—and really when I came in, I hadn't any idea you were here, or Billy either."

"Then," said Billy, moderating the defiant attitude, "you actually weren't dodging around and trying to find out what Lottie and I were about on the sly? Well, I'll believe you. I'm sure you couldn't be as mean as that, when I'm the only brother you have got, that always brings you oranges when you're sick, and never plays ball on the stairs when you've got a headache. Now, then, I'll trust you. I've been asking Lottie to marry me, and I want you to help me. Ask her if she won't, Daniel—see if she won't do it for you!"

Miss Pilgrim had been trying to find words, but her face was too much for her and she was obliged to seek retirement in her handkerchief. As she drew it from her pocket, a well-worn piece of paper followed it and fell upon the floor. Billy picked it up before she noticed it, and was about to hand it to her, when his jealous eye fell upon a withered rosebud sewed to its margin. As he looked at it, with his little brows knit into a precocious sternness, he recognized his brother's nandwriting immediately beneath the flower. It was one of the daily anonymous sonnets, of which Daniel had told me, and the bud a relic of the bouquet accompanying it. Still Daniel was silent. What else could he be?

"Very well, very well, Master Daniel!" exclaimed Billy, in a voice trembling with grief and indignation, "there's good enough reason why you·won't speak a word for me. You want her yourself—here it is in your own writing. No wonder you won't tell Lottie to be my wife, when you're trying to take her away from me. Oh, Lottie, dear Lottie! I love you just as much as he does, though I don't know everything and can't write you poetry like it was out of the Fifth Reader! Daniel, how could you go and write to my Lottie this way: 'My churner'—no, it isn't churner, it's charmer,—'let me call thee mine'?"

Forgetting the sacredness of private MS. in that of private grief, he would have gone on, with a pause here and there for certainty of spelling, to the conclusion of the poem, had not Lottie sprung up, with her imploring face suffused by her discovery, for the first time, of the identity of her secret lover and the escape of his sonnet from her pocket. It was too late! There he stood before her unmistakably proved, and herself unmistakably proving in what estimation she held his verses and bouquets.

"Oh Billy, dear Billy! If you do love me, don't do so!" So exclaiming, she held out her hand, and Billy put the MS. into it with all the dignity of a wounded spirit.

"Mr. Lovegrove," said Miss Pilgrim, "I don't know what to say."

"I feel very much that way myself," said Daniel.

"*I* don't," said Billy, now in command of his voice. "I'll tell you what it is: perhaps Daniel didn't know how much I wanted you, Lottie—and perhaps he wants you 'most as bad as I do. But whatever way it is, I want you to choose between us, fair and square, and no dodging. Come now! You can take just whichever one of us you please, and the other won't lay up any grudge, though I know if that's me, or like me, he'll feel awful. You can have till to-morrow morning to make up your mind between me and Daniel, and if he won't say anything about it to pa and ma till then, *I* won't. Good-by, *dear* Lottie!"

He drew her face down to his, kissed her almost affectionately and then marched out of the door, feeling, as he afterward told me, as if he had blackened his boots all for nothing. Ah me! my dear Billy, how many times we do that in this world! Of what followed when Daniel and Miss Pilgrim were left alone, I have never had full details.

. . . .

But I do know that the young lady obeyed Billy and made her choice. Six months after that both my nephews stood up in Mrs. Rumbullion's parlor to take their several shares in a ceremony in which Miss Pilgrim was the central figure when it began, and Mrs. Daniel Lovegrove when it concluded. Time and elasticity of boyhood had so closed the sharp but evanescent wound in Billy's heart that he could stand the trial of being groomsman where he had wanted to be groom—more especially since he was supported through the emergency by a little sister of Lottie's who promised to be wondrously like her by the time Billy could stand up in the more enviable capacity. Neither Daniel nor Lottie would listen to any objection to such a groomsman on the score of his extreme youth, for, as they said, Billy had been quite as instrumental in bringing them together as any agent, save the divinity shaping the ends and tying all the knots in which there are heartstrings concerned, as well as white ribbon.

Since then Lu has stopped wishing that Billy were like Daniel, for she says that if he had been, there would never have been any Mrs. Daniel Lovegrove in the world.

THE MAN WHO STOLE A MEETING-HOUSE

BY J. T. TROWBRIDGE

John Townsend Trowbridge (born in Ogden, N. Y., in 1827) began his literary career in 1857 with a realistic novel of New England life entitled "Neighbor Jackwood." During the Civil War he wrote several stories dealing with that great event, such as "The Drummer Boy" and "Cudjo's Cave." Popular as these were, he will be remembered chiefly for his subsequent work in juvenile fiction, of which "The Jack Hazard Series" is a type. He has published seven volumes of verse, beginning with "The Vagabonds and Other Poems" (1869), and ending with a complete edition of his poems (1903); and an autobiography, "My Own Story" (1903). He has written many short stories of which in homely theme, direct narrative style, and plain moral purpose the present selection is thoroughly representative.

THE MAN WHO STOLE A MEETING-HOUSE

BY J. T. TROWBRIDGE

O N a recent journey to the Pennsylvania oil regions, I stopped one evening with a fellow-traveler at a village which had just been thrown into a turmoil of excitement by the exploits of a horse-thief. As we sat around the tavern hearth, after supper, we heard the particulars of the rogue's capture and escape fully discussed; then followed many another tale of theft and robbery, told amid curling puffs of tobacco-smoke; until, at the close of an exciting story, one of the natives turned to my traveling acquaintance, and, with a broad laugh, said, "Kin ye beat that, stranger?"

"Well, I don't know—maybe I could if I should try. I never happened to fall in with any such tall horse-stealing as you tell of, but I knew a man who stole a meeting-house once."

"Stole a meetin'-house! That goes a little beyant anything yit," remarked another of the honest villagers. "Ye don't mean he stole it and carried it away?"

"Stole it and carried it away," repeated my traveling companion, seriously, crossing his legs, and resting his arm on the back of his chair. "And, more than all that, I helped him."

"How happened that?—for you don't look much like a thief yourself."

All eyes were now turned upon my friend, a plain New England farmer, whose honest homespun appearance and candid speech commanded respect.

"I was his hired man, and I acted under orders. His name was Jedwort—Old Jedwort, the boys called him, although he wasn't above fifty when the crooked little circumstance happened which I'll make as straight a story of as I can, if the company would like to hear it."

"Sartin, stranger! sartin! about stealin' the meetin'-house!" chimed in two or three voices.

My friend cleared his throat, put his hair behind his ears, and with a grave, smooth face, but with a merry twinkle in his shrewd gray eye, began as follows:

"Jedwort I said his name was; and I shall never forget how he looked one particular morning. He stood leaning on the front gate—or rather on the post, for the gate itself was such a shackling concern a child couldn't have leaned on't without breaking it down. And Jedwort was no child. Think of a stoutish, stooping, duck-legged man, with a mountainous back, strongly suggestive of a bag of grist under his shirt, and you have him. That imaginary grist had been growing heavier and heavier, and he more and more bent under it, for the last fifteen years and more, until his head and neck just came forward out from between his shoulders like a turtle's from its shell. His arms hung, as he walked, almost to the ground. Being curved with the elbows outward, he looked for all the world, in a front view, like a waddling interrogation-point inclosed in a parenthesis. If man was ever a quadruped, as I've heard some folks tell, and rose gradually from four legs to two, there must have been a time, very early in his history, when he went about like Old Jedwort.

"The gate had been a very good gate in its day. It had even been a genteel gate when Jedwort came into possession of the place by marrying his wife, who inherited it from her uncle. That was some twenty years before, and everything had been going to rack and ruin ever since.

"Jedwort himself had been going to rack and ruin, morally speaking. He was a middling decent sort of man when I first knew him; and I judge there must have been something about him more than common, or he never could have got such a wife. But then women do marry, sometimes, unaccountably. I've known downright ugly and disagreeable fellows to work around, till by and by they would get a pretty girl fascinated by something in them which nobody else could see, and then marry her in spite of everything;—just as you may have seen a magnetizer on the stage make his subjects do just what he pleased, or a black snake charm a bird. Talk about women marrying with their eyes open, under such circumstances! They don't marry with their eyes open: they are put to sleep, in one sense, and a'n't more than half responsible for what they do, if they are that. Then rises the question that has puzzled wiser heads than any of ours here, and will puzzle more yet, till society is different from what it is now—how much a refined and sensitive woman is bound to suffer from a coarse and disgusting master, legally called her husband, before she is entitled to break off a bad bargain she scarce had a hand in making. I've sat here to-night and heard about men getting goods under false pretences; you've told some astonishing big stories, gentlemen, about rogues stealing horses and sleighs; and I'm going to tell you about the man who stole a meeting-house; but, when all is said, I guess it will be found that more extraordinary thieving than all that often goes on under our own eyes, and nobody takes any notice of it. There's such a thing, gentlemen, as getting hearts under false pretences. There's such a thing as a man's stealing a wife.

"I speak with feeling on this subject, for I had an opportunity of seeing what Mrs. Jedwort had to put up with from a man no woman of her stamp could do anything but detest. She was the patientest creature you ever saw. She was even too patient. If I had been tied to such a cub, I think I should have cultivated the beautiful and benignant qualities of a wildcat; there would have been one good fight, and one of us would have been living, and the other would have been dead, and that would have been the end of it. But Mrs. Jedwort bore and bore untold miseries and a large number of children. She had had nine of these, and three were under the sod and six above it when Jedwort ran off with the meeting-house in the way I am going on to tell you. There was Maria, the oldest girl, a perfect picture of what her mother had been at nineteen. Then there were the two boys, Dave and

Dan, fine young fellows, spite of their father. Then came Lottie, and Susie, and then Willie, a little four-year-old.

"It was amazing to see what the mother would do to keep her family looking decent with the little means she had. For Jedwort was the tightest screw ever you saw. It was avarice that had spoiled him, and came so near turning him into a beast. The boys used to say he grew so bent looking in the dirt for pennies. That was true of his mind, if not of his body. He was a poor man, and a pretty respectable man, when he married his wife; but he had no sooner come into possession of a little property than he grew crazy for more. There are a good many men in the world, that nobody looks upon as monomaniacs, who are crazy in just that sort of way. They are all for laying up money, depriving themselves of comforts, and their families of the advantages of society and education, just to add a few dollars to their hoard every year; and so they keep on till they die and leave it to their children, who would be much better off if a little more had been invested in the cultivation of their minds and manners, and less in stocks and bonds.

"Jedwort was just one of that class of men, although perhaps he carried the fault I speak of a little to excess. A dollar looked so big to him, and he held it so close, that at last he couldn't see much of any-thing else. By degrees he lost all regard for decency and his neighbor's opinions. His children went bare-foot, even after they got to be great boys and girls, because he was too mean to buy them shoes. It was pitiful to see a nice, interesting girl, like Maria, go about looking as she did, while her father was piling his money into the bank. She wanted to go to school and learn music, and be somebody; but he wouldn't keep a hired girl, and so she was obliged to stay at home and do housework; and she could no more have got a dollar out of him to pay for clothes and tuition than you could squeeze sap out of a hoe-handle.

"The only way his wife could ever get anything new for the family was by stealing butter from her own dairy, and selling it behind his back. 'You needn't say anything to Mr. Jedwort about this batch of butter,' she would hint to the storekeeper; 'but you may hand the money to me, or I will take my pay in goods.' In this way a new gown, or a piece of cloth for the boys' coats, or something else the family needed, would be smuggled into the house, with fear and trembling lest old Jedwort should make a row and find where the money came from.

"The house inside was kept neat as a pin; but everything around it looked terribly shiftless. It was built originally in an ambitious style, and painted white. It had four tall front pillars, supporting the portion of the roof that came over the porch—lifting up the eyebrows of the house, if I may so express my-self, and making it look as if it was going to sneeze. Half the blinds were off their hinges, and the rest flapped in the wind. The front doorstep had rotted away. The porch had once a good floor, but for years Jedwort had been in the habit of going to it whenever he wanted a board for the pig-pen, until not a bit of floor was left.

"But I began to tell about Jedwort leaning on the gate that morning. We had all noticed him; and as Dave and I brought in the milk, his mother asked, 'What is your father planning now? Half the time he stands there, looking up the road; or else he's walking up that way in a brown study.'

" 'He's got his eye on the old meeting-house,' says Dave, setting down his pail. 'He has been watching it and walking round it, off and on, for a week.'

"That was the first intimation I had of what the old fellow was up to. But after breakfast he followed me out of the house, as if he had something on his mind to say to me.

" 'Stark,' says he, at last, 'you've always insisted on't that I wasn't an enterprisin' man.'

" 'I insist on't still,' says I; for I was in the habit of talking mighty plain to him, and joking him pretty hard sometimes. 'If I had this farm, I'd show you enterprise. You wouldn't see the hogs in the garden half the time, just for want of a good fence to keep 'em out. You wouldn't see the very best strip of land lying waste, just for want of a ditch. You wouldn't see that stone wall by the road tumbling down year after year, till by and by you won't be able to see it for the weeds and thistles.'

" 'Yes,' says he, sarcastically, 'ye'd lay out ten times as much money on the place as ye'd ever git back agin, I've no doubt. But I believe in economy.'

"That provoked me a little, and I said, 'Economy!

You're one of the kind of men that'll skin a flint for sixpence and spoil a jack-knife worth a shilling. You waste fodder and grain enough every three years to pay for a bigger barn—to say nothing of the inconvenience.'

" 'Wal, Stark,' says he, grinning and scratching his head, 'I've made up my mind to have a bigger barn, if I have to steal one.'

" 'That won't be the first thing you've stole, neither,' says I.

"He flared up at that. 'Stole?' says he. 'What did I ever steal?'

" 'Well, for one thing, the rails the freshet last spring drifted off from Talcott's land onto yours, and you grabbed: what was that but stealing?'

" 'That was luck. He couldn't swear to his rails. By the way, they'll jest come in play now.'

" 'They've come in play already,' says I. 'They've gone on to the old fences all over the farm, and I could use a thousand more without making much show.'

" 'That's 'cause you're so dumbed extravagant with rails, as you are with everything else. A few loads can be spared from the fences here and there, as well as not. Harness up the team, boys, and git together enough to make about ten rods o' zigzag, two rails high.'

" 'Two rails?' says Dave, who had a healthy contempt for the old man's narrow, contracted way of doing things. 'What's the good of such a fence as that?'

" 'It'll be,' says I, 'like the single bar in music. When our old singing master asked his class once what a single bar was, Bill Wilkins spoke up and said, "It's a bar that horses and cattle jump over, and pigs and sheep run under." What do you expect to keep out with two rails?'

" 'The *law*, boys, the *law*,' says Jedwort. 'I know what I'm about. I'll make a fence the *law* can't run under nor jump over; and I don't care a cuss for the cattle and pigs. You git the rails, and I'll rip some boards off'n the pig-pen to make stakes.'

" 'Boards a'n't good for nothin' for stakes,' says Dave. 'Besides, none can't be spared from the pig-pen.'

" 'I'll have boards enough in a day or two for forty pig-pens,' says Jedwort. 'Bring along the rails and dump 'em out in the road for the present, and say nothin' to nobody.'

"We got the rails, and he made his stakes; and right away after dinner he called us out. 'Come, boys,' says he, 'now we'll astonish the natives.'

"The wagon stood in the road, with the last jag of rails still on it. Jedwort piled on his stakes, and threw on the crowbar and axe, while we were hitching up the team.

" 'Now, drive on, Stark,' says he.

" 'Yes; but where shall I drive to?'

" 'To the old meetin'-house,' says Jedwort, trudging on ahead.

"The old meeting-house stood on an open common,

at the northeast corner of his farm. A couple of
cross-roads bounded it on two sides; and it was
bounded on the other two by Jedwort's overgrown
stone wall. It was a square, old-fashioned building,
with a low steeple, that had a belfry, but no bell in it,
and with a high, square pulpit and high, straight-
backed pews inside. It was now some time since
meetings had been held there; the old society that
used to meet there having separated, one division of
it building a fashionable chapel in the North Village,
and the other a fine new church at the Centre.

"Now, the peculiarity about the old church property was, that nobody had any legal title to it. A
log meeting-house had been built there when the
country was first settled and the land was of no account. In the course of time that was torn down, and
a good frame house put up in its place. As it belonged to the whole community, no title, either to the
house or land, was ever recorded; and it wasn't until
after the society dissolved that the question came
up as to how the property was to be disposed of.
While the old deacons were carefully thinking it over,
Jedwort was on hand, to settle it by putting in his
claim.

"'Now, boys,' says he, 'ye see what I'm up to.'

"'Yes,' says I, provoked as I could be at the mean
trick, 'and I knew it was some such mischief all along.
You never show any enterprise, as you call it, unless it
is to get the start of a neighbor. Then you are wide
awake; then you are busy as the Devil in a gale of
wind.'

" 'But what *are* you up to, pa?' says Dan, who didn't see the trick yet.

"The old man says, 'I'm goin' to fence in the rest part of my farm.'

" 'What rest part?'

" 'This part that never was fenced; the old meetin'-house common.'

" 'But, pa,' says Dave, disgusted as I was, 'you've no claim on that.'

" 'Wal, if I ha'n't, I'll make a claim. Give me the crowbar. Now, here's the corner, nigh as I can squint'; and he stuck the bar into the ground. 'Make a fence to here from the wall, both sides.'

" 'Sho, pa!' says Dan, looking bewildered; 'ye a'n't goin' to fence in the old meetin'-house, be ye?'

" 'That's jest what I'm goin' to do. Go and git some big stuns from the wall—the biggest ye can find, to rest the corners of the fence on. String the rails along by the road, Stark, and go for another load. Don't stand gawpin' there!'

" '*Gawpin'?*' says I; 'it's enough to make anybody *gawp*. You do beat all the critters I ever had to deal with. Haven't ye disgraced your family enough already, without stealing a meeting-house?'

" 'How have I disgraced my family?' says he.

"Then I put it to him. 'Look at your children; it's all your wife can do to prevent 'em from growing up in rags and dirt and ignorance, because you are too close-fisted to clothe 'em decently or send 'em to school. Look at your house and yard. To see an Irishman's shanty in such a condition seems appropriate enough, but a genteel place, a house with pillars, run down and gone to seed like that, is an eyesore to the community. Then look at your wife. You never would have had any property to mismanage if it hadn't been for her; and see the way you show your gratitude for it. You won't let her go into company, nor have company at home; you won't allow a hired girl in the house, but she and Maria have to do all the drudgery. You make perfect slaves of 'em. I swear, if it wa'n't for your wife, I wouldn't work for you an hour longer; but she's the best woman in the world, after all you've done to break her spirit, and I hate to leave her.'

"The old fellow squirmed, and wrenched the crowbar in the ground, then snarled back: 'Yes! you're waitin' for me to die; then you mean to step into my shoes.'

" 'I hope you'll have a decenter pair than them you've got on, if I'm to step into 'em,' says I.

" 'One thing about it,' says he, 'she won't have ye.'

" 'I should think,' says I, 'a woman that would marry you would have 'most anybody.'

"So we had it back and forth, till by and by he left me to throw off the rails, and went to show the boys how to build the fence.

" 'Look here,' says he; 'jest put a thunderin' big stun to each corner; then lay your rail on; then drive your pair of stakes over it like a letter X.' He drove a pair. 'Now put on your rider. There's your letter X, ridin' one length of rails and carryin' another. That's what I call puttin' yer alphabet to a practical use; and I say there a'n't no sense in havin' any more edication than ye *can* put to a practical use. I've larnin' enough to git along in the world; and if my boys have as much as I've got, they'll git along. Now work spry, for there comes Deacon Talcott.'

" 'Wal, wal!' says the Deacon, coming up, puffing with excitement; 'what ye doin' to the old meetin'-house?'

" 'Wal,' says Jedwort, driving away at his stakes, and never looking up, 'I've been considerin' some time what I should do with't, and I've concluded to make a barn on't.'

" 'Make a barn! make a barn!' cries the Deacon. 'Who give ye liberty to make a barn of the house of God?'

" 'Nobody; I take the liberty. Why shouldn't I do what I please with my own prop'ty?'

" 'Your own property—what do you mean? 'Ta'n't your meetin'-house.'

" 'Whose is't, if 'ta'n't mine?' says Jedwort, lifting his turtle's head from between his horizontal shoulders, and grinning in the Deacon's face.

" 'It belongs to the society,' says the Deacon.

" 'But the s'ciety's pulled up stakes and gone off.'

" 'It belongs to individooals of the society—to individooals.'

" 'Wal, I'm an individooal,' says Jedwort.

" 'You! you never went to meetin' here a dozen times in your life!'

" 'I never did have my share of the old meetin'-

house, that's a fact,' says Jedwort; 'but I'll make it up now.'

" 'But what are ye fencin' up the common for?' says the Deacon.

" 'It'll make a good calf-pastur'. I've never had my share o' the vally o' that, either. I've let my neighbors' pigs and critters run on't long enough; and now I'm jest goin' to take possession o' my own.'

" 'Your own!' says the Deacon, in perfect consternation. 'You've no deed on't.'

" 'Wal, have you?'

" 'No—but—the society—'

" 'The s'ciety, I tell ye,' says Jedwort, holding his head up longer than I ever knew him to hold it up at a time and grinning all the while in Talcott's face— 'the s'ciety is split to pieces. There a'n't no s'ciety now—any more'n a pig's a pig arter you've butchered and e't it. You've e't the pig amongst ye, and left me the pen. The s'ciety never had a deed o' this 'ere prop'ty; and no man never had a deed o' this 'ere prop'ty. My wife's gran'daddy, when he took up the land here, was a good-natered sort of man, and he allowed a corner on't for his neighbors to put up a temp'rary meetin'-house. That was finally used up—the kind o' preachin' they had them days was enough to use up in a little time any house that wa'n't fire-proof; and when that was preached to pieces, they put up another shelter in its place. This is it. And now't the land a'n't used no more for the puppose 'twas lent for, it goes back nat'rally to the estate 'twas took from, and the buildin's along with it.'

" 'That's all a sheer fabrication,' says the Deacon. 'This land was never a part of what's now your farm, any more than it was a part of mine.'

" 'Wal,' says Jedwort, 'I look at it in my way, and you've a perfect right to look at it in your way. But I'm goin' to make sure o' my way, by puttin' a fence round the hull concern.'

" 'And you're usin' some of my rails for to do it with!' says the Deacon.

" 'Can you swear they're your rails?'

" 'Yes, I can; they're the rails the freshet carried off from my farm last spring, and landed on to yourn.'

" 'So I've heard ye say. But can you swear to the partic'lar rails? Can you swear, for instance, 't this 'ere is your rail? or this 'ere one?'

" 'No; I can't swear to precisely them two—but—'

" 'Can you swear to these two? or to any one or two?' says Jedwort. No, ye can't. Ye can swear to the lot in general, but you can't swear to any partic'lar rail, and that kind o' swearin' won't stand law, Deacon Talcott. I don't boast of bein' an edicated man, but I know suthin' o' what law is, and when I know it, I dror a line there, and I toe that line, and I make my neighbors toe that line, Deacon Talcott. Nine p'ints of the law is possession, and I'll have possession o' this 'ere house and land by fencin' on't in; and though every man 't comes along should say these 'ere rails belong to them, I'll fence it in with these 'ere very rails.'

"Jedwort said this, wagging his obstinate old head, and grinning with his face turned up pugnaciously at the Deacon; then went to work again as if he had settled the question, and didn't wish to discuss it any further.

"As for Talcott, he was too full of wrath and boiling indignation to answer such a speech. He knew that Jedwort had managed to get the start of him with regard to the rails, by mixing a few of his own with those he had stolen, so that nobody could tell 'em apart; and he saw at once that the meeting-house was in danger of going the same way, just for want of an owner to swear out a clear title to the property. He did just the wisest thing when he swallowed his vexation, and hurried off to alarm the leading men of the two societies, and to consult a lawyer.

" 'He'll stir up the old town like a bumble-bee's nest,' says Jedwort. 'Hurry up, boys, or there'll be a buzzin' round our ears 'fore we git through!'

" 'I wish ye wouldn't, pa!' says Dave. 'Why don't we 'tend to our own business, and be decent, like other folks? I'm sick of this kind of life.'

" 'Quit it, then,' says Jedwort.

" 'Do you tell me to quit it?' says Dave, dropping the end of a rail he was handling.

" 'Yes, I do; and do it dumbed quick, if ye can't show a proper respect to your father!'

"Dave turned white as a sheet, and he trembled as he answered back, 'I should be glad to show you respect, if you was a man I could feel any respect for.'

"At that Jedwort caught hold of the iron bar that was sticking in the ground, where he had been making a hole for a stake, and pulled away at it. 'I'll make a stake-hole in you!' says he. 'It's enough to have a sassy hired man round, without bein' jawed by one's own children!'

"Dave was out of reach by the time the bar came out of the ground.

"'Come here, you villain!' says the old man.

"'I'd rather be excused,' says Dave, backing off. 'I don't want any stake-holes made in me to-day. You told me to quit, and I'm going to. You may steal your own meeting-houses in future; I won't help.'

"There was a short race. Dave's young legs proved altogether too smart for the old waddler's, and he got off. Then Jedwort, coming back, wheezing and sweating, with his iron bar, turned savagely on me.

"'I've a good notion to tell you to go too!'

"'Very well, why don't ye?' says I. 'I'm ready.'

"'There's no livin' with ye, ye're gettin' so dumbed sassy! What I keep ye for is a mystery to me.'

"'No, it a'n't; you keep me because you can't get another man to fill my place. You put up with my sass for the money I bring ye in.'

"'Hold your yawp,' says he, 'and go and git another load of rails. If ye see Dave, tell him to come back to work.'

"I did see Dave, but, instead of telling him to go

back, I advised him to put out from the old home and get his living somewhere else. His mother and Maria agreed with me; and when the old man came home that night Dave was gone.

"When I got back with my second load, I found the neighbors assembling to witness the stealing of the old meeting-house, and Jedwort was answering their remonstrances.

" 'A meetin'-house is a respectable kind o' prop'ty to have round,' says he. 'The steeple'll make a good show behind my house. When folks ride by, they'll stop and look, and say, "There's a man keeps a private meetin'-house of his own." I can have preachin' in't, too, if I want. I'm able to hire a preacher of my own, or I can preach myself and save the expense.'

"Of course, neither sarcasm nor argument could have any effect on such a man. As the neighbors were going away, Jedwort shouted after 'em: 'Call agin. Glad to see ye. There'll be more sport in a few days, when I take the dumbed thing away.' (The dumbed thing was the meeting-house.) 'I invite ye all to see the show. Free gratis. It'll be good as a circus, and a 'tarnal sight cheaper. The women can bring their knittin', and the gals their everlastin' tattin'. As it'll be a pious kind o' show, bein' it's a meetin'-house, guess I'll have notices gi'n out from the pulpits the Sunday afore.'

"The common was fenced in by sundown; and the next day Jedwort had over a house-mover from the North Village to look and see what could be done with the building. 'Can ye snake it over, and drop it back of my house?' says he.

"It'll be a hard job,' says old Bob, 'without you tear down the steeple fust.'

"But Jedwort said, 'What's a meetin'-house 'thout a steeple? I've got my heart kind o' set on that steeple, and I'm bound to go the hull hog on this 'ere concern, now I've begun.'

" 'I vow,' says Bob, examining the timbers, 'I won't warrant but the old thing'll all tumble down.'

" 'I'll resk it.'

" 'Yes; but who'll resk the lives of me and my men?'

" 'O, you'll see if it's re'ly goin' to tumble, and look out. I'll engage 't me and my boys'll do the most dangerous part of the work. Dumbed if I wouldn't agree to ride in the steeple and ring the bell if there was one.'

"I've never heard that the promised notices were read from the pulpits; but it wasn't many days before Bob came over again, bringing with him this time his screws and ropes and rollers, his men and timbers, horse and capstan; and at last the old house might have been seen on its travels.

"It was an exciting time all around. The societies found that Jedwort's fence gave him the first claim to house and land unless a regular siege of the law was gone through to beat him off—and then it might turn out that he would beat them. Some said fight him; some said let him be—the thing a'n't worth going to law for; and so, as the leading men couldn't agree as to what should be done, nothing was done. That was just what Jedwort had expected, and he laughed in his sleeve while Bob and his boys screwed up the old meeting-house, and got their beams under it, and set it on rollers, and slued it around, and slid it on the timbers laid for it across into Jedwort's field, steeple foremost, like a locomotive on a track.

"It was a trying time for the women folks at home. Maria had declared that, if her father did persist in stealing the meeting-house, she would not stay a single day after it, but would follow Dave.

"That touched me pretty close, for, to tell the truth, it was rather more Maria than her mother that kept me at work for the old man. 'If you go,' says I, 'then there is no object for me to stay; I shall go too.'

" 'That's what I supposed,' says she; 'for there's no reason in the world why you should stay. But then Dan will go; and who'll be left to take sides with mother? That's what troubles me. Oh, if she could only go too! But she won't; and she couldn't if she would, with the other children depending on her. Dear, dear! what shall we do?'

"The poor girl put her head on my shoulder, and cried; and if I should own up to the truth, I suppose I cried a little too. For where's the man that can hold a sweet woman's head on his shoulder, while she sobs out her trouble, and he hasn't any power to help her —who, I say, can do any less, under such circumstances, than drop a tear or two for company?

" 'Never mind; don't hurry,' says Mrs. Jedwort. 'Be patient, and wait awhile, and it'll all turn out right, I'm sure.'

" 'Yes, you always say, "Be patient, and wait!" '
says Maria, brushing back her hair. 'But, for my
part, I'm tired of waiting, and my patience has given
out long ago. We can't always live in this way, and
we may as well make a change now as ever. But I
can't bear the thought of going and leaving you.'

"Here the two younger girls came in; and, seeing
that crying was the order of the day, they began to
cry; and when they heard Maria talk of going, they
declared they would go; and even little Willie, the four-
year-old, began to howl.

" 'There, there! Maria! Lottie! Susie!' said Mrs.
Jedwort, in her calm way; 'Willie, hush up! I don't
know what we are to do; but I feel that something is
going to happen that will show us the right way, and
we are to wait. Now go and wash the dishes, and
set the cheese.'

"That was just after breakfast, the second day of
the moving; and sure enough, something like what
she prophesied did happen before another sun.

"The old frame held together pretty well till along
toward night, when the steeple showed signs of seced-
ing. 'There she goes! She's falling now!' sung out
the boys, who had been hanging around all day in hopes
of seeing the thing tumble.

"The house was then within a few rods of where
Jedwort wanted it; but Bob stopped right there, and
said it wasn't safe to haul it another inch. 'That
steeple's bound to come down, if we do,' says he.

" 'Not by a dumbed sight, it a'n't,' says Jedwort.
'Them cracks a'n't nothin'; the j'ints is all firm yit.'

He wanted Bob to go up and examine; but Bob shook
his head—the concern looked too shaky.   Then he
told me to go up; but I said I hadn't lived quite long
enough, and had a little rather be smoking my pipe on
terra firma.   Then the boys began to hoot.   'Dumbed
if ye a'n't all a set of cowards,' says he.   'I'll go up
myself.'

"We waited outside while he climbed up inside.   The
boys jumped on the ground to jar the steeple, and
make it fall.   One of them blew a horn—as he said,
to bring down the old Jericho—and another thought
he'd help things along by starting up the horse, and
giving the building a little wrench.   But Bob put a
stop to that; and finally out came a head from the
belfry window.   It was Jedwort, who shouted down
to us: 'There ain't a j'int or brace gi'n out.   Start the
hoss, and I'll ride.   Pass me up that 'ere horn, and—'

"Just then there came a cracking and loosening of
timbers; and we that stood nearest had only time to
jump out of the way, when down came the steeple
crashing to the ground, with Jedwort in it."

"I hope it killed the cuss," said one of the village
story-tellers.

"Worse than that," replied my friend; "it just
cracked his skull—not enough to put an end to his
miserable life, but only to take away what little sense
he had.   We got the doctors to him, and they patched
up his broken head; and, by George, it made me mad
to see the fuss the women folks made over him.   It
would have been my way to let him die; but they were
as anxious and attentive to him as if he had been the

kindest husband and most indulgent father that ever
lived; for that's women's style: they're unreasoning
creatures.

"Along toward morning, we persuaded Mrs. Jedwort, who had been up all night, to lie down a spell
and catch a little rest, while Maria and I sat up and
watched with the old man. All was still except our
whispers and his heavy breathing; there was a lamp
burning in the next room; when all of a sudden a
light shone into the windows, and about the same time
we heard a roaring and crackling sound. We looked
out, and saw the night all lighted up, as if by some
great fire. As it appeared to be on the other side of
the house, we ran to the door, and there what did we
see but the old meeting-house all in flames! Some
fellows had set fire to it to spite Jedwort. It must
have been burning some time inside; for when we
looked out the flames had burst through the roof.

"As the night was perfectly still, except a light wind
blowing away from the other buildings on the place,
we raised no alarm, but just stood in the door and saw
it burn. And a glad sight it was to us, you may be
sure. I just held Maria close to my side, and told her
that all was well—it was the best thing that could
happen. 'O yes,' says she, 'it seems to me as though a
kind Providence was burning up his sin and shame
out of our sight.'

"I had never yet said anything to her about mar-
riage—for the time to come at that had never seemed
to arrive; but there's nothing like a little excitement
to bring things to a focus. You've seen water in a

tumbler just at the freezing-point, but not exactly able to make up its mind to freeze, when a little jar will set the crystals forming, and in a minute what was liquid is ice. It was the shock of events that night that touched my life into crystals—not of ice, gentlemen, by any manner of means.

"After the fire had got along so far that the meeting-house was a gone case, an alarm was given, probably by the very fellows that set it, and a hundred people were on the spot before the thing had done burning.

"Of course these circumstances put an end to the breaking up of the family. Dave was sent for, and came home. Then, as soon as we saw that the old man's brain was injured so that he wasn't likely to recover his mind, the boys and I went to work and put that farm through a course of improvement it would have done your eyes good to see. The children were sent to school, and Mrs. Jedwort had all the money she wanted now to clothe them, and to provide the house with comforts, without stealing her own butter. Jedwort was a burden; but, in spite of him, that was just about the happiest family, for the next four years, that ever lived on this planet.

"Jedwort soon got his bodily health, but I don't think he knew one of us again after his hurt. As near as I could get at his state of mind, he thought he had been changed into some sort of animal. He seemed inclined to take me for a master, and for four years he followed me around like a dog. During that time he never spoke, but only whined and growled.

When I said, 'Lie down,' he'd lie down; and when I whistled he'd come.

"I used sometimes to make him work; and certain simple things he would do very well, as long as I was by. One day I had a jag of hay to get in; and, as the boys were away, I thought I'd have him load it. I pitched it on to the wagon about where it ought to lie, and looked to him only to pack it down. There turned out to be a bigger load than I had expected, and the higher it got, the worse the shape of it, till finally, as I was starting it toward the barn, off it rolled, and the old man with it, head foremost.

"He struck a stone heap, and for a moment I thought he was killed. But he jumped up and spoke for the first time. *'I'll blow it,'* says he, finishing the sentence he had begun four years before, when he called for the horn to be passed up to him.

"I couldn't have been much more astonished if one of the horses had spoken. But I saw at once that there was an expression in Jedwort's face that hadn't been there since his tumble in the belfry; and I knew that, as his wits had been knocked out of him by one blow on the head, so another blow had knocked 'em in again.

" 'Where's Bob?' says he, looking all round.

" 'Bob?' says I, not thinking at first who he meant. Oh, Bob is dead—he has been dead these three years.'

"Without noticing my reply, he exclaimed: 'Where did all that hay come from? Where's the old meetin'-house?'

" 'Don't you know?' says I. 'Some rogues set fire to it the night after you got hurt, and burnt it up.'

"He seemed then just beginning to realize that something extraordinary had happened.

" 'Stark,' says he, 'what's the matter with ye? You're changed.'

" 'Yes,' say I, 'I wear my beard now, and I've grown older!'.

" 'Dumbed if 'ta'n't odd!' says he. 'Stark, what in thunder's the matter with *me?*'

" 'You've had meeting-house on the brain for the past four years,' says I; 'that's what's the matter.'

"It was some time before I could make him understand that he had been out of his head, and that so long a time had been a blank to him.

"Then he said, 'Is this my farm?'

" 'Don't you know it?' says I.

" 'It looks more slicked up than ever it used to,' says he.

" 'Yes,' says I; 'and you'll find everything else on the place slicked up in about the same way.'

" 'Where's Dave?' says he.

" 'Dave has gone to town to see about selling the wool.'

" 'Where's Dan?'

" 'Dan's in college. He takes a great notion to medicine; and we're going to make a doctor of him.'

" 'Whose house is that?' says he, as I was taking him home.

" 'No wonder you don't know it,' says I. 'It has been painted, and shingled, and had new blinds put on; the gates and fences are all in prime condition; and that's a new barn we put up a couple of years ago.'

" 'Where does the money come from, to make all these improvements?'

" 'It comes off the place,' says I. 'We haven't run in debt the first cent for anything, but we've made the farm more profitable than it ever was before.'

" 'That *my* house?' he repeated wonderingly, as we approached it. 'What sound is that?'

" 'That's Lottie practicing her lesson on the piano.'

" 'A pianer in my house?' he muttered. 'I can't stand that!' He listened. 'It sounds pooty, though!'

" 'Yes, it does sound pretty, and I guess you'll like it. How does the place suit you?'

" 'It *looks* pooty.' He started. 'What young lady is that?'

"It was Lottie, who had left her music and stood by the window.

" 'My dahter! ye don't say! Dumbed if she a'n't a mighty nice gal.'

" 'Yes,' says I; 'she takes after her mother.'

"Just then Susie, who heard talking, ran to the door.

" 'Who's that agin?' says Jedwort.

"I told him.

" 'Wal, *she's* a mighty nice-lookin' gal!'

" 'Yes,' says I, *she* takes after her mother.'

"Little Willie, now eight years old, came out of the woodshed with a bow-and-arrow in his hand, and stared like an owl, hearing his father talk.

" 'What boy is that?' says Jedwort. And when I told him, he muttered, 'He's an ugly-looking brat!'

" 'He's more like his father,' says I.

"The truth is, Willie was such a fine boy the old man was afraid to praise him, for fear I'd say of him, as I'd said of the girls, that he favored his mother.

"Susie ran back and gave the alarm; and then out came mother, and Maria with her baby in her arms, for I forgot to tell you that we had been married now nigh on to two years.

"Well, the women folks were as much astonished as I had been when Jedwort first spoke, and a good deal more delighted. They drew him into the house; and I am bound to say he behaved remarkably well. He kept looking at his wife, and his children, and his grandchild, and the new paper on the walls, and the new furniture, and now and then asking a question or making a remark.

" 'It all comes back to me now,' says he at last. 'I thought I was living in the moon, with a superior race of human bein's; and this is the place, and you are the people.'

"It wasn't more than a couple of days before he began to pry around, and find fault, and grumble at the expense; and I saw there was danger of things relapsing into something like their former condition. So I took him one side, and talked to him.

" 'Jedwort,' says I, 'you're like a man raised from the grave. You was the same as buried to your neighbors, and now they come and look at you as they would at a dead man come to life. To you, it's like coming into a new world, and I'll leave it to you now, if you don't rather like the change from the old state of things to what you see around you to-day. You've

seen how the family affairs go on—how pleasant everything is, and how we all enjoy ourselves. You hear the
piano, and like it; you see your children sought after
and respected, your wife in finer health and spirits than
you've ever known her since the day she was married;
you see industry and neatness everywhere on the premises; and you're a beast if you don't like all that. In
short, you see that our management is a great deal
better than yours; and that we beat you even in the
matter of economy. Now, what I want to know is
this: whether you think you'd like to fall into our
way of living, or return like a hog to your wallow.'

" 'I don't say but what I like your way of livin' very
well,' he grumbled.

" 'Then,' says I, 'you must just let us go ahead, as
we have been going ahead. Now's the time for you to
turn about and be a respectable man, like your neighbors. Just own up, and say you've not only been out
of your head the past four years, but that you've been
more or less out of your head the last four-and-twenty
years. But say you're in your right mind now,
and prove it by acting like a man in his right
mind. Do that, and I'm with you; we're all with
you. But go back to your old dirty ways, and you go
alone. Now I sha'n't let you off till you tell me what
you mean to do.'

"He hesitated some time, then said, 'Maybe you're
about right, Stark; you and Dave and the old woman
seem to be doin' pooty well, and I guess I'll let you
go on.' "

Here my friend paused, as if his story was done;

when one of the villagers asked, "About the land where the old meetin'-house stood—what ever was done with that?"

"That was appropriated for a new schoolhouse; and there my little shavers go to school."

"And old Jedwort, is he alive yet?"

"Both Jedwort and his wife have gone to that country where meanness and dishonesty have a mighty poor chance—where the only investments worth much are those recorded in the Book of Life. Mrs. Jedwort was rich in that kind of stock; and Jedwort's account, I guess, will compare favorably with that of some respectable people, such as we all know. I tell ye, my friends," continued my fellow-traveler, "there's many a man, both in the higher and lower ranks of life, that 't would do a deal of good, say nothing of the mercy 'twould be to their families, just to knock 'em on the head, and make Nebuchadnezzars of 'em—then, after they'd been turned out to grass a few years, let 'em come back again, and see how happy folks have been, and how well they have got along without 'em.

"I carry on the old place now," he added. "The younger girls are married off; Dan's a doctor in the North Village; and as for Dave, he and I have struck ile. I'm going out to look at our property now."

A RIDE WITH A MAD HORSE IN A FREIGHT-CAR

W. H. H. MURRAY

William Henry Harrison Murray (born April 26, 1840, in Guilford, Ct.; died March 3, 1904) is generally known by the sobriquet of "Adirondack" Murray, because of his fascinating and authoritative works on hunting, fishing, and camp life in the great North Woods of New York State. He also wrote an authoritative book on "The Perfect Horse." That deep sympathy with our noblest animal which invariably accompanies profound discernment of its nature is displayed in the present selection, which is unquestionably not only Mr. Murray's masterpiece, but also the one great classic story of the horse in English literature.

A RIDE WITH A MAD HORSE IN A FREIGHT-CAR

BY W. H. H. MURRAY

IT was at the battle of Malvern Hill—a battle where the carnage was more frightful, as it seems to me, than in any this side of the Alleghanies during the whole war—that my story must begin. I was then serving as Major in the —th Massachusetts Regiment—the old —th, as we used to call it—and a bloody time the boys had of it too. About 2 P. M. we had been sent out to skirmish along the edge of the wood in which, as our generals suspected, the Rebs lay massing for a charge across the slope, upon the crest of which our army was posted. We had barely entered the underbrush when we met the heavy formations of Magruder in the very act of charging. Of course, our thin line of skirmishers was no impediment to those onrushing masses. They were on us and over us before we could get out of the way. I do not think that half of those running, screaming masses of men ever knew that they had passed over the remnants of as plucky a regiment as ever came out of the old Bay State. But many of the boys had good reason to remember that afternoon at the base of Malvern Hill, and I among the number; for when the last line of Rebs had passed over me, I was left among the bushes with the breath nearly trampled

out of me and an ugly bayonet-gash through my
thigh; and mighty little consolation was it for me at
that moment to see the fellow who ran me through
lying stark dead at my side, with a bullet-hole in his
head, his shock of coarse black hair matted with
blood, and his stony eyes looking into mine. Well, I
bandaged up my limb the best I might, and started
to crawl away, for our batteries had opened, and the
grape and canister that came hurtling down the slope
passed but a few feet over my head. It was slow and
painful work, as you can imagine, but at last, by dint
of perseverance, I had dragged myself away to the
left of the direct range of the batteries, and, creeping
to the verge of the wood, looked off over the green
slope. I understood by the crash and roar of the guns,
the yells and cheers of the men, and that hoarse murmur which those who have been in battle know, but
which I can not describe in words, that there was hot
work going on out there; but never have I seen, no,
not in that three days' desperate *mêlée* at the Wilder-
ness, nor at that terrific repulse we had at Cold Harbor, such absolute slaughter as I saw that afternoon
on the green slope of Malvern Hill. The guns of the
entire army were massed on the crest, and thirty thousand of our infantry lay, musket in hand, in front.
For eight hundred yards the hill sank in easy declen-
sion to the wood, and across this smooth expanse the
Rebs must charge to reach our lines. It was nothing
short of downright insanity to order men to charge
that hill; and so his generals told Lee, but he would
not listen to reason that day, and so he sent regiment

after regiment, and brigade after brigade, and division after division, to certain death. Talk about Grant's disregard of human life, his effort at Cold Harbor—and I ought to know, for I got a minie in my shoulder that day—was hopeful and easy work to what Lee laid on Hill's and Magruder's divisions at Malvern. It was at the close of the second charge, when the yelling mass reeled back from before the blaze of those sixty guns and thirty thousand rifles, even as they began to break and fly backward toward the woods, that I saw from the spot where I lay a riderless horse break out of the confused and flying mass, and, with mane and tail erect and spreading nostril, come dashing obliquely down the slope. Over fallen steeds and heaps of the dead she leaped with a motion as airy as that of the flying fox when, fresh and unjaded, he leads away from the hounds, whose sudden cry has broken him off from hunting mice amid the bogs of the meadow. So this riderless horse came vaulting along. Now from my earliest boyhood I have had what horsemen call a 'weakness' for horses. Only give me a colt of wild, irregular temper and fierce blood to tame, and I am perfectly happy. Never did lash of mine, singing with cruel sound through the air, fall on such a colt's soft hide. Never did yell or kick send his hot blood from heart to head deluging his sensitive brain with fiery currents, driving him into frenzy or blinding him with fear; but touches, soft and gentle as a woman's, caressing words, and oats given from the open palm, and unfailing kindness, were the means I used to 'subjugate'

him. Sweet subjugation, both to him who subdues
and to him who yields! The wild, unmannerly, and
unmanageable colt, the fear of horsemen the country
round, finding in you not an enemy, but a friend, receiving his daily food from you, and all those little
'nothings' which go as far with a horse as a woman,
to win and retain affection, grows to look upon you
as his protector and friend, and testifies in countless
ways his fondness for you. So when I saw this
horse, with action so free and motion so graceful,
amid that storm of bullets, my heart involuntarily
went out to her, and my feelings rose higher and
higher at every leap she took from amid the whirlwind of fire and lead. And as she plunged at last
over a little hillock out of range and came careering
toward me as only a riderless horse might come, her
head flung wildly from side to side, her nostrils
widely spread, her flank and shoulders flecked with
foam, her eye dilating, I forgot my wound and all the
wild roar of battle, and, lifting myself involuntarily to
a sitting posture as she swept grandly by, gave her a
ringing cheer.

"Perhaps in the sound of a human voice of happy
mood amid the awful din she recognized a resemblance to the voice of him whose blood moistened her
shoulders and was even yet dripping from saddle and
housings. Be that as it may, no sooner had my voice
sounded than she flung her head with a proud upward
movement into the air, swerved sharply to the left,
neighed as she might to a master at morning from her
stall, and came trotting directly up to where I lay,

and, pausing, looked down upon me as it were in compassion. I spoke again, and stretched out my hand caressingly. She pricked her ears, took a step forward and lowered her nose until it came in contact with my palm. Never did I fondle anything more tenderly, never did I see an animal which seemed to so court and appreciate human tenderness as that beautiful mare. I say 'beautiful.' No other word might describe her. Never will her image fade from my memory while memory lasts.

"In weight she might have turned, when well conditioned, nine hundred and fifty pounds. In color she was a dark chestnut, with a velvety depth and soft look about the hair indescribably rich and elegant. Many a time have I heard ladies dispute the shade and hue of her plush-like coat as they ran their white, jeweled fingers through her silken hair. Her body was round in the barrel and perfectly symmetrical. She was wide in the haunches, without projection of the hipbones, upon which the shorter ribs seemed to lap. High in the withers as she was, the line of her back and neck perfectly curved, while her deep, oblique shoulders and long, thick forearm, ridgy with swelling sinews, suggested the perfection of stride and power. Her knees across the pan were wide, the cannon-bone below them short and thin; the pasterns long and sloping; her hoofs round, dark, shiny, and well set on. Her mane was a shade darker than her coat, fine and thin, as a thoroughbred's always is whose blood is without taint or cross. Her ear was thin, sharply pointed, delicately curved, nearly black

around the borders, and as tremulous as the leaves of
an aspen. Her neck rose from the withers to the head
in perfect curvature, hard, devoid of fat, and well cut
up under the chops. Her nostrils were full, very full,
and thin almost as parchment. The eyes, from which
tears might fall or fire flash, were well brought out,
soft as a gazelle's, almost human in their intelligence,
while over the small bony head, over neck and shoulders, yea, over the whole body and clean down to the
hoofs, the veins stood out as if the skin were but
tissue-paper against which the warm blood pressed,
and which it might at any moment burst asunder. 'A
perfect animal,' I said to myself as I lay looking her
over—'an animal which might have been born from
the wind and the sunshine, so cheerful and so swift
she seems; an animal which a man would present as
his choicest gift to the woman he loved, and yet one
which that woman, wife or lady-love, would give him
to ride when honor and life depended on bottom and
speed.'

"All that afternoon the beautiful mare stood over
me, while away to the right of us the hoarse tide of
battle flowed and ebbed. What charm, what delusion
of memory held her there? Was my face to her as the
face of her dead master, sleeping a sleep from which
not even the wildest roar of battle, no, nor her cheerful
neigh at morning, would ever wake him? Or is there
in animals some instinct, answering to our intuition,
only more potent, which tells them whom to trust and
whom to avoid? I know not, and yet some such sense
they may have, they must have; or else why should

this mare so fearlessly attach herself to me? By what
process of reason or instinct I know not, but there she
chose me for her master; for when some of my men
at dusk came searching, and found me, and, laying
me on a stretcher, started toward our lines, the mare,
uncompelled, of her own free will, followed at my
side; and all through that stormy night of wind and
rain, as my men struggled along through the mud
and mire toward Harrison's Landing, the mare followed, and ever after, until she died, was with me,
and was mine, and I, so far as man might be, was
hers. I named her Gulnare.

"As quickly as my wound permitted, I was trans-
ported to Washington, whither I took the mare with
me. Her fondness for me grew daily, and soon became so marked as to cause universal comment. I
had her boarded while in Washington at the corner of
—— Street and —— Avenue. The groom had instructions to lead her around to the window against
which was my bed, at the hospital, twice every day,
so that by opening the sash I might reach out my
hand and pet her. But the second day, no sooner had
she reached the street, than she broke suddenly from
the groom and dashed away at full speed. I was
lying, bolstered up in bed, reading, when I heard the
rush of flying feet, and in an instant, with a loud,
joyful neigh, she checked herself in front of my window. And when the nurse lifted the sash, the beautiful creature thrust her head through the aperture, and
rubbed her nose against my shoulder like a dog. I am
not ashamed to say that I put both my arms around

her neck, and, burying my face in her silken mane, kissed her again and again. Wounded, weak, and away from home, with only strangers to wait upon me, and scant service at that, the affection of this lovely creature for me, so tender and touching, seemed almost human, and my heart went out to her beyond any power of expression, as to the only being, of all the thousands around me, who thought of me and loved me. Shortly after her appearance at my window, the groom, who had divined where he should find her, came into the yard. But she would not allow him to come near her, much less touch her. If he tried to approach she would lash out at him with her heels most spitefully, and then, laying back her ears and opening her mouth savagely, would make a short dash at him, and, as the terrified African disappeared around the corner of the hospital, she would wheel, and, with a face bright as a happy child's, come trotting to the window for me to pet her. I shouted to the groom to go back to the stable, for I had no doubt but that she would return to her stall when I closed the window. Rejoiced at the permission, he departed. After some thirty minutes, the last ten of which she was standing with her slim, delicate head in my lap, while I braided her foretop and combed out her silken mane, I lifted her head, and, patting her softly on either cheek, told her that she must 'go.' I gently pushed her head out of the window and closed it, and then, holding up my hand, with the palm turned toward her, charged her, making the appropriate motion, to 'go away right straight back to her stable.'

For a moment she stood looking steadily at me, with an indescribable expression of hesitation and surprise in her clear, liquid eyes, and then, turning lingeringly, walked slowly out of the yard.

"Twice a day for nearly a month, while I lay in the hospital, did Gulnare visit me. At the appointed hour the groom would slip her headstall, and, without a word of command, she would dart out of the stable, and, with her long, leopard-like lope, go sweeping down the street and come dashing into the hospital yard, checking herself with the same glad neigh at my window; nor did she ever once fail, at the closing of the sash, to return directly to her stall. The groom informed me that every morning and evening, when the hour of her visit drew near, she would begin to chafe and worry, and, by pawing and pulling at the halter, advertise him that it was time for her to be released.

"But of all exhibitions of happiness, either by beast or man, hers was the most positive on that afternoon when, racing into the yard, she found me leaning on a crutch outside the hospital building. The whole corps of nurses came to the doors, and all the poor fellows that could move themselves—for Gulnare had become a universal favorite, and the boys looked for her daily visits nearly, if not quite, as ardently as I did—crawled to the windows to see her. What gladness was expressed in every movement! She would come prancing toward me, head and tail erect, and, pausing, rub her head against my shoulder, while I patted her glossy neck; then suddenly, with a sidewise spring,

she would break away, and with her long tail elevated
until her magnificent brush, fine and silken as the
golden hair of a blonde, fell in a great spray on either
flank, and, her head curved to its proudest arch, pace
around me with that high action and springing step
peculiar to the thoroughbred. Then like a flash, dropping her brush and laying back her ears and stretch-
ing her nose straight out, she would speed away with
that quick, nervous, low-lying action which marks
the rush of racers, when side by side and nose to nose
lapping each other, with the roar of cheers on either
hand and along the seats above them, they come
straining up the home stretch. Returning from one
of these arrowy flights, she would come curvetting
back, now pacing sidewise as on parade, now dashing
her hind feet high into the air, and anon vaulting up
and springing through the air, with legs well under
her, as if in the act of taking a five-barred gate, and
finally would approach and stand happy in her reward
—my caress.

"The war, at last, was over. Gulnare and I were
in at the death with Sheridan at the Five Forks. Together we had shared the pageant at Richmond and
Washington, and never had I seen her in better spirits
than on that day at the capital. It was a sight indeed
to see her as she came down Pennsylvania Avenue.
If the triumphant procession had been all in her honor
and mine, she could not have moved with greater
grace and pride. With dilating eye and tremulous
ear, ceaselessly champing her bit, her heated blood
bringing out the magnificent lacework of veins over

her entire body, now and then pausing, and with a
snort gathering herself back upon her haunches as
for a mighty leap, while she shook the froth from
her bits, she moved with a high, prancing step down
the magnificent street, the admired of all beholders.
Cheer after cheer was given, huzza after huzza rang
out over her head from roofs and balcony, bouquet
after bouquet was launched by fair and enthusiastic
admirers before her; and yet, amid the crash and
swell of music, the cheering and tumult, so gentle
and manageable was she, that, though I could feel
her frame creep and tremble under me as she moved
through that whirlwind of excitement, no check or
curb was needed, and the bridle-lines—the same she
wore when she came to me at Malvern Hill—lay un-
lifted on the pommel of the saddle. Never before had
I seen her so grandly herself. Never before had the
fire and energy, the grace and gentleness, of her blood
so revealed themselves. This was the day and the
event she needed. And all the royalty of her ances-
tral breed—a race of equine kings—flowing as without taint or cross from him that was the pride and
wealth of the whole tribe of desert rangers, expressed
itself in her. I need not say that I shared her mood.
I sympathized in her every step. I entered into all
her royal humors. I patted her neck and spoke loving
and cheerful words to her. I called her my beauty,
my pride, my pet. And did she not understand me?
Every word! Else why that listening ear turned
back to catch my softest whisper; why the responsive
quiver through the frame, and the low, happy neigh?

'Well,' I exclaimed, as I leaped from her back at the close of the review—alas! that words spoken in lightest mood should portend so much!—'well, Gulnare, if you should die, your life has had its triumph. The nation itself, through its admiring capital, has paid tribute to your beauty, and death can never rob you of your fame.' And I patted her moist neck and foam-flecked shoulders, while the grooms were busy with head and loins.

"That night our brigade made its bivouac just over Long Bridge, almost on the identical spot where four years before I had camped my company of three months' volunteers. With what experiences of march and battle were those four years filled! For three of these years Gulnare had been my constant companion. With me she had shared my tent, and not rarely my rations, for in appetite she was truly human, and my steward always counted her as one of our 'mess.' Twice had she been wounded—once at Fredericksburg, through the thigh; and once at Cold Harbor, where a piece of shell tore away a part of her scalp. So completely did it stun her, that for some moments I thought her dead, but to my great joy she shortly recovered her senses. I had the wound carefully dressed by our brigade surgeon, from whose care she came in a month with the edges of the wound so nicely united that the eye could with difficulty detect the scar. This night, as usual, she lay at my side, her head almost touching mine. Never before, unless when on a raid and in face of the enemy, had I seen her so uneasy. Her movements during the night compelled wakefulness on my part.

The sky was cloudless, and in the dim light I lay and watched her. Now she would stretch herself at full length, and rub her head on the ground. Then she would start up, and, sitting on her haunches, like a dog, lift one foreleg and paw her neck and ears. Anon she would rise to her feet and shake herself, walk off a few rods, return and lie down again by my side. I did not know what to make of it, unless the excitement of the day had been too much for her sensitive nerves. I spoke to her kindly and petted her. In response she would rub her nose against me, and lick my hand with her tongue—a peculiar habit of hers —like a dog. As I was passing my hand over her head, I discovered that it was hot, and the thought of the old wound flashed into my mind, with a momentary fear that something might be wrong about her brain, but after thinking it over I dismissed it as incredible. Still I was alarmed. I knew that something was amiss, and I rejoiced at the thought that I should soon be at home where she could have quiet, and, if need be, the best of nursing. At length the morning dawned, and the mare and I took our last meal together on Southern soil—the last we ever took together. The brigade was formed in line for the last time, and as I rode down the front to review the boys she moved with all her old battle grace and power. Only now and then, by a shake of the head, was I reminded of her actions during the night. I said a few words of farewell to the men whom I had led so often to battle, with whom I had shared perils not a few, and by whom, as I had reason to think, I was loved, and then gave, with a voice slightly unsteady, the last order they would ever receive from me: 'Brigade, Attention, Ready to break ranks, *Break Ranks.*' The order was obeyed. But ere they scattered, moved by a common impulse, they gave first three cheers for me, and then, with the same heartiness and even more power, three cheers for Gulnare. And she, standing there, looking with her bright, cheerful countenance full at the men, pawing with her forefeet, alternately, the ground, seemed to understand the compliment; for no sooner had the cheering died away than she arched her neck to its proudest curve, lifted her thin, delicate head into the air, and gave a short, joyful neigh.

"My arrangements for transporting her had been made by a friend the day before. A large, roomy car had been secured, its floor strewn with bright, clean straw, a bucket and a bag of oats provided, and everything done for her comfort. The car was to be attached to the through express, in consideration of fifty dollars extra, which I gladly paid, because of the greater rapidity with which it enabled me to make my journey. As the brigade broke up into groups, I glanced at my watch and saw that I had barely time to reach the cars before they started. I shook the reins upon her neck, and with a plunge, startled at the energy of my signal, away she flew. What a stride she had! What an elastic spring! She touched and left the earth as if her limbs were of spiral wire. When I reached the car my friend was standing in front of it, the gang-plank was ready, I leaped from the saddle

and, running up the plank into the car, whistled to
her; and she, timid and hesitating, yet unwilling to be
separated from me, crept slowly and cautiously up the
steep incline and stood beside me. Inside I found a
complete suit of flannel clothes with a blanket and, better than all, a lunch-basket. My friend explained that
he had bought the clothes as he came down to the
depot, thinking, as he said, 'that they would be much
better than your regimentals,' and suggested that I doff
the one and don the other. To this I assented the
more readily as I reflected that I would have to pass
one night at least in the car, with no better bed than
the straw under my feet. I had barely time to un-
dress before the cars were coupled and started. I
tossed the clothes to my friend with the injunction to
pack them in my trunk and express them on to me,
and waved him my adieu. I arrayed myself in the
nice, cool flannel and looked around. The thoughtful-
ness of my friend had anticipated every want. An old
cane-seated chair stood in one corner. The lunch-
basket was large and well supplied. Amid the oats I
found a dozen oranges, some bananas, and a package
of real Havana cigars. How I called down blessings
on his thoughtful head as I took the chair and, lighting one of the fine-flavored *figaros,* gazed out on the
fields past which we were gliding, yet wet with morning dew. As I sat dreamily admiring the beauty before
me, Gulnare came and, resting her head upon my shoulder, seemed to share my mood. As I stroked her
fine-haired, satin-like nose, recollection quickened and
memories of our companionship in perils thronged into

my mind. I rode again that midnight ride to Knoxville, when Burnside lay intrenched, desperately holding his own, waiting for news from Chattanooga of which I was the bearer, chosen by Grant himself because of the reputation of my mare. What riding that was! We started, ten riders of us in all, each with the same message. I parted company the first hour out with all save one, an iron-gray stallion of Messenger blood. Jack Murdock rode him, who learned his horsemanship from buffalo and Indian hunting on the plains— not a bad school to graduate from. Ten miles out of Knoxville the gray, his flanks dripping with blood, plunged up abreast of the mare's shoulders and fell dead; and Gulnare and I passed through the lines alone. *I had ridden the terrible race without whip or spur.* With what scenes of blood and flight she would ever be associated! And then I thought of home, unvisited for four long years—that home I left a stripling, but to which I was returning a bronzed and brawny man. I thought of mother and Bob—how they would admire her!—of old Ben, the family groom, and of that one who shall be nameless, whose picture I had so often shown to Gulnare as the likeness of her future mistress; had they not all heard of her, my beautiful mare, she who came to me from the smoke and whirlwind, my battle-gift? How they would pat her soft, smooth sides, and tie her mane with ribbons, and feed her with all sweet things from open and caressing palm! And then I thought of one who might come after her to bear her name and repeat at least some portion of her beauty—a horse honored and renowned the country through, because of the transmission of the mother's fame.

"About three o'clock in the afternoon a change came over Gulnare. I had fallen asleep upon the straw, and she had come and awakened me with a touch of her nose. The moment I started up I saw that something was the matter. Her eyes were dull and heavy. Never before had I seen the light go out of them. The rocking of the car as it went jumping and vibrating along seemed to irritate her. She began to rub her head against the side of the car. Touching it, I found that the skin over the brain was hot as fire. Her breathing grew rapidly louder and louder. Each breath was drawn with a kind of gasping effort. The lids with their silken fringe drooped wearily over the lustreless eyes. The head sank lower and lower, until the nose almost touched the floor. The ears, naturally so lively and erect, hung limp and widely apart. The body was cold and senseless. A pinch elicited no motion. Even my voice was at last unheeded. To word and touch there came, for the first time in all our intercourse, no response. I knew as the symptoms spread what was the matter. The signs bore all one way. She was in the first stages of phrenitis, or inflammation of the brain. In other words, *my beautiful mare was going mad*.

"I was well versed in the anatomy of the horse. Loving horses from my very childhood, there was little in veterinary practice with which I was not familiar. Instinctively, as soon as the symptoms had developed themselves, and I saw under what frightful disorder

Gulnare was laboring, I put my hand into my pocket for my knife, in order to open a vein. *There was no knife there.* Friends, I have met with many surprises. More than once in battle and scout have I been nigh death; but never did my blood desert my veins and settle so around the heart, never did such a sickening sensation possess me, as when, standing in that car with my beautiful mare before me marked with those horrible symptoms, I made that discovery. My knife, my sword, my pistols even, were with my suit in the care of my friend, two hundred miles away. Hastily, and with trembling fingers, I searched my clothes, the lunch-basket, my linen; not even a pin could I find. I shoved open the sliding door, and swung my hat and shouted, hoping to attract some brakeman's attention. The train was thundering along at full speed, and none saw or heard me. I knew her stupor would not last long. A slight quivering of the lip, an occasional spasm running through the frame, told me too plainly that the stage of frenzy would soon begin. 'My God,' I exclaimed in despair, as I shut the door and turned toward her, 'must I see you die, Gulnare, when the opening of a vein would save you? Have you borne me, my pet, through all these years of peril, the icy chill of winter, the heat and torment of summer, and all the thronging dangers of a hundred bloody battles, only to die torn by fierce agonies, when so near a peaceful home?'

"But little time was given me to mourn. My life was soon to be in peril, and I must summon up the utmost power of eye and limb to escape the violence of my frenzied mare. Did you ever see a mad horse when his madness is on him? Take your stand with me in that car, and you shall see what suffering a dumb creature can endure before it dies. In no malady does a horse suffer more than in phrenitis, or inflammation of the brain. Possibly in severe cases of colic, probably in rabies in its fiercest form, the pain is equally intense. These three are the most agonizing of all the diseases to which the noblest of animals is exposed. Had my pistols been with me, I should then and there, with whatever strength Heaven granted, have taken my companion's life, that she might be spared the suffering which was so soon to rack and wring her sensitive frame. A horse laboring under an attack of phrenitis is as violent as a horse can be. He is not ferocious as is one in a fit of rabies. He may kill his master, but he does it without design. There is in him no desire of mischief for its own sake, no cruel cunning, no stratagem and malice. A rabid horse is conscious in every act and motion. He recognizes the man he destroys. There is in him an insane *desire* to *kill*. Not so with the phrenetic horse. He is unconscious in his violence. He sees and recognizes no one. There is no method or purpose in his madness. He kills without knowing it.

"I knew what was coming. I could not jump out, that would be certain death. I must abide in the car, and take my chance of life. The car was fortunately high, long, and roomy. I took my position in front of my horse, watchful, and ready to spring. Suddenly her lids, which had been closed, came open with a snap, as if an electric shock had passed through her, and the eyes, wild in their brightness, stared directly at me. And what eyes they were! The membrane grew red and redder until it was of the color of blood, standing out in frightful contrast with the transparency of the cornea. The pupil gradually dilated until it seemed about to burst out of the socket. The nostrils, which had been sunken and motionless, quivered, swelled, and glowed. The respiration became short, quick and gasping. The limp and dripping ears stiffened and stood erect, pricked sharply forward, as if to catch the slightest sound. Spasms, as the car swerved and vibrated, ran along her frame. More horrid than all, the lips slowly contracted, and the white, sharp-edged teeth stood uncovered, giving an indescribable look of ferocity to the partially opened mouth. The car suddenly reeled as it dashed around a curve, swaying her almost off her feet, and, as a contortion shook her, she recovered herself, and rearing upward as high as the car permitted, plunged directly at me. I was expecting the movement, and dodged. Then followed exhibitions of pain which I pray God I may never see again. Time and again did she dash herself upon the floor, and roll over and over, lashing out with her feet in all directions. Pausing a moment, she would stretch her body to its extreme length, and, lying upon her side, pound the floor with her head as if it were a maul. Then like a flash she would leap to her feet, and whirl round and round until from very giddiness she would stagger and fall. She would lay hold of the straw with her teeth, and shake it as a dog shakes a

struggling woodchuck; then dashing it from her mouth,
she would seize hold of her own sides, and rend herself. Springing up, she would rush against the end
of the car, falling all in a heap from the violence of the
concussion. For some fifteen minutes without intermission the frenzy lasted. I was nearly exhausted.
My efforts to avoid her mad rushes, the terrible ten-
sion of my nervous system produced by the spectacle
of such exquisite and prolonged suffering, were weak-
ening me beyond what I should have thought it possible an hour before for anything to weaken me. In
fact, I felt my strength leaving me. A terror such as
I had never yet felt was taking possession of my mind.
I sickened at the sight before me, and at the thought
of agonies yet to come. 'My God,' I exclaimed, 'must
I be killed by my own horse in this miserable car!'
Even as I spoke the end came. The mare raised herself until her shoulders touched the roof, then dashed
her body upon the floor with a violence which threatened the stout frame beneath her. I leaned, panting
and exhausted, against the side of the car. Gulnare
did not stir. She lay motionless, her breath coming
and going in lessening respirations. I tottered toward
her, and, as I stood above her, my ear detected a low
gurgling sound. I can not describe the feeling that
followed. Joy and grief contended within me. I
knew the meaning of that sound. Gulnare, in her frenzied violence, had broken a blood-vessel, and was bleeding internally. Pain and life were passing away together. I knelt down by her side. I laid my head upon
her shoulders, and sobbed aloud. Her body moved a lit-

tle beneath me. I crawled forward, and lifted her beautiful head into my lap. O, for one more sign of recognition before she died! I smoothed the tangled masses of her mane. I wiped, with a fragment of my coat, torn in the struggle, the blood which oozed from her nostril. I called her by name. My desire was granted. In a moment Gulnare opened her eyes. The redness of frenzy had passed out of them. She saw and recognized me. I spoke again. Her eye lighted a moment with the old and intelligent look of love. Her ear moved. Her nostril quivered slightly as she strove to neigh. The effort was in vain. Her love was greater than her strength. She moved her head a little, as if she would be nearer me, looked once more with her clear eyes into my face, breathed a long breath, straightened her shapely limbs, and died. And there, holding the head of my dead mare in my lap, while the great warm tears fell one after another down my cheeks, I sat until the sun went down, the shadows darkened in the car, and night drew her mantle, colored like my grief, over the world.

BALACCHI BROTHERS

BY REBECCA HARDING DAVIS

Rebecca (Blaine) Harding (born June 24, 1831, in Washington, Pa.) wrote in 1861 a short story entitled "Life in the Iron Mills," which attracted general and favorable notice for its realistic picture of labor conditions. In 1863 she married L. Clark Davis, a Philadelphia journalist, and her subsequent stories, in connection with those of her son Richard, have made the name of "Harding Davis" stand as a hall mark of sterling literary merit to two generations of readers. She has selected for the present volume, as representative of her work in brief fiction, "Balacchi Brothers." This falls in the separate categories of love romance, tale of action, and story of character, and excels in each. As a study of a special temperament it was far in advance of contemporary stories

BALACCHI BROTHERS

BY REBECCA HARDING DAVIS

"THERE'S a man, now, that has been famous in his time," said Davidge as we passed the mill, glancing in at the sunny gap in the side of the building.

I paused incredulously: Phil's lion so often turned out to be Snug the joiner. Phil was my chum at college, and in inviting me home to spend the vacation with him I thought he had fancied the resources of his village larger than they proved. In the two days since we came we had examined the old doctor's cabinet, listened superciliously to a debate in the literary club upon the Evils of the Stage, and passed two solid afternoons in the circle about the stove in the drugshop, where the squire and the Methodist parson, and even the mild, white-cravated young rector of St. Mark's, were wont to sharpen their wits by friction. What more was left? I was positive that I knew the mental gauge of every man in the village.

A little earlier or later in life a gun or fishing-rod would have satisfied me. The sleepy, sunny little market-town was shut in by the bronzed autumn meadows, that sent their long groping fingers of grass or parti-colored weeds drowsily up into the very streets: there were ranges of hills and heavy stretches of oak and beech woods, too, through which crept glittering creeks full of trout. But I was just at that age when the soul disdains all aimless pleasures: my game was Man. I was busy in philosophically testing, weighing, labeling human nature.

"Famous, eh?" I said, looking after the pursy figure of the miller in his flowery canvas roundabout and corduroy trousers, trotting up and down among the bags.

"That is one of the Balacchi Brothers," Phil answered as we walked on. "You've heard of them when you were a boy?"

I had heard of them. The great acrobats were as noted in their line of art as Ellsler and Jenny Lind in theirs. But acrobats and danseuses had been alike brilliant, wicked impossibilities to my youth, for I had been reared a Covenanter of the Covenanters. In spite of the doubting philosophies with which I had clothed myself at college, that old Presbyterian training clung to me in every-day life close as my skin.

After that day I loitered about the mill, watching this man, whose life had been spent in one godless theatre after another, very much as the Florentine peasants looked after Dante when they knew he had come back from hell. I was on the lookout for the taint, the abnormal signs, of vice. It was about that time that I was fevered with the missionary enthusiasm, and in Polynesia, where I meant to go (but where I never did go), I declared to Phil daily that I should find in every cannibal the half-effaced image of God, only waiting to be quickened into grace and virtue. That was quite conceivable. But that a flashy, God-defying actor could be the same man at heart as this fat, good-tempered, gossiping miller, who jogged to the butcher's every morning for his wife, a basket on one arm and a baby on the other, was not conceivable. He was a close dealer at the butcher's, too, though dribbling gossip there as everywhere; a regular attendant at St. Mark's, with his sandy-headed flock about him, among whom he slept comfortably enough, it is true, but with as pious dispositions as the rest of us.

I remember how I watched this man, week in and week out. It was a trivial matter, but it irritated me unendurably to find that this circus-rider had human blood precisely like my own: it outraged my early religion.

We talk a great deal of the rose-colored illusions in which youth wraps the world, and the agony it suffers as they are stripped from its bare, hard face. But the fact is, that youth (aside from its narrow, passionate friendships) is usually apt to be acrid and watery and sour in its judgment and creeds—it has the quality of any other unripe fruit: it is middle age that is just and tolerant, that has found room enough in the world for itself and all human flies to buzz out their lives good-humoredly together. It is youth who can see a tangible devil at work in every party or sect opposed to its own, whose enemy is always a villain, and who finds treachery and falsehood in the friend who is occasionally bored or indifferent: it is middle age that has discovered the reasonable sweet *juste*

milieu of human nature—who knows few saints perhaps, but is apt to find its friend and grocer and shoe-
maker agreeable and honest fellows.   It is these vehe-
ment illusions, these inherited bigotries and prejudices,
that tear and cripple a young man as they are taken
from him one by one.   He creeps out of them
as a crab from the shell that has grown too small
for him, but he thinks he has left his identity behind him.

It was such a reason as this that made me follow
the miller assiduously, and cultivate a quasi intimacy
with him, in the course of which I picked the following story from him.   It was told at divers times, and
with many interruptions and questions from me.   But
for obvious reasons I have made it continuous.   It had
its meaning to me, coarse and common though it was
—the same which Christ taught in the divine beauty
of His parables.   Whether that meaning might not be
found in the history of every human life, if we had
eyes to read it, is matter for question.

Balacchi Brothers?   And you've heard of them,
eh?   Well, well! (with a pleased nod, rubbing his
hands on his knees).   Yes, sir.   Fifteen years ago
they were known as The Admirable Crichtons of the
Ring.   It was George who got up that name: I did
not see the force of it.   But no name could claim too
much for us.   Why, I could show you notices in the
newspapers that— I used to clip them out and stuff
my pocketbook with them as we went along, but after
I quit the business I pasted them in an old ledger, and

I often now read them of nights. No doubt I lost a good many, too.

Yes, sir: I was one of Balacchi Brothers. My name *is* Zack Loper. And it was then, of course.

You think we would have plenty of adventures? Well, no—not a great many. There's a good deal of monotony in the business. Towns seem always pretty much alike to me. And there was such a deal of rehearsing to be done by day and at night. I looked at nothing but the rope and George: the audience was nothing but a packed flat surface of upturned, staring eyes and half-open mouths. It was an odd sight, yes, when you come to think of it. I never was one for adventures. I was mostly set upon shaving close through the week, so that when Saturday night came I'd have something to lay by: I had this mill in my mind, you see. I was married, and had my wife and a baby that I'd never seen waiting for me at home. I was brought up to milling, but the trapeze paid better. I took to it naturally, as one might say.

But George!—he had adventures every week. And as for acquaintances! Why, before we'd be in a town two days he'd be hail-fellow-well-met with half the people in it. That fellow could scent a dance or a joke half a mile off. You never see such wide-awake men nowadays. People seem to me half dead or asleep when I think of him.

Oh, I thought you knew. My partner Balacchi. It was Balacchi on the bills: the actors called him Signor, and people like the manager, South, and we, who knew him well, George. I asked him his real name once or twice, but he joked it off. "How many names must a man be saddled with?" he said. I don't know it to this day, nor who he had been. They hinted there was something queer about his story, but I'll go my bail it was a clean one, whatever it was.

You never heard how "Balacchi Brothers" broke up? That was as near to an adventure as I ever had. Come over to this bench and I'll tell it to you. You don't dislike the dust of the mill? The sun's pleasanter on this side.

It was early in August of '56 when George and I came to an old town on the Ohio, half city, half village, to play an engagement. We were under contract with South then, who provided the rest of the troupe, three or four posture-girls, Stradi, the pianist, and a Madame Somebody, who gave readings and sang. "Concert" was the heading in large caps on the bills, "Balacchi Brothers will give their æsthetic *tableaux vivants* in the interludes," in agate below.

"I've got to cover you fellows over with respectability here," South said. "Rope-dancing won't go down with these aristocratic church-goers."

I remember how George was irritated. "When I was my own agent," he said, "I only went to the cities. Educated people can appreciate what we do, but in these country towns we rank with circus-riders."

George had some queer notions about his business. He followed it for sheer love of it, as I did for money. I've seen all the great athletes since, but I never saw one with his wonderful skill and strength, and with

the grace of a woman too, or a deer. Now that takes
hard, steady work, but he never flinched from it, as I
did; and when night came, and the people and lights,
and I thought of nothing but to get through, I used
to think he had the pride of a thousand women in
every one of his muscles and nerves: a little applause
would fill him with a mad kind of fury of delight and
triumph. South had a story that George belonged to
some old Knickerbocker family, and had run off from
home years ago. I don't know. There was that wild
restless blood in him that no home could have kept
him.

We were to stay so long in this town that I found
rooms for us with an old couple named Peters, who had
but lately moved in from the country, and had half a
dozen carpenters and masons boarding with them.
It was cheaper than the hotel, and George preferred
that kind of people to educated men, which made me
doubt that story of his having been a gentleman. The
old woman Peters was uneasy about taking us, and
spoke out quite freely about it when we called, not
knowing that George and I were Balacchi Brothers
ourselves.

"The house has been respectable so far, gentlemen,"
she said. "I don't know what about taking in them
half-naked, drunken play-actors. What do you say,
Susy?" to her granddaughter.

"Wait till you see them, grandmother," the girl
said gently. "I should think that men whose lives depended every night on their steady eyes and nerves
would not dare to touch liquor."

"You are quite right—nor even tobacco," said George. It was such a prompt, sensible thing for the little girl to say that he looked at her attentively a minute, and then went up to the old lady, smiling: "We don't look like drinking men, do we, madam?"

"No, no, sir. I did not know that you were the I-talians." She was quite flustered and frightened, and said cordially enough how glad she was to have us both. But it was George she shook hands with. There was something clean and strong and inspiring about that man that made most women friendly to him on sight.

Why, in two days you'd have thought he'd never had another home than the Peters's. He helped the old man milk, and had tinkered up the broken kitchen-table, and put in half a dozen window-panes, and was intimate with all the boarders; could give the masons the prices of job-work at the East, and put Stoll, the carpenter, on the idea of contract-houses, out of which he afterward made a fortune. It was nothing but jokes and fun and shouts of laughter when he was in the house: even the old man brightened up and told some capital stories. But from the first I noticed that George's eye followed Susy watchfully wherever she went, though he was as distant and respectful with her as he was with most women. He had a curious kind of respect for women, George had. Even the Slingsbys, that all the men in the theatre joked with, he used to pass by as though they were logs leaning against the wall. They were the posture-girls, and anything worse besides the name *I* never saw.

There was a thing happened once on that point which I often thought might have given me a clew to his history if I'd followed it up. We were playing in one of the best theatres in New York (they brought us into some opera), and the boxes were filled with fine ladies beautifully dressed, or, I might say, half dressed.

George was in one of the wings. "It's a pretty sight," I said to him.

"It's a shameful sight!" he said with an oath. "The Slingsbys do it for their living, but these women—"

I said they were ladies, and ought to be treated with respect. I was amazed at the heat he was in.

"I had a sister, Zack, and there's where I learned what a woman should be."

"I never heard of your sister, George," said I. I knew he would not have spoken of her but for the heat he was in.

"No. I'm as dead to her, being what I am, as if I were six feet under ground."

I turned and looked at him, and when I saw his face I said no more, and I never spoke of it again. It was something neither I nor any other man had any business with.

So, when I saw how he was touched by Susy and drawn toward her, it raised her in my opinion, though I'd seen myself how pretty and sensible a little body she was. But I was sorry, for I knew 'twan't no use. The Peters were Methodists, and Susy more strict than any of them; and I saw she looked on the theatre as the gate of hell, and George and me swinging over it.

I don't think, though, that George saw how strong her feeling about it was, for after we'd been there a week or two he began to ask her to go and see us perform, if only for once. I believe he thought the girl would come to love him if she saw him at his best. I don't wonder at it, sir. I've seen those pictures and statues they've made of the old gods, and I reckon they put in them the best they thought a man could be; but I never knew what real manhood was until I saw my partner when he stood quiet on the stage waiting the signal to begin, the light full on his keen blue eyes, the gold-worked velvet tunic and his perfect figure.

He looked more like other men in his ordinary clothing. George liked a bit of flash, too, in his dress —a red necktie or gold chain stretched over his waistcoat.

Susy refused at first, steadily. At last, however, came our final night, when George was to produce his great leaping feat, never yet performed in public. We had been practicing it for months, and South judged it best to try it first before a small, quiet audience, for the risk was horrible. Whether because it was to be the last night, and her kind heart disliked to hurt him by refusal, or whether she loved him better than either she or he knew, I could not tell, but I saw she was strongly tempted to go. She was an innocent little thing, and not used to hide what she felt. Her eyes were red that morning, as though she had been crying all the night. Perhaps, because I was a married man, and quieter than George, she acted more freely with me than him.

"I wish I knew what to do," she said, looking up to me with her eyes full of tears. There was nobody in the room but her grandmother.

"I couldn't advise you, Miss Susy," says I. "Your church discipline goes against our trade, I know."

"I know what's right myself: I don't need church discipline to teach me," she said sharply.

"I think I'd go, Susy," said her grandmother. "It is a concert, after all: it's not a play."

"The name don't alter it."

Seeing the temper she was in, I thought it best to say no more, but the old lady added, "It's Mr. George's last night. Dear, dear! how I'll miss him!"

Susy turned quickly to the window. "Why does he follow such godless ways, then?" she cried. She stood still a good while, and when she turned about her pale little face made my heart ache. "I'll take home Mrs. Tyson's dress now, grandmother," she said, and went out of the room. I forgot to tell you Susy was a seamstress. Well, the bundle was large, and I offered to carry it for her, as the time for rehearsal did not come till noon. She crept alongside of me without a word, looking weak and done-out: she was always so busy and bright, it was the more noticeable. The house where the dress was to go was one of the largest in the town. The servant showed us into a back parlor, and took the dress up to her mistress. I looked around me a good deal, for I'd

never been in such a house before; but very soon I
caught sight of a lady who made me forget carpets
and pictures. I only saw her in the mirror, for she
was standing by the fireplace in the front room. The
door was open between. It wasn't that she was especially pretty, but in her white morning-dress, with
the lace about her throat and her hair drawn back from
her face, I thought she was the delicatest, softest,
finest thing of man or woman kind I ever saw.

"Look there, Susy! look there!" I whispered.

"It is a Mrs. Lloyd from New York. She is here
on a visit. That is her husband;" and then she went
down into her own gloomy thoughts again.

The husband was a grave, middle-aged man. He
had had his paper up before his face, so that I had
not seen him before.

"You will go for the tickets, then, Edward?" she
said.

"If you make a point of it, yes," in an annoyed
tone. "But I don't know why you make a point of
it. The musical part of the performance is beneath
contempt, I understand, and the real attraction is the
exhibition of these mountebanks of trapezists, which
will be simply disgusting to you. You would not en-
courage such people at home: why would you do it
here?"

"They are not necessarily wicked." I noticed there
was a curious unsteadiness in her voice, as though
she was hurt and agitated. I thought perhaps she
knew I was there.

"There is very little hope of any redeeming qualities in men who make a trade of twisting their bodies like apes," he said. "Contortionists and ballet-dancers and clowns and harlequins—" he rattled all the names over with a good deal of uncalled-for sharpness, I thought, calling them "dissolute and degraded, the very offal of humanity." I could not understand his heat until he added, "I never could comprehend your interest and sympathy for that especial class, Ellinor."

"No, you could not, Edward," she said quietly. "But I have it. I never have seen an exhibition of the kind. But I want to see this to-night, if you will gratify me. I have no reason," she added when he looked at her curiously. "The desire is unaccountable to myself."

The straightforward look of her blue eyes as she met his seemed strangely familiar and friendly to me.

At that moment Susy stood up to go. Her cheeks were burning and her eyes sparkling. "Dissolute and degraded!" she said again and again when we were outside. But I took no notice.

As we reached the house she stopped me when I turned off to go to rehearsal. "You'll get seats for grandmother and me, Mr. Balacchi?" she said.

"You're going, then, Susy?"

"Yes, I'm going."

Now the house in which we performed was a queer structure. A stock company, thinking there was a field for a theatre in the town, had taken a four-story building, gutted the interior, and fitted it up with tiers of seats and scenery. The stock company was starved

out, however, and left the town, and the theatre was
used as a gymnasium, a concert-room or a church by
turns. Its peculiarity was, that it was both exceedingly lofty and narrow, which suited our purpose
exactly.

It was packed that night from dome to pit. George
and I had rehearsed our new act both morning and
afternoon, South watching us without intermission.
South was terribly nervous and anxious, half disposed, at the last minute, to forbid it, although it had
been announced on the bills for a week. But a feat
which is successful in an empty house, with but one
spectator, when your nerves are quiet and blood cool,
is a different thing before an excited, terrified, noisy
audience, your whole body at fever heat. However,
George was cool as a cucumber, indeed almost indifferent about the act, but in a mad boyish glee all day
about everything else. I suppose the reason was that
Susy was going.

South had lighted the house brilliantly and brought
in a band. And all classes of people poured into the
theatre until it could hold no more. I saw Mrs. Peters
in one of the side-seats, with Susy's blushing, frightened little face beside her. George, standing back
among the scenes, saw her too: I think, indeed, it was
all he did see.

There were the usual readings from Shakespeare at
first.

While Madame was on, South came to us. "Boys,"
said he, "let this matter go over a few weeks. A
little more practice will do you no harm. You can

substitute some other trick, and these people will be none the wiser."

George shrugged his shoulders impatiently: "Nonsense! When did you grow so chicken-hearted, South? It is I who have to run the risk, I fancy."

I suppose South's uneasiness had infected me. "I am quite willing to put it off," I said. I had felt gloomy and superstitious all day. But I never ventured to oppose George more decidedly than that.

He only laughed by way of reply, and went off to dress. South looked after him, I remember, saying what a magnificently-built fellow he was. If we could only have seen the end of that night's work!

As I went to my dressing-room I saw Mrs. Lloyd and her husband in one of the stage-boxes, with one or two other ladies and gentlemen. She was plainly and darkly dressed, but to my mind she looked like a princess among them all. I could not but wonder what interest she could have in such a rough set as we, although her husband, I confess, did judge us hardly.

After the readings came the concert part of the performance, and then what South chose to call the Moving Tableaux, which was really nothing in the world but ballet-dancing. George and I were left to crown the whole. I had some ordinary trapeze-work to do at first, but George was reserved for the new feat, in order that his nerves might be perfectly unshaken. When I went out alone and bowed to the audience, I observed that Mrs. Lloyd was leaning eagerly forward, but at the first glance at my face she sank back with a look of relief, and turned away, that she might not see my exploits. It nettled me a little, I think, yet they were worth watching.

Well, I finished, and then there was a song to give me time to cool. I went to the side-scenes, where I could be alone, for that five minutes. I had no risk to run in the grand feat, you see, but I had George's life in my hands. I haven't told you yet—have I?—what it was he proposed to do.

A rope was suspended from the centre of the dome, the lower end of which I held, standing in the highest gallery opposite the stage. Above the stage hung the trapeze on which George and the two posture-girls were to be. At a certain signal I was to let the rope go, and George springing from the trapeze across the full width of the dome, was to catch it in mid-air, a hundred feet above the heads of the people. You understand? The mistake of an instant of time on either his part or mine, and death was almost certain. The plan we had thought surest was for South to give the word, and then that both should count— One, Two, Three! At Three the rope fell and he leaped. We had practiced so often that we thought we counted as one man.

When the song was over the men hung the rope and the trapeze. Jenny and Lou Slingsby swung themselves up to it, turned a few somersaults, and then were quiet. They were only meant to give effect to the scene in their gauzy dresses and spangles. Then South came forward and told the audience what we meant to do. It was a feat, he said, which had never

been produced before in any theatre, and in which
failure was death. No one but that most daring of
all acrobats, Balacchi, would attempt it. Now, I knew
South so well that I saw under all his confident, brag-
ging tone he was more anxious and doubtful than he
had ever been. He hesitated a moment, and then requested that after we took our places the audience
should preserve absolute silence, and refrain from
even the slightest movement until the feat was over.
The merest trifle might distract the attention of the
performers and render their eyes and hold unsteady,
he said. He left the stage, and the music began.

I went round to take my place in the gallery.
George had not yet left his room. As I passed
I tapped at the door and called, "Good luck, old
fellow!"

"That's certain now, Zack," he answered with a
joyous laugh. He was so exultant, you see, that Susy
had come.

But the shadow of death seemed to have crept over
me. When I took my stand in the lofty gallery, and
looked down at the brilliant lights and the great mass
of people, who followed my every motion as one man,
and the two glittering, half-naked girls swinging in
the distance, and heard the music rolling up thunders
of sound, it was all ghastly and horrible to me, sir.
Some men have such presentiments, they say: I never
had before or since. South remained on the stage perfectly motionless, in order, I think, to maintain his
control over the audience.

The trumpets sounded a call, and in the middle of

a burst of triumphant music George came on the stage.
There was a deafening outbreak of applause, and then
a dead silence, but I think every man and woman felt
a thrill of admiration of the noble figure. Poor
George! the new, tight-fitting dress of purple velvet
that he had bought for this night set off his white
skin, and his fine head was bare, with no covering
but the short curls that Susy liked.

It was for Susy! He gave one quick glance up at
her, and a bright, boyish smile, as if telling her not
to be afraid, which all the audience understood, and
answered by an involuntary, long-drawn breath. I
looked at Susy. The girl's colorless face was turned
to George, and her hands were clasped as though she
saw him already dead before her; but she could be
trusted, I saw. *She* would utter no sound. I had
only time to glance at her, and then turned to my
work. George and I dared not take our eyes from
each other.

There was a single bugle note, and then George
swung himself up to the trapeze. The silence was like
death as he steadied himself and slowly turned so
as to front me. As he turned he faced the stage-box
for the first time. He had reached the level of the
posture-girls, who fluttered on either side, and stood
on the swaying rod poised on one foot, his arms
folded, when in the breathless stillness there came a
sudden cry and the words, "Oh, Charley! Charley!"

Even at the distance where I stood I saw George
start and a shiver pass over his body. He looked
wildly about him.

"To me! to me!" I shouted.

He fixed his eye on mine and steadied himself. There was a terrible silent excitement in the people, in the very air.

There was the mistake. We should have stopped then, shaken as he was, but South, bewildered and terrified, lost control of himself: he gave the word.

I held the rope loose—held George with my eyes— One!

I saw his lips move: he was counting with me.

Two!

His eye wandered, turned to the stage-box.

Three!

Like a flash, I saw the white upturned faces below me, the posture-girls' gestures of horror, the dark springing figure through the air, that wavered—and fell a shapeless mass on the floor.

There was a moment of deathlike silence, and then a wild outcry—women fainting, men cursing and crying out in that senseless, helpless way they have when there is sudden danger. By the time I had reached the floor they had straightened out his shattered limbs, and two or three doctors were fighting their way through the great crowd that was surging about him.

Well, sir, at that minute what did I hear but George's voice above all the rest, choked and hollow as it was, like a man calling out of the grave: "The women! Good God! don't you see the women?" he gasped.

Looking up then, I saw those miserable Slingsbys hanging on to the trapeze for life. What with the scare and shock, they'd lost what little sense they had, and there they hung helpless as limp rags high over our heads.

"Damn the Slingsbys!" said I. God forgive me! But I saw this battered wreck at my feet that had been George. Nobody seemed to have any mind left. Even South stared stupidly up at them and then back at George. The doctors were making ready to lift him, and half of the crowd were gaping in horror, and the rest yelling for ladders or ropes, and scrambling over each other, and there hung the poor flimsy wretches, their eyes starting out of their heads from horror, and their lean fingers losing their hold every minute. But, sir—I couldn't help it—I turned from them to watch George as the doctors lifted him.

"It's hardly worth while," whispered one.

But they raised him and, sir—the body went one way and the legs another.

I thought he was dead. I couldn't see that he breathed, when he opened his eyes and looked up for the Slingsbys. "Put me down," he said, and the doctors obeyed him. There was that in his voice that they had to obey him, though it wasn't but a whisper.

"Ladders are of no use," he said. "Loper!"

"Yes, George."

"You can swing yourself up. Do it."

I went. I remember the queer stunned feeling I had: my joints moved like a machine.

When I had reached the trapeze, he said, as cool as

if he were calling the figures for a Virginia reel,
"Support them, you—Loper. Now lower the trapeze, men—carefully!"

It was the only way their lives could be saved, and
he was the only man to see it. He watched us until
the girls touched the floor more dead than alive,
and then his head fell back and the life seemed to go
suddenly out of him like the flame out of a candle,
leaving only the dead wick.

As they were carrying him out I noticed for the
first time that a woman was holding his hand. It
was that frail little wisp of a Susy, that used to blush
and tremble if you spoke to her suddenly, and here she
was quite quiet and steady in the midst of this great
crowd.

"His sister, I suppose?" one of the doctors said
to her.

"No, sir. If he lives I will be his wife." The old
gentleman was very respectful to her after that, I
noticed.

Now, the rest of my story is very muddled, you'll
say, and confused. But the truth is, I don't understand it myself. I ran on ahead to Mrs. Peters's to
prepare his bed for him, but they did not bring him
to Peters's. After I waited an hour or two, I found
George had been taken to the principal hotel in the
place, and a bedroom and every comfort that money
could buy were there for him. Susy came home sob-
bing late in the night, but she told me nothing, except that those who had a right to have charge of him
had taken him. I found afterward the poor girl was

driven from the door of his room, where she was waiting like a faithful dog. I went myself, but I fared no
better. What with surgeons and professional nurses,
and the gentlemen that crowded about with their solemn looks of authority, I dared not ask to see him.
Yet I believe still George would rather have had old
Loper by him in his extremity than any of them.
Once, when the door was opened, I thought I saw Mrs.
Lloyd stooping over the bed between the lace curtains, and just then her husband came out talking to
one of the surgeons.

He said: "It is certain there were here the
finest elements of manhood. And I will do my part
to rescue him from the abyss into which he has
fallen."

"Will you tell me how George is, sir?" I asked,
pushing up. "Balacchi? My partner?"

Mr. Lloyd turned away directly, but the surgeon
told me civilly enough that if George's life could be
saved, it must be with the loss of one or perhaps both
of his legs.

"He'll never mount a trapeze again, then," I said,
and I suppose I groaned; for to think of George
helpless—

"God forbid!" cried Mr. Lloyd, sharply. "Now
look here, my good man: you can be of no possible
use to Mr.—Balacchi, as you call him. He is in the
hands of his own people, and he will feel, as they
do, that the kindest thing you can do is to let him
alone."

There was nothing to be done after that but to

touch my hat and go out, but as I went I heard him
talking of "inexplicable madness and years of wasted
opportunities."

Well, sir, I never went again: the words hurt like
the cut of a whip, though 'twan't George that spoke
them. But I quit business, and hung around the town
till I heard he was going to live, and I broke up my
contract with South. I never went on a trapeze
again. I felt as if the infernal thing was always
dripping with his blood after that day. Anyhow, all
the heart went out of the business for me with George.
So I came back here and settled down to the milling,
and by degrees I learned to think of George as a rich
and fortunate man.

I've nearly done now—only a word or two more.
About six years afterward there was a circus came to
town, and I took the wife and children and went.
I always did when I had the chance. It was the old
Adam in me yet, likely.

Well, sir, among the attractions of the circus was
the great and unrivaled Hercules, who could play with
cannon-balls as other men would with dice. I don't
know what made me restless and excited when I read
about this man. It seemed as though the old spirit
was coming back to me again. I could hardly keep
still when the time drew near for him to appear. I
don't know what I expected. But when he came out
from behind the curtain I shouted out like a madman,
"Balacchi! George! George!"

He stopped short, looked about, and catching sight
of me tossed up his cap with his old boyish shout: then

he remembered himself, and went on with his performance.

He was lame—yes, in one leg. The other was gone altogether. He walked on crutches. Whether the strength had gone into his chest and arms, I don't know; but there he stood tossing about the cannon-balls as I might marbles. So full of hearty good-humor too, joking with his audience, and so delighted when they gave him a round of applause.

After the performance I hurried around the tent, and you may be sure there was rejoicing that made the manager and other fellows laugh.

George haled me off with him down the street. He cleared the ground with that crutch and wooden leg like a steam-engine. "Come! come along!" he cried: "I've something to show you, Loper."

He took me to a quiet boarding-house, and there, in a cozy room, was Susy with a four-year-old girl.

"We were married as soon as I could hobble about," he said, "and she goes with me and makes a home wherever I am."

Susy nodded and blushed and laughed. "Baby and I," she said. "Do you see Baby? She has her father's eyes, do you see?"

"She *is* her mother, Loper," said George—"just as innocent and pure and foolish—just as sure of the Father in heaven taking care of her. They've made a different man of me in some ways—a different man," bending his head reverently.

After a while I began, "You did not stay with—?"

But Balacchi frowned. "I knew where *I* belonged," he said.

Well, he's young yet. He's the best Hercules in the profession, and has laid up a snug sum. Why don't he invest it and retire? I doubt if he'll ever do that, sir. He may do it, but I doubt it. He can't change his blood, and there's that in Balacchi that makes me suspect he will die with the velvet and gilt on, and in the height of good-humor and fun with his audience.

RND OF VOLUME ONB